The Other Team

Felix Fowler

Felix Fowler

First Edition

ISBN 979-8-9923377-1-6

To my grandmother, for your love of books and endless support and pride in all that I do.

Chapter One

I tried to sleep in the backseat, but the road was bumpy, and not truly knowing the way I was going kept me awake.

That, and I swear Dad was trying to hit every rough patch along the way.

And Patrick had to make some stupid comment every time I almost got calm enough to try to sleep.

And Mom kept trying to give me helpful tips that were the least helpful things I'd ever heard.

I hate road trips.

A few hours in, we'd passed the turn to Camp Brightbirch. Everyone would've moved in two or three days ago, but we still could've turned around and gone. I could've taken a sleeping bag on the floor if all the beds in Cabin Nine were full, and Jason and Guillermo and Alex would've been thrilled.

Instead, we drove past, and I told myself to remember to write letters. Some of those guys I'd been going to camp with for six or seven years. I knew absolutely no one at Weltmeister. I wasn't even entirely, 100% sure how to *say* Weltmeister.

The back seat was cramped, and I couldn't get a good look at where we were going. *Another year,* I told myself, *and you'll have a license, then you can go yourself. If they even remember you in another year.*

"Man, this is a drive," Patrick said, glancing up at the front seat to make sure Mom and Dad's eyes were on the road and then sprawling his legs out over my bag. I was tall for my age but Patrick was just straight up tall. Annoyingly tall, mostly in the form of ensuring I never had the space to get comfortable. "Sure hope you don't mess up the suspension or anything, Dad."

Dad's eyebrow twitched. "Son, I don't think I could make this car's suspension worse if I drove it straight off the mountain."

"Well, I'm only saying we want my car to be in top shape when we have to come pick Kit up tomorrow. Going to be an even longer drive back, you know."

I threw an elbow at his ribs, but he was ready and took it on the bicep. He snickered as Mom told him to hush and looked back out the window.

"With you driving from the backseat I'm sure this car will be fine," Dad said, sighing.

I kept annoying Mom by putting my knees in the back of her seat. She'd tell me to take them down and I'd tell her the backseat was too small and that was the only way for my legs to fit.

We'd repeat the whole seat-kicking ordeal every fifteen minutes or so. I reread the first three paragraphs of the mystery book I'd brought with me a dozen times (Patrick kept asking if there were enough pictures for me. I kept asking him to name a single book he'd read this year), never absorbing a single detail of what was going on. I went through the duffel bag beside me. *Cleats, shin guards, socks, shorts, more socks, extra cleats.* I did it every few miles. As soon as I was sure it was squared away, there'd be a little voice that told me I'd forgotten something big, and I'd have to go to the coaches on the very first day and tell them I'd shown up without any shoes or pants or something.

Or, the little voice whispered, *maybe you just want something to be missing so you'll have to turn around.*

"It says here," Mom said, glasses far down her nose and index finger jabbing at her phone, "That '*Wie geht es dir?*' means 'how are you'. I bet if you learned a little the coaches would really appreciate that."

I didn't speak German but I was pretty sure Mom had mispronounced every single word in that sentence.

"Um, I think I'll be okay, Mom. Thanks, though."

"Besides if he needs to know something, his boyfriend can come bail him out like he always does. Unless he got grounded too?"

"What do you mean, always does? I never get grounded," I muttered, counting how many socks I had. How often did they do laundry? Was I going to be the only one having to re-wear stuff? Or could I just go without if that happened? Which one was weirder? "And you just think it's gay because you don't have any friends." Also, Kyle didn't even get grounded which is completely unfair.

"I know he's not your boyfriend," Patrick said, "because you don't have the game to get him even if you were gay."

"Whatever. You still don't have any friends."

"Yeah, sure. You have *one* friend, how is that any better?"

"It's literally infinitely better. If you had better stuff to do you wouldn't have come on this road trip."

Patrick snorted. "I had to keep an eye on the Beast, dude, don't flatter yourself." When our parents got a new car about a year ago he had inherited the Beast, a Honda Odyssey built before either of us had been born that the dealer wouldn't even take as a trade-in.

Dad gave an extremely skeptical glance at the rearview mirror but said nothing.

"Settle down, you two," Mom said, licking a finger and going to the next page. "Stop trying to get a rise out of your little brother. This is a stressful day."

"Sorry, Mom," Patrick said, pushing his long hair back out of his face. "Just trying to help. Kit's grounded for the first time ever, and all. Gotta watch out for my little brother. Make sure he doesn't fall off the straight-and-narrow path like his way cooler big bro."

"Don't you have summer classes to be failing?"

"Don't worry about the German," Dad said, entirely bypassing the bickering. He had one hand on the wheel and the other lifting up the thermos of coffee he'd been sipping from for six hours straight. We'd had no bathroom stops. I had no idea how that was possible. "He won't need the German once he drops a hat trick on the first day."

Mom and Dad started discussing whether or not learning German in the last half hour of the drive would be useful. Mom said it would help me make the coaches feel at home; Dad said unless the college recruiters were German there wasn't much point. I checked through my duffel bag two more times and tried to remember if I had ever even pulled off a hat trick.

At a certain point Mom started asking Patrick questions about the upcoming semester which at least gave me a minute to breathe. I sorted through my stuff, trying to brush the dirt from Patrick's Converses off them. I'd been too busy trying to deal with Patrick's stupid comments I hadn't taken a second to notice everything else that had been going on. My hands were already sweating even though Dad had the A/C on full blast. I kept dropping the stuff in my bag as I double-checked everything. Well, I guess I was octuple-checking at this point. *There's probably at least a few other sophomores who are going to be there,* I thought, trying to remember back to the pictures I'd seen on the website and ballpark how old they had looked. *You just need to find one or two other people who are halfway normal and you'll be fine. You can still write to Kyle and the Brightbirch guys.*

"Almost here!" Dad announced, making me snap my head up. Weltmeister Academy came into view. Well, I guess technically Weltmeister

Academy didn't come into view. St. Michael's Preparatory School for Young Men came into view, but that was where Weltmeister Academy was going to be hosted for the summer. The road finally grew smoother as we passed under oak trees taller than any house I'd ever been in. Big bright signs had been put up directing us along the way, and a few older kids—dressed in school uniforms—smirked at more soccer players who were coming to run in circles and dribble the ball on their campus for six weeks while they enjoyed their summer break.

"This is so nice!" Mom said, nearly putting her nose to the window to look up at the tall brick buildings.

I glanced down at the running shoes on my feet. I'd only had them for a year, but there were a lot of miles in that time. They were muddy—the kind of muddy where it just gets pounded into the shoe and never comes out—and one of the laces had lost the little plastic thing on the end, so if it got fully untied, you needed a half hour to get it back in place. From what I'd read, Weltmeister was pretty serious. I mean, there were going to be people from all over there. Elite colleges looking into them and everything.

I looked down at the fraying shoelaces. "It is extremely nice," I said. "Do you think we were supposed to, like, dress up?" I asked, wiping the mud off my shoe on the floor. *Oh, crap, hope Patrick didn't see that or I'll never hear the end of it.*

"Don't say like," Dad said reflexively. "And it never hurts to dress up. Makes a good first impression."

"Yeah Kit if you want we can turn around and get you fitted for a suit."

"You didn't need to dress up, Kit. You're fine." I caught Mom's glance in the rearview mirror, but my eyes wandered up to my own reflection. Mom had insisted on a good haircut before I left, since I probably wouldn't get one for the rest of the summer. The haircutter had trimmed it too short—my own fault for telling her to go up another inch—and it hadn't quite grown back in where I wanted it yet. I tried to smooth it into place. It was supposed to look the same as Messi's. Instead, it was like a badger crawled up on my head and died. I knew it was bad because even Patrick hadn't said anything about it, and Patrick was happy to remind me of how much taller he was. And more filled out. And less acne-prone. And able to drive. You know, how supportive brothers always do.

Dad rolled down the window to ask where we were supposed to park, and I checked everything in my duffel bag one more time. Dad swung into the parking lot, backing the van into a spot while still drinking coffee.

I took a long deep breath, tried to guess how many miles back the exit for Camp Brightbirch had been, and opened the door to Weltmeister Academy.

There were at least a hundred other campers I could see out there, but probably even more. Maybe two hundred? Apparently, AP Statistics had not given me any help when it came to plain old counting. It was hard to tell with everybody's parents running around. I saw a couple of middle-aged guys in athletic polos with clipboards and whistles checking people in, getting signatures from parents, handing out folders with dorm keys and campus maps. I saw a few kids standing next to a minivan finishing up some pizza they'd brought with them, and a nearby coach was looking at them with a wolfish smile, saying nothing.

Wait. Something wasn't right.

I looked back through the crowd again, at all the other campers, and I got that big sinking feeling like when you remember there's a test next period you'd completely forgotten about. Everybody else was stepping out of cars onto the pavement, cleats click-clacking on the ground, in short soccer shorts, shin guards and socks on.

"Uh, Mom," I said, trying to speak quietly enough that the very tall and very German guy talking to Dad about what dorm I was supposed to be in couldn't hear. "Why, um—why's everybody else already dressed in clothes to practice?"

Mom opened her mouth to say something and then stopped. She looked around, pulling my suitcase out and putting it on the asphalt. I was too busy looking for any single person who hadn't dressed up to remind her not to carry my stuff for me in front of all these people, who were definitely all dressed ready to go. "I'm sure it's not everyone," Mom said, the same way she said my haircut looked good. She paused, blinking. "Um, why don't you—"

"Can I see the email they sent you guys?" I asked.

Mom pulled out her phone and had to slide her glasses back on to punch in her lock code (it was just her birthday. That was her password for everything).

"Hurry," I said.

"Deep breaths, Kit." She read to herself under her breath. *"Hello, welcome to Weltmeister Academy, the only—"*

"Further down!"

"I'm getting there!"

Patrick was failing to stifle his laughter in the back seat and I had to remind myself very forcefully that I had just counted over a hundred potential eyewitnesses in the area.

"There a problem?" Dad asked. I turned over to look. The coach in the athletic shirt was looking over as well, and I wasn't sure who looked more annoyed. The coach was a little under six feet, and he had a bit of a belly, but he also looked like he could probably pick up the Beast and do a few squats with it if he had to. He had a hooked nose and a thick walrus mustache.

"Yes," he said, with a thick German accent. His name tag said "WILHELM" which had somehow been written angrily. "Is there?"

"Not at all," Mom said, before I could say anything. She furrowed up her brows, thinking for a minute. Remembering something and taking that little half-breath before you say something.

Oh, no.

"Ah, we get is deer?"

The coach stared at Mom like he was worried she was having a stroke. I looked at the ground trying to see if I could squeeze in the storm drain, crawl somewhere underground, and not come out until the summer was over. Patrick was howling inside the car.

"Honey?" Dad asked.

"Ah, sorry. *Wie geht es dir?*"

Coach Wilhelm's eyebrows, thick as tree trunks, furrowed. "I am confused, that is how I am." He poked his clipboard at me, which felt like the judge pointing the gavel at you when they sentence you to death row. "Why is this one not dressed?"

"We didn't, uh, we didn't see that. In the e-mail. That's my fault." Mom gave a sheepish smile. "I thought, um, I just didn't see it. Surely he can go and change, real fast?

I saw maybe fifty or sixty yards away the other kids were getting lined and sorted up to start warming up and running drills. They were already chatting and laughing, like they'd known each other before coming. The parking lot was thinning out, too: people were finishing up with signing in, and that meant there was not any cover for my jeans and old shoes. I could feel people looking at me not ready to play, and it felt like when you walk through a spiderweb and it's suddenly all over you. There was absolutely no way I was going to change in the car in front of everyone.

"Why did *he* not read the email?" the coach asked, looking from Mom to me. I wanted to look away but figured that wouldn't be manly enough. I tried to stand up straighter. "Can he not read? He looks old enough to read. The email says we start as soon as you arrive—'excellence from the first day!'"

I could feel my stomach curling up and cringing inside my chest. I took a deep breath. This was not going to go over well but I also couldn't just lie to him in front of my family. I wasn't even sure I could lie to him if it had just been me. "I, uh. I was grounded, sir. So I didn't see it. I didn't have my phone or anything. Not even for the ride up."

The coach blinked.

I would've given up both my kidneys and probably a leg just to get back in that car and leave.

"Grounded? Is he a troublemaker?" the coach asked, looking to Dad. I guess that was fair. Mom hadn't given the impression she had a thorough command of either English or German. "I don't have time for trouble. I have time for football."

"No," Dad said, looking at me. Our eyes met. He gave me a half-grimace in solidarity. "He's a good kid. He'll be one of your best."

I tried to keep my back straight and not think about anything forgotten in the duffel bag or my tennis shoes or the sound of Patrick snickering. "I wasn't—I was hanging out with my friend Kyle. He was moving away, and I was out past curfew. It was just once. I won't cause any problems, sir."

The coach sighed and rubbed at his forehead. "Well, fine. Do not—no more mistakes. Go take your bag to your dorm, change and come back down as quickly as you can. We will be starting immediately."

"Yes sir," all three of us muttered in varying degrees of meekness.

He turned and walked to the next family, shaking his head and scratching at his bald spot.

"Sorry," Mom said, once he was out of earshot. "I'm super sorry, Kit, I didn't—"

"It's okay, Mom." I had been so mad at her a second ago, but she was blinking hard trying not to cry, and that was worse. "It's fine, it's fine."

"Nobody'll even remember in a few days, and we'll go real fast so you'll be back down before they notice, okay? A few people are still getting unpacked too, okay?"

Dad nodded and immediately moved into overtime, grabbing the last of the bags from The Beast, which was still hissing and popping from the exertion of getting up those hills. Patrick watched, idly looking out the window at a few of the moms. Always helpful, Patrick. Always helpful.

Around us, there were still a few families getting unpacked, but not many. I turned and noticed somebody looking right at me: a kid about my age, maybe a little older. Probably a little older—I was supposed to be too young to be here, but Dad had gotten the ear of one of the recruiters, and I think they let me in just to make him stop talking. He had a jersey that was a little too big on him and curly blonde hair that hung down over his face a bit. He had a small nose, wide eyes and a wider smile. For a second, I felt the urge to look for that drain grate to crawl through again—but it wasn't a leering grin or anything mocking. It was warmer. Like a laughing with and not a laughing at. He glanced from me to Wilhelm, and back over to my outfit, and I saw the gears turning behind his eyes. His mom and dad were still getting things sorted out: there was some sort of confusion over who to give his prescriptions too, best I could eavesdrop.

As Dad slammed the door on the back of the Beast (the car rattled like a skeleton when this happened and I heard Patrick's muffled voice telling him to be gentler), I noticed the blonde kid glance over his shoulder, back at me, and begin rummaging through his bag—an old U.S. Army rucksack—and pulled out a bag of clearly labelled medications that he took to his parents and the coach talking with them. I couldn't make out what they were saying.

"Hurry up, Kit," Dad said, jolting me back to reality. I nodded and grabbed my backpack, slinging it over my shoulder and following him away. Up ahead, I could see people beginning to take warm-up laps. I grabbed my other bags from Mom, who didn't put up a fight over it. Her face was still a deeper red than I'd ever seen.

Patrick rolled down one of the windows. "Hey, I hear you're supposed to punch the biggest guy you see today so everybody else knows to respect you."

"You're the biggest guy I can see out here, Patrick."

Patrick smirked. "Heh. Good luck. I'm not getting out of the A/C but you guys have fun."

"Thanks."

Before we were out of earshot, I could hear Coach Wilhelm sighing as he approached the blonde boy near us. "Fine, go and drop them off then come straight back."

We moved past them and Dad led me on the way up to the dorm, machine-gun-firing facts and advice at me as he fumbled out my key card for the building. Of course, my I.D. picture was post-haircut and not pre-.

"Make sure you remember to drink as much water as you can."

"Yes, I'll hydr—"

"But not too much, okay? You don't want to cramp. Boxers, they just get a little sprayed in their mouths in-between rounds to not cramp."

"I'm not going to be boxing anyone, Dad." Wait, what if someone tried to fight me. That had never really happened before, but what if—

"I know, I know, but soccer's even tougher, if you ask me. Now you watch the angles on your shots, they're—"

"Honey," Mom said, "I think his dorm room was back there."

Dad stopped, blinking at the folder's pages in one hand and hauling a suitcase in the other. "...Eh. It was. Yeah, back there."

We filed into the dorm, where at the least I got to claim a bed before my roommate (a dude called Richard Laskins, if the door tag was right) could. I dropped my suitcase on the ground and had it unzipped and half the clothes out before Mom was even in the room, snatching shorts and a jersey.

"I'm gonna go change," I said, standing up and looking around. There were two beds, a ceiling low enough to make me feel the need to hunch a bit, a desk that looked like it was built in the 80s, and a dresser. There was a window, but no door other than the one we'd come through. "Uh—where's the bathroom?"

"Hall bathroom," Dad said, not looking up from the duffel bag. He was laying out my soccer gear for when I came back in. "That's how dorms are. I pity the guys who had to share one with your brother. Now hurry up!"

I looked around the room one more time, as if a bathroom I could close the door on and have to myself would appear if I checked again. "Uh, yeah, yeah." I swallowed. I'd never had a bathroom situation like that—I'd either come ready for practice before or snagged a bathroom stall right after my last class.

I ducked into the bathroom, which felt like a white-tile prison. There were a few sinks and urinals on the left wall, then five or six showers with curtains that were barely hanging on the rods. They didn't look like they would stay closed, or even close at all for that matter, and were short enough you could still see at least half of whoever was in there. It felt so open, like I may as well be changing in the middle of the field everyone who came prepared was already playing on.

I took a deep breath. That was a later problem. I needed to focus and get back to that field as fast as I possibly could, if not faster. I stepped into one of the stalls and ripped off my t-shirt pulling it up over my head at the same time I was trying to kick my jeans off. Normally I tried not to let any of my stuff touch the bathroom floor when I was changing, but I figured death by Wilhelm would be a lot worse than death by staph infection. I scooped everything up and bolted back around to the room, where Dad had put all my stuff neatly to the side and Mom was fretting changing the sheets. I had to twist my shirt around the right way as I dropped my outfit on the floor.

Something's off, thought that back part of my brain that seizes upon every little odd detail when I'm panicked. Here mom and dad were, unloading all my stuff, but I hadn't seen anybody else in the hallway, even though it for sure looked like other people had gotten there and started unloading before we did. There's no way they were all in one of the other dorms, either.

I shook my head. *Focus. The logistics of move-in day are not really top priority here, Kit.*

"It's okay, it's okay," I said, my heart thundering far too fast for the short distance I'd run. "I—I gotta get going, I love you, but I gotta go."

"Gear," Dad said, nodding down at the duffel bag.

I grimaced. Of course. I was so dumb. I sat down and shoved shin guards under socks and laced my cleats as fast as I possibly could. It only took a minute, but it felt like every second was dragging on and on and on, the same way as when you get asked a question in front of the class and have no idea what the answer is. And I was still in the dorm—I wasn't even out there yet. It was going to be so much worse jogging out there in front of everyone. I tried breathing as deep as I could. I just had to get down and play well enough and nobody would remember. Just like Mom had said.

Dad offered me a hand up and gave me a clasp on the shoulder. I swallowed.

"You're gonna do great, kid." He said, smiling.

"Thanks, Dad, I—"

"I know, I love you, but you gotta go. We'll find our way out."

I nodded, turning to give Mom a big hug. She squeezed back with the mom strength that threatens to break ribs. "I left you something in your bag," she said quietly, and gave me a quick pat on the back.

"Thanks," I whispered. "Love you."

"Love you too, Kit Kat."

I winced, but at least it was just the three of us in the room. I nodded and scrambled to the hallway, feeling like a deer skidding on an icy road as I stumbled across the tile floor in cleats meant for muddy fields.

"Hey!" a voice said from behind me. I was so focused on remembering my way back out the building I nearly ruined the shorts I'd just changed into.

"Uh," I said. Real smart. Real cool, Kit. I turned and looked. It was the kid I'd seen unloading the car next to ours—the blonde curly haired one. He gave me a wide grin. "Hi."

"Hey," he said. "Didn't come dressed? It's totally fine. Don't sweat it, man."

I knew the clock was ticking, but the field could wait for a second. "You had to drop off meds or something? Sorry, I mean—I wasn't trying to be nosy."

He shrugged, "No worries. I'm an open book. I had to drop some off before we got going. I'm Freddie, by the way."

"Kit." I took a moment to think—I wasn't entirely sure, but I was pretty sure something didn't quite add up there. Not in the sense that I thought Freddie was lying to me or being a jerk or anything, but more...I was pretty sure he could've dropped his meds off and gotten back to the field way before now.

I gave Freddie a smile. *Well, at least one person at this camp isn't judging me already.* "Thanks, man. Glad you got your stuff squared away. Let's get going."

We did a fist bump while trying to keep moving, which meant we only got like half our knuckles to connect, and Freddie almost slipped and fell. We jogged out the building. I went slightly slower than I wanted—Freddie wasn't moving as fast as me—and we only made two wrong turns finding our way out the maze that was St. Michael's boys' dorm.

I think I could've gotten it right the first time if I'd been paying attention. Instead, I was trying to figure out why anyone would risk getting read the riot act by Coach Wilhelm on the first day to be late with me.

Chapter Two

Somewhere between the seventieth and eightieth burpee, I could no longer feel my cheeks burning. They'd been red for ten straight minutes after I had to walk out across the open field with Freddie while everybody stared at us. Now at least, nobody was thinking about my being unfashionably late, but I think that was also because we all felt like we were about to die.

We were lined up in rows of ten. They'd finished jumping jacks and high knees by the time we got to the field, and I did my best to shake my legs loose as I found the first open spot I could and tried my best to make it seem like I'd been there all along.

"If you have a heart attack, are you supposed to stop or just push through it?" I heard someone say, two or three rows back—it sounded like Freddie, but my brain did not have enough oxygen to think and keep doing push-ups at the same time. There were a few people that snickered. I smiled but kept my face firmly toward the mud while I did it. I knew how getting caught messing around during conditioning played out.

"IF YOU CAN TALK, YOU AREN'T GOING FAST ENOUGH!" came a bellowing voice from the front of the column, followed by another whistle blast. The whistles came every three or four seconds, and we were supposed to have hammered out another rep by the time the next one came through. I remember in one of my history classes they taught us that in World War One, the commanders would blow whistles before the guys had to get up over the trenches and charge. I honestly felt like they had a better deal than we did.

The guy next to me had been pale and skinny even before he sweated half his body weight out. "Are—" he huffed, "—the recruiters here today?" he talked low enough to avoid Wilhelm's notice.

"Devil's the only one watching us right now, mate," came an entirely-too-cheery British voice from the other side of him. I didn't say a word. I'd gotten enough attention for one day. Each rep made my arms and chest burn a little bit more, and I could feel the stitches in my sides getting sharper.

"NINETY-FOUR, NINETY-FIVE..." roared the coach up front. I guess the fastest way to describe him is to say he looked fully capable of eating Coach Wilhelm if he had to, and then have some room leftover to have one or two of us for dessert. He was burly, with what looked like old military tattoos poking out from under his shirt sleeves, and I got a glimpse of cauliflower ear on one side as he paced back and forth, looking for anyone who couldn't match the whistle's pace. I didn't look at his nametag, because I felt like making eye contact with him was probably going to end with me doing thirty more burpees.

"NINETY-SEVEN, NINETY-EIGHT..."

I was wheezing hard. I'm in pretty good shape, and I'm pretty good at soccer, but I don't think I could've cranked out any past a hundred if they'd had a gun to my head. Granted, I'm not sure how much worse a gun to my head would've been compared to the burpees.

"ONE HUNDRED!" There were three sharp whistle blasts and I heard no less than four kids flop onto the dirt. I didn't quite flop, but I definitely stayed on my hands and knees, burpee half-finished, until I could suck some wind back into my lungs. I tried to look like I was stretching and not just dying.

"You have one minute, then we start the next drill!"

Each time my heart beat, it felt like a hand grenade was going off in my chest. Fifteen minutes ago I was standing in the AC hugging my mom goodbye. Now, I was pretty sure my shirt was more sweat than fabric.

I sucked in as much air as I could while we had a free minute and tried to figure out if it was going to get any hotter this afternoon or if it would start cooling down at any point. *They have ice cream at Camp Brightbirch, you know.*

"Scare tactics," muttered a kid to my right. He hadn't said anything so far, no whining or groaning or cursing under his breath or anything. Nearly everybody else had.

He had long brown hair that looked like a mop on top of his head, and dark eyes peeking out from under the mane. He must've been as gassed as the rest of us, but he pulled himself up to his feet.

"What do you mean?" I asked, trying to do the same. I didn't want to be the only one on the ground. No blood in the water in front of the sharks. I already felt like I made myself look dumb by being late without my gear on. I wasn't going to shoot myself in the foot a second time or remind them of that if I could help.

He frowned, looking at me. His chest was rising and falling sharply, but as he studied me, I could tell the gears whirring behind his eyes didn't seem to be slowing down. "Wait, you were the one who forgot his stuff."

Cool. So the feeling of my skin crawling *could* get worse. "Um, yeah, I..."

He furrowed his brow. "So did they already pick you, then?"

"I don't know what you're talking about."

The messy-haired kid nodded to where the cars had been to unload. I saw everybody's bags and stuff were still there. Nobody else's stuff had been brought inside. *I knew all those dorms being empty was weird!*

"If you flunk these conditioning trials, they call your parents to swing back around and come pick you up before you even unpack." I saw his eyes dart over to the scrawny guy who had been beside me, still wheezing for air as hard as if he hadn't stopped doing burpees at all. He shook his head. "Not going to be me." He eyed me up one more time, and I felt a bit like one of the lobsters in the tank at the store when a customer sticks his face to the glass. "Looks like it's not going to be you, either. Is your dad a scout or something?"

"Oh." I said. I wanted to try to think of something smarter, but I was doing all I could to huff out monosyllables. I definitely heard at least one person puke. *Probably those idiots who ate pizza before showing up to a German soccer camp.* At least he did it after he was done having to get on the ground and do push-ups.

"LINE UP!" bellowed the rough-looking coach. Wilhelm had taken up the rear of the field. I'm not entirely sure which one I'd rather have mad at me, or which one was supposed to be the rock and which one was the hard place. There were a few others swarming around, but mercifully, I hadn't been honed in on and chewed out yet. "TWO BY TWO! WE SPLIT INTO THREE COLUMNS!"

I heard more than a few groans from the kids who were dumb enough to do it audibly.

"WE HAVE VOLUNTEERS!" he pointed out the whiners with a finger that looked as thick as three of mine and paired them up at the back of the line.

"Any idea what this is?" the pale kid beside me asked.

"First circle of hell, baby!" the jokester a few rows back answered, just audibly enough to be heard by us but not by the coaches.

"Column sprints," the messy-haired kid said. I caught his eye. He had some acne, and needed a trim—maybe with a weed whacker—but it somehow made him seem more intense. "Try to save your strength," he said to me, barely above a whisper.

I frowned, trying to assess the different columns. I couldn't really see any particular one, mine included, that looked really athletic or something to figure out if this is part of how they choose to send home.

I motioned to pair up with him, but he'd already snagged the kid in the row in front of me. That guy looked really strong, but he was shorter and stockier. *He can't possibly sprint that fast,* I thought. He was built like a silverback.

The pale kid moved up beside me, and I was too tired to scout for anybody else, or really to care that much. The whistle blew again and we took off at a jog. Well, the coaches said it was a jog. It felt suspiciously like full-speed running to me.

Each time the whistle blew, the kids at the back had to sprint to the front of the column. I couldn't begin to tell you the number of curse words—or the number of languages those curses were in—as people blitzed past me.

One foot in front of the other, I told myself, trying to breathe as deeply as I could before I was at the back of the line.

I could hear Dad's voice chiming in my ears. *Remember to breathe deep so you don't cramp!*

Thanks, Dad. Always helpful.

The line in front of us grew longer and longer, and finally we were at the back of the column. I took one last deep breath, trying to stretch my lungs as far as they'd go. I watched a pair of guys muttering to each other in Spanish sprint up and out of sight, and then we took off.

The jogging had given me just enough time to catch some of my breath back. I felt bad for the idiots who'd gotten forced to sprint first, right after the burpees. But it was like the kids who'd puked—better them than me.

I had no idea how you were supposed to keep up with everyone else after hurling.

After all, the drive up had been long enough without needing to make it twice in one day.

It turns out a line of maybe sixty people, even going two-by-two, is pretty long when it comes to sprinting past them. I could feel myself going steady the first quarter, holding strong the second, then starting to lose energy at the halfway point. I could feel a few people's eyes on me, trying to see who was going to fall behind and who was going to keep up.

Focus, Kit, I snapped at myself. *You already made everybody notice you, you can't be the slowest kid at the camp now, or nobody will want you on their team. It wasn't your fault you were late, but it's going to be your fault if you're slow.*

That did the trick. I put everything I had into going as hard as I could and had to hope I didn't wipe out in the mud. I cleared the front of the column, slowed to a jog, and tried to hide just how bad my legs were hurting from the coaches until they turned their focus to the kids sprinting up from the back.

"Nice," the messy-haired kid behind me said. It was another two or three full seconds before my partner stumbled up to the front and joined up in-step with me. I realized I'd wound up looking better by comparison.

As I felt a wave of relief from knowing I had at least another forty-five seconds before I had to do that again, something about the messy-haired kid clicked for me: he'd picked the short stocky guy on purpose. He wanted a partner he could outsprint to make himself look way better by comparison. He must've thought I'd done the same thing.

I couldn't figure out if I was impressed or a little concerned by that.

I turned to the pale kid beside me and sucked in enough air between steps to say, "Good job, man, keep it up."

He gave me something between a grimace and a grin and we kept going.

The whistle blasts came steady as war drums. There was barely any time to think, just the feeling of my feet pounding into the dirt, whistles screeching, wheezing for air, and repeat.

The column grew longer and longer ahead of us again. I took my last good, deep breath. Back home, I'd gotten promoted to junior varsity after three games on the freshman team. The other guys here looked older, taller, better. I wasn't sure I was the best, but I wasn't going to be the worst.

I glanced over at the pale kid, who was about thirty more seconds of running away from cardiac arrest.

Maybe it was the sweat soaking through into my brain, or the lack of oxygen, or, I don't know. Paying it forward. Freddie had stuck his neck out for me. Besides, it would be nice to have at least one other person here think of me as something other than the guy who was late to the first practice.

"I'm going to go a little slower," I whispered to him, burning half the air I'd pulled into my lungs. "Give it all you've got, we'll go together."

He looked up, eyes wide, and nodded right as the whistle blew.

We took off. Slower than the first sprint, but steady. Neck and neck. I could've gotten to the front faster than him, maybe by another second or two on top of the first go. But I didn't. I could feel the coaches' eyes on us as we settled into the front of the line once more.

The messy-haired kid was quiet behind me as we got back to the front.

After that it was a bit of a haze. There were other drills, more running, leg lifts and squats, running, another round of column sprints, and then a little more running to end it. By the end, even the guys who looked like they could've been a stunt double for Captain America were swaying on their feet during the cool-down and stretching. Even the coaches looked tired, and they'd just been standing there.

"Okay," Coach Wilhelm said. "That's it for now. Welcome to Weltmeister Academy. Go grab your bags, get settled in, then dining hall in an hour. You all need to eat so you can be ready for real conditioning tomorrow morning."

At least half the guys cried with relief and pretended it was sweat. Everybody staggered like a zombie horde to their luggage. A few people just stood in place or sat down, completely uncaring if they looked slow in front of the coaches. A couple guys were teetering a bit, like their Gatorade had fermented.

In the part of my brain that wasn't focused on the cramps in my thighs, I realized something. Once everybody got back to their rooms, there was going to be a stampede to get to the showers. It was going to make the column sprints look like a morning jog. Nobody had escaped the burpees without mud—or for a few poor suckers, puke. Thinking about having to go in there while everybody and their brother came through felt like, well, about as bad as having to jog out to get in line on the field in front of everyone. *Maybe everyone's so tired they won't remember,* a little voice that sounded a whole lot like Mom telling me to try speaking German said.

I'd like to say I jogged really athletically and smoothly back to the dorms, but instead I looked more like Frankenstein trying to power walk. I stopped to guzzle down at least two gallons of the sweetest, coldest water I'd ever had from the hall fountain, then showered top to bottom in Guinness World Record time. The water pressure was like a leak in a gardening hose, and the temperature went from lukewarm to scalding to frigid every thirty seconds. *Cool, Mom and Dad found me the one summer camp on earth with worse showers than Brightbirch.*

Outside, the noise in the hall was getting steadily louder, people shouting and hollering, doors opening and slamming. I turned the water off, got maybe 40% of me properly dried off, and scrambled into my bathing suit as the first few people started coming into the showers. It seemed like almost all the guys coming in were taller, or in better shape, or walking in groups of twos or threes. Once I made it back to my room, I collapsed on my bed and tried to regain feeling in my legs for a minute. I wasn't sure if it was possible to get a full REM cycle of sleep before we were expected down in the dining hall, but I was going to try.

"Hey," a voice said.

I blinked. "Huh?"

"You...Christopher?" The kid below me glanced at the nametag on the door.

"Yeah. Everybody calls me Kit, though. You must be Richard?"

He nodded. He was a slender black kid who looked almost bored to be here. I had seen many expressions during the wind sprints, but not boredom. "Yeah. Hey, uh, you mind if we swap roommates?"

It took me a second to process. *Did I already make somebody mad?* For a second I thought it must've been the fact I'd showed up unprepared, that he wouldn't want to be dormmates with the idiot that couldn't even read basic instructions, but...it didn't seem like he recognized me. Did he? "Uh, what?"

"Me and a few of my friends from our varsity team came here together, but they kinda split us up into a few different dorms, so I figured we'd swap if that's cool."

I pushed myself up onto my elbows and thought about it. They'd come together as a group? Had everybody else come here with a few other members from their team? *Mom, what else was in that email you didn't read?* "Wait, you—you came here with your team?"

Richard's expression had switched from boredom to whatever the look on your face is called when you're staring at a crazy guy. I think I preferred boredom. "Uh, yeah. Didn't you?"

"Uh, no, I came by myself."

"Oh."

There was a pause. I wasn't really sure what to tell him, because I was definitely not about to go ask the Coaches if, on top of being late to the first day's conditioning, if I could change dorm rooms. At the same time, I really did not want to spend the next six weeks being stuck with a guy who resented me.

"I'm happy to help with your—with swapping, and all, but I don't really know if the coaches will let us."

Richard frowned. Wasn't sure if it was at me or the situation. "Yeah, I guess."

"Sorry."

Richard shrugged and grabbed his towel to go shower without saying much else. The door shut behind him. I sat up and rubbed at my temples. Cool. This was great. This was really great.

There wasn't any point in sitting around and waiting for Richard to come back just so I could do something else that would annoy him, so I went ahead and got dressed to go down to the dining hall. I wasn't really sure what exactly they wanted us to wear in our off-time. I figured shorts and a jersey was safe. Nobody was going to have brought actual nice clothes to this, right?

With the way things had gone so far, I didn't really want to roll the dice on that. I walked down the hall, where things had only gotten louder, and I saw three kids cackling as they tried to see how hard they could kick a ball all the way down the hallway. One of them was adamantly arguing it was possible to open the door to the outside of the dorm if they aimed it just right. The other two seemed to think this was pretty stupid, but were bored enough to try it. I guess that wasn't the worst way to kill time waiting for the showers. I was lucky I'd gotten in early, but I felt dumb when I realized I could've also just waited everybody else out and had the showers to myself. Then again, looking at the line, that may have been a while.

The hallways in the summer weren't decorated with a whole lot, just bulletin boards that had leftover stuff pinned up from the spring. There were notices about signing out of your dorm for the summer, stuff going on throughout campus. There were study groups for final exams, a big Shakespeare play coming up, a spring recital, information on football tryouts for the fall, info on a spring dance with what I guessed was St. Michael's sister school, somebody desperately attempting to get a last-minute roommate before the deadline passed—

"You and me both," I muttered. I read over the board again, just in case there was anything interesting, and one more time before I had to admit to myself stalling for time wasn't going to help me. I double-checked that I had my room keys, that I remembered which one was my room, how to get back—

"Okay, for real this time." I took a deep breath and made my way down the steps (my thighs burned in protest) and followed the little print-out map that they'd given us. The sun wasn't quite setting yet, but it was close enough to make the sky full of warm orange light with some pinks around the edges.

It was pretty. It would've been a strong contender for Best Sunset of the Week at Brightbirch.

The walk was short enough, and a few people had already started making their way there first. Completely fine by me. You always let somebody else test out cafeteria food before you get in line.

We scanned in with I.D. cards (I couldn't tell if the lady at the cashier's desk smirked at my picture or not, but I was pretty sure she had. Whatever. She was so old she probably didn't know who Messi was) and stepped into a dining hall that made my high school's look like a food truck. There were four or five different stations that I could see just from the entrance, and enough tables to seat at least a few hundred on this half of the hall alone. There was a second story where I saw what looked like maybe some regular high school kids taking some summer classes or something—they didn't have any soccer camp lanyards on—and what looked to be one or two teachers and a few coaches. I could smell hibachi from where one short woman was furiously trying to make six or seven stir fries at once, another counter had somebody rolling burritos like their life depended on it, and the guy at the salad station was on his phone because no one was in line.

I circled the hall for a minute or two, seeing what all there was. I thought I would wait until I saw somebody I recognized—Freddie, maybe, or even that messy-haired kid—but after about thirty seconds of smelling food on the grill I was waiting in line. Running suicides does not lend itself to fasting afterwards.

As the line inched forward I tried to see if the room looked like it had as many people as the field. Did anybody get axed right off the bat? It seemed like there weren't as many kids around...but it was hard to tell. People kept moving in groups, which made it tough to get a read on their numbers. I saw Richard howling at something a short kid in his squad had said, and five or six guys a little older than me parked at a long table, pizzas forgotten as they furiously argued in Spanish.

I scanned the room one more time, and it was like realizing I'd come without my gear on all over again. Everybody in that room looked like they had come here together. They had that energy you have when you're talking with your teammates rather than trying to awkwardly fumble your way through a conversation. The tables were filling up, and there didn't look to be very many people sitting on their own, or asking if they could sit down, or anything like that.

"What do you want?"

"Huh?"

The burrito lady stared at me. "What do you want on your burrito?"

"Let him take his time!" the guy behind her rolling tortillas pleaded.

She rolled her eyes. "Hurry up and order or get out of line."

"Uh, um—the—just some of everything, I guess."

I felt bad as soon as I said it. I'd just meant to buy myself some time, but I think the guy making them almost cried when he heard me say it. The cook shoved it all in half-heartedly, tortilla tearing, and dropped it on my plate. I mouthed "sorry" at him and turned away.

It felt like standing in midfield right after the ball got absolutely rocketed back over your head, towards your own goal. Just the sense of being completely out of position. Or like the other team was getting to play offsides and never get called. Everyone else had come here with at least two or three people from their own teams. Maybe their whole teams—I saw at least fifteen or sixteen guys walk in as a group together, some even with matching haircuts.

And theirs actually did look like Messi's.

I circled and got in another line and got a sandwich, and my burrito was cold by the time I got through the pizza line and got a slice draped across them both (the pizza lady gave me a very concerned stare before putting the slice on my plate). Still didn't see Freddie. There wasn't even anyone I recognized playing against at a tournament or something. Not even the pale kid. He may have gotten kicked out already, for all I knew. I hadn't seen him after the column sprints.

I killed about ten more minutes before I looked for a table by the windows, tucked behind a wide column, where flyers for a summer trip to Nicaragua were peeling off a bulletin board. I sat down and stared at my cold, bursting burrito. My section stayed empty for five or six minutes, but then two or three separate groups came through and settled at the tables around me. A few grabbed chairs from where I was and slid them over to make room.

Six more weeks.

I ate as fast as I could and walked back to the dorms while some of the kids were still walking in.

It was barely eight thirty. I didn't really care. I got dressed for bed and sat in the chair at my desk, which creaked any time you moved half an inch or shifted at all. I strongly considered swapping it with Richard's, since he was so keen on the idea of changing things out. I figured he'd be out of the dorm hanging with friends so often it wouldn't really matter.

I took my backpack and the few books I'd brought to read out. It didn't really seem like most of the guys I'd seen so far would want to read in their free time, but that was very far down on the list of things I'd done to make an idiot out of myself today. I reached in to grab my glasses case and felt my hands brush against something that crinkled. Under all twenty pairs of socks Dad had made me pack ("You never know when you'll get blisters, and what if it's the day the scouts are there?"), there was a package wrapped up in brown paper and tied with string. It was Mom's signature present knot that was no one had been able to untie at any Christmas in living memory. I sat on the floor with my legs crossed and tore at the paper, pulling the box out from around the string.

A little note fell out.

Kit Kat,

I got this for you so you could get in touch with everybody. You're going to do amazing! Dad and I know it. Love you.

Mom

Inside was a package of stationery, some pens, thirty or forty stamps, and an index card that had the address to Camp Brightbirch on it. It had Kyle's new address, too. And home. I guess in case I'd forget.

I sat and stared at the little box until it stopped being blurry.

Then I got in bed and pretended to be asleep when Richard came in a few hours later, laughing.

Chapter Three

I won't lie and say I wasn't winded at all when we finished the next morning's conditioning, because I was pretty tired. But I was able to force myself to wait a few seconds before walking over to the shade of the massive oak trees that littered St. Michael's campus, and make it look like I wasn't wheezing when the coaches were watching. The sun was near the center of the sky and we had been doing everything from windsprints to ball control drills to mini-scrimmages all morning. I definitely wasn't the best at Weltmeister.

But I wasn't the worst. I for sure wasn't the worst. As the last whistles blew, I caught myself grinning.

"LUNCH!" Wilhelm shouted, his voice as loud as cannon fire. "YOU HAVE TWO HOURS, THEN COME BACK HERE. YOU SHOULD FINISH EATING WITHIN AN HOUR AND HAVE TIME TO LET YOUR FOOD SETTLE!"

I thought of the pizza kids from yesterday. Apparently, that was advice people needed to be told.

We took off our pinnies to toss them back into the boxes. As I dropped mine in, Ludwig—the cauliflower-eared coach—made eye contact with me and gave me a nod. I think the lines in his face looked more chiseled than the ones on Mt. Rushmore. "Good."

Maybe this is a bit too forward, but I was pretty sure that was the most positive emotion he'd shown to another human in at least ten years. There was already a rumor going around that Ludwig was German for Lucifer.

"Uh, thank you, sir."

He frowned. "You should be going and getting lunch. Go."

I nodded, turning and looking through the crowd. Everyone was crushing their water bottles, putting pinnies away, and taking a minute to recover before heading inside. Through the crowd, I caught eyes with Freddie, who seemed to be talking with a few guys like he already knew them. He noticed me and gave me a grin, which I returned.

In doing so, I wasn't watching out for, say, the roots of those giant oak trees, and I nearly faceplanted in front of all the coaches I'd spent the last three hours trying to impress. I managed to catch myself without breaking anything or anyone, but Wilhelm for sure noticed.

He gave me a level stare. "Do not do that."

That was about right. "Yes, sorry, sir." I turned and jogged off.

After a moment, I noticed somebody had jogged up beside me. It was the pale scrawny kid—which, I mean, I don't know if I was in a position to be throwing stones about being scrawny—from the column runs yesterday. He'd called dibs on me when we had to form teams for 3 v 3s.—number 83—jogged over to join me. "Hey, man, you were awesome out there, dude."

I gave him a grin. "Thanks, man. You played well too."

"I'm, uh, Bryan. Nice to meet you."

"Kit," I said. I paused. "We're both super sweaty so I don't know if I'm supposed to try to shake your hand or not, honestly."

He laughed and took a second to breathe before talking. "Yeah, no worries. Are you going to get lunch?"

I glanced around, trying to see if I could catch Freddie's eye again. "Yeah, I was headed there."

"Sweet."

Bryan proceeded to unload on all the little mistakes he'd made, and how he didn't think they were entirely his fault—his cleats had been tied too tight, the sun had been in our eyes consistently, he hadn't slept well—and I was totally fine to let him ramble. I got one or two annoyed stares from guys I'd dribbled around. We walked past the aides, who were holding clipboards, comparing notes, and talking in low tones. Everybody else seemed to be doing the same thing I was, which was trying to eavesdrop on what they were saying, but they weren't letting anything juicy slip.

We had a few more sessions to go through, but I was pretty sure I'd done okay. Maybe not the best, but I'd made a name for myself other than "guy who had to change within the first forty-five seconds of camp starting".

"...but, I mean, other than that, I think I did pretty good."

Pretty well, I thought. "Yeah, me too man. I mean—I think you did well, too."

Bryan flashed me a grin. He had braces. That was fine, but he'd picked lime green for the colored part of the braces, which I had a ton of questions about from an aesthetics standpoint. It was probably rude to open with those. "So, anyway, where are you thinking of going to college and stuff? Where are you from?"

"Oh, I'm a sophomore. So I'm not touring anywhere for a while." Huh. Was I supposed to be touring colleges already? *Make it through one thing at a time, Kit. And definitely make sure any college emails don't go to Mom.*

Bryan blinked. "Dude, for real? I thought you were a senior for sure." He looked me up and down. "Like, a senior only halfway through puberty or something, but a senior for sure."

"No—thanks, though." I paused. "I think?"

Bryan scratched at his head. "Wow. I'm aiming for anywhere in-state, I guess, unless this camp gets me somewhere cool. Do you have, like, any ideas or anything, though?"

"Guess anywhere that gives me a good scholarship," I said, mostly truthfully. I mean, I had some ideas, but I feel like telling somebody you want to go to academically tough colleges makes you come off as a know-it-all, and like I said, I was really not in the position to start burning bridges yet. "But, you know, somewhere I can get a good job after."

"Wait, do you mean like academic scholarships? Are you smart?"

"I mean, hopefully I'm not stupid?"

Bryan nodded. "Yeah. But you have good grades and stuff?"

We'd gotten in line to swipe into the cafeteria, which meant I didn't have any real easy retreat from this conversation. I could feel where it was going, like watching something spiral around and around the sink before it goes totally down the drain. And I felt like crap for even thinking that way because, I mean, this morning I'd eaten the tire-tread-consistency eggs that Weltmeister considered breakfast alone, and now that I had somebody to eat with I was immediately just wishing they'd stop talking. *Kyle would be amused.* "I mean, I guess so."

"Huh." Maybe I sound crazy saying it, but I'd experienced that sort of reaction before. When people found out you scored better than them on something, you could feel a stiffness or aloofness start to creep in. This guy had been asking me to be on his team an hour ago and now I couldn't shake the feeling he was trying to size me up to find something I sucked at. It wasn't even like I thought I was better than Bryan at anything other than 3v3s and knowing to pick better colors to wear on your teeth.

I should've just told him I was an idiot. If Kyle was here, he would've told him I'm an idiot for me.

"Yeah, uh, so, where are you from?" I asked.

The conversation got back rolling again, but it didn't fully feel like it went back to something normal. Maybe that was just in my head. Bryan kept trying to slip in questions about where I was applying to, which was especially annoying because we wouldn't even be applying at the same time, so it wouldn't even matter if my grades were better.

Couldn't someone who has normal conversational skills have asked to be my teammate?

We'd finished lunch and I was brainstorming ways to politely go back to my room when somebody else walked up to the table. He was taller than me by an inch or two. The guy had older cleats that he had clearly painted himself hanging from his athletic bag, which looked to be held together by duct tape and a dream. Best I could tell, the paint had faded, then been painted over again. He had a buzz cut of brown hair, light brown skin, and the veins in his arms were popping enough that I wondered if he'd gone and lifted weights before trials today.

"You were 64," he said. I couldn't make heads or tails of his tone. It wasn't really a question. It didn't seem angry enough to be a threat, but it didn't seem friendly enough to be an icebreaker, either.

"Yeah," I said. I tried to remember for a minute—we'd rotated against a number of other 3v3 teams. I think we'd played against him, but I had been so fixated on what I was doing that I didn't remember a ton of specific details. I couldn't have told you much beyond the nuances of what I was doing—when I hit the ball a moment too early, or when I timed a shot on goal just right.

"I was on his team," Bryan added.

The other kid looked over at him. "Yeah, something like that. What's your name?"

"Bryan."

"No, I meant 64."

"Oh." Bryan scowled. Couldn't really blame him, but he did walk into that one.

"Kit," I said.

"I'm Oliver. You played well out there."

"Uh, thanks, you too."

He nodded for a moment, looking me over again. I felt a bit like I was in a police line-up. "See you around." He turned and walked off. I followed him for a minute as Bryan started rambling again, and I didn't see him go and sit back down with a team of his own. He looked like he left the dining hall to go back to the dorms, though one on a different side of campus from mine.

"—so it really would've been a 4 on the exam, but—"

I caught him taking a half-second break to pause for a breath and seized the moment. "Hey, I'm gonna go crash before afternoon drills, Bryan, but I'll catch up with you later."

Bryan continued his story for a full sentence before that registered. I was already standing and grabbing my tray. "Oh, yeah, for sure, catch you later, man. Thanks for grabbing lunch with me. I'll see you at conditioning later."

I wandered back to my dorm—it felt weird thinking of it as my dorm, when yesterday it had been an eight-by-ten box I was stuck in for the summer—trying to figure out if, gun to my head, I'd rather everyone else at camp that summer be nonstop talking my head off like Bryan or say weirdly little like Oliver.

I was snoring about thirty seconds after telling myself I was just going to lay down for a second before doing some stretches and woke up to the stampede of people heading back out to the fields. *I should set an alarm next time,* I thought, and just the hypothetical of being late two days in a row had me up and awake in a matter of heartbeats.

Meanwhile, the sun had not stopped for a power nap. Most everybody was already sweating and we were standing still. There was a quick round of stretches, mandatory sunscreen passed out, and then the whistles came.

Just like that, I was back into the flow of it. I caught glimpses of faces or players and numbers, but my brain was focused on only the details that matter. Who was left or right-footed, who had ball control to watch out for, if someone opened each feint the same way.

Stations rotated. We ran sprints for the beep test (we went inside for that; a few people were almost brought to tears by the air conditioning). More 3v3s. Goal kicks. Corner kicks. Juggling. 1v1's. Sit-ups.

By the time late afternoon rolled around and mosquitoes were swarming around anyone who slowed down below a jog, the whistles blew three times in succession, and the skills test was over. I think nearly everyone had started off the day nervous, but at a certain point, your brain didn't have enough energy to keep your legs running and be anxious about what your ranking would be. As I caught my breath, I could feel the thoughts come racing again. *Did I do well enough?* I thought that I had—I'd won most of my matchups, been able to juggle the longest of anyone in my station. I hadn't been able to see any other groups, however. It was possible I was just a small fish in a microscopic pond.

"OKAY!" Ludwig shouted. "You all go inside and shower. You smell very bad."

There were a few laughs at that.

"After you shower. We will have dinner, no evening session. This gives us time to compare notes, calculate scores, ranks, and put together teams. You will meet your team at breakfast tomorrow. Are there any questions?"

"Will we be able to change teams?" someone asked.

Ludwig's eye twitched. You could feel people slowly shift away from the guy who asked that to avoid being caught in the collateral damage of the death glare. "No. That's the whole point of us making teams. Do not be stupid."

There was nothing but tense, thick quiet interrupted by huffing for air for a few moments.

A lanky American coach beside Ludwig who seemed to have not gotten the memo about never smiling piped up. His name was Bronson. He'd been in charge of most of the running drills we'd done. "Um," Coach Bronson said, as if he was also slightly anxious to break the silence, "You guys can go shower now. Great work everyone!"

We broke off and split up, everyone immediately beginning to talk shop on who'd done well, who'd screwed up, who they thought teams and top contenders would be. I was too tired to join in and didn't have anybody I really knew to talk with, anyway. I sat underneath one of the massive trees, not bothering to swat at the mosquitoes that hovered around, and waited until the crowds had thinned out and the noise died down. I figured I would have the showers to myself while everybody else was at dinner. I didn't know anybody to sit with, bar Bryan. And honestly, I figured the mosquitoes were going to be just as annoying to sit with, so I might as well wait.

It was my last night eating alone at Weltmeister.

The next morning, I would have a team.

Chapter Four

"I have known you for all of thirty minutes, and I am one hundred percent, would-bet-my-life-on-it sure you are lying to me right now," Chandler said. Chandler had been the snarky, messy-haired one from the column runs. His demeanor at the breakfast table was basically the same as it had been during sprints.

"No, I'm serious," Martin said, his German accent thick. He looked like he should've been going to a camp for the other kind of football with how wide his shoulders and biceps were, and he held the unique title of being the only guy at the table—maybe the entire camp—with a worse haircut than mine. He didn't seem bothered. I wasn't sure if he just didn't care, or didn't realize his haircut was awful, or maybe he even thought it looked good, but whatever it was the guy's confidence almost let him pull it off. "Neither of them know about each other."

Chandler spouted the first real grin I'd seen on him, which quickly vanished as he took another sip of the coffee he insisted on drinking black. I don't think anybody else noticed, but he grimaced every time he took a sip. "You're absolutely not dating two girls right now, Martin."

"I am! Why don't you believe me!"

"Martin, Martin, listen—it's not that I think you're too ugly to pull it off," a kid from down the table by Freddie said, leaning halfway over his plates to shout down at him. He had a scar on his face, "I just don't think you're smart enough to keep it going."

There were some laughs at the table—including from Martin, who did a quick glance to make sure no coaches were watching and threw his empty milk carton in response.

Unfortunately, Martin chucked the carton not at the guy with the scar, but the guy with the scar's *twin*. I knew they were named Charles and Damian, but I couldn't remember which one was which. Also, I wasn't totally sure they were twins because I didn't want to be the guy staring at them like a creep trying to figure out, and there was no way to ask without sounding like a total idiot. So, I was staying quiet and hopefully un-creepy and un-idiotic.

Beside me, a hand flickered out and caught the milk carton mid-air before it could hit the wrong twin. Mateo put the empty carton down on the table, brushing his hair back with his free hand. "I hope you aim better with your feet than your hands."

"I wasn't trying," Martin said with the exact same tone he'd used to insist he had two girlfriends.

"Uh huh," Chandler muttered.

"Speaking of disasters with women," the kid with the scar continued. He had a slightly nasal voice. He turned and looked at Freddie, smirking. "You don't have this guy beat, Martin. If you want to talk about true womanizing, look no further."

"Oh my God," Freddie muttered, immediately blushing. "Dude, no, it's—"

"Freddie is too nice to be a player," Mateo said, tossing the empty milk carton back and forth in his hands. "Does he get girls? Yes, I'm sure. Does he play them? No. Freddie's not a player."

"Exactly the problem," the kid with the scar said. "There's this girl at home who has been head-over-heels for Freddie for, like, two years. Maybe since middle school."

"We're just friends," Freddie said, his face going steadily redder.

"And he is just absolutely not interested. It's a real power move. Freddie's just playing hard to get. She must put love letters in his locker, like—"—I could hear my dad saying *"Don't say like"*—"twice a semester. Actually, no, it was like twice a week."

"It was not twice a week. I mean, maybe twice a month, but—ugh. You're the worst," Freddie said, shaking his head. "I didn't want to hurt her feelings, okay? I'm just not really into her. Also, the letters thing was just one time. I knew I shouldn't have told you guys."

I was glad I got a lucky break and got at least one nice person on my team. I didn't think I'd wind up liking these guys as much as my cabin at Brightbirch but there's no worse feeling than joining a new team and them already knowing and liking each other and not wanting anyone coming in to shake that up. Even though Freddie had come with some of the guys here, he was cool. Given how my first day here had gone, this felt like winning the lottery.

The non-scarred twin was laughing at this, as well as one other guy from Freddie's home team I hadn't been able to get a good look at. Both of the maybe-twins were in pretty solid shape—they were a bit shorter than me but looked like they lifted weights or something. "Yeah, man, you can give Martin those love letters she writes you and maybe he can actually get a girl."

Martin started looking for another milk carton while Freddie did his best to turn invisible and slide under the table.

"If you guys want help with love letters, just ask Kit," The boy with the scar said. "I saw him writing some earlier."

It was my turn to feel my face go red. *Why did I think writing letters before breakfast here was a good idea? Don't write in your dorm, Kit, Richard might think you're weird, just do it in the cafeteria in front of everyone. The brilliant Kit Cook, everyone.* "Not love letters," I said, "Just writing home to one of my friends."

"Is she cute at least?" Martin asked.

"No, it's my buddy since like second grade. Sorry to disappoint."

"No girlfriend, huh?" Chandler asked. "Personally, I say that's a smart move, you'll save money being single. But if you're dead-set on one, maybe if you ask Martin really nice you can see if one of his imaginary girlfriends has a sister or something."

"No one believes in me," Martin sighed with faux despair. "Here I thought my team had my back, yet all they do is call me a liar—"

"I think writing letters is pretty neat, Kit," Miles said, giving me a clap on the back. I'm not great with names—you may have noticed—but I could remember Miles easily because he was the only guy with a British accent. He'd come over from London. He was lanky, with dark brown skin and a very cheery smile. I think he was trying to keep me from feeling singled out but it kinda just made it feel more like the spotlight was on me.

"Um, thanks," I said. "And not on my radar at the moment, Chandler. I've got too much schoolwork to really look at any relationship stuff."

There was a round of boos, which I took with a sheepish grin.

"I do not understand," said a Korean boy from the end of the table by Martin. His real name was Ye-Joon, but everyone just called him Slick. He had more pomade in his hair than the entire Outsiders crew put together. "Maybe it is different here. But why are you playing soccer if you're not trying to get girls? Literally the only reason I learned."

There were a few laughs at that. Including from me, but mine was mostly relief. Even Alejandro cracked a grin. He was seated at the far end of the table and seemed pretty shy. Or maybe his English just wasn't great—either way, the guy hadn't said a word.

I had more immediate concerns. Thank God they hadn't lingered on the letters stuff. The next six weeks were going to be long if I was getting roasted every day. I was just glad I hadn't mentioned my mom got the writing stuff for me. I mean, I love her, it was really nice of her, but oh man would that have made impressing these guys an uphill battle.

"He has a good point," Mateo said. "I met my girlfriend because she played on the girl's team."

"You'd date someone on your own team?" Martin asked.

"Low hanging fruit, Martin," Chandler said.

Martin scowled. "What does that mean?" He glanced at Slick and Alejandro, who both shrugged.

"Never mind."

Mateo ignored it. Most of us were just wearing standard athletic clothes, but he had on a pretty nice jersey from some club in Argentina I didn't immediately recognize. "But seriously, you—"

"Um, hey, Kit," I heard a voice say from the walkway beside the table.

It took me a second to register. When the other guys at the table went quiet and Mateo elbowed me I startled and turned to see who it was.

Bryan was standing there, tray in hand. His brown hair was still wet, like maybe he'd slept in and just now gotten out the shower and gotten down to the cafeteria. "Hey, uh, I didn't know if I could sit with you, if that's—"

His voice trailed off a bit and I could feel that pressure ratcheting back up, the same way it had been when Chandler had made his stupid comment earlier. "Hey, Bryan, uh, I think—first breakfast as a team and all, are you sure you don't want to be with yours?"

There was a pregnant pause as I realized that...if Bryan's team had wanted to be with him, he would already have been there. Had he already pissed them off this fast or something? Maybe he didn't even piss them off. Maybe he was just being too Bryan.

He didn't really have a great poker face. I felt like I kicked a puppy. He nodded, almost spilling his tray in the process. "Yeah, of course, I'll uh—yeah. See you around, man."

"Yeah, I—" I tried to think of what I was supposed to say there, if I should've walked it back and asked him to sit with us or if that would be worse, but he'd already walked off, head hunched down a bit. *Nice going, Kit.*

I had meant what I said, right? I wanted to just have time with my new team?

"That was tactful," said one of the other guys near Freddie, who I think had come with him. He had whatever those genes were that give you facial hair at, like, age thirteen, because he had a full-on five o'clock shadow. "Guy seemed kinda...."

"Annoying," Mateo said. "Anyway, as I was saying, we—"

We heard a whistle blow and the coaches started motioning for us to put dishes away and get ready for the day. *If Bryan's just now sitting down to eat, he's either going to be hungry all morning or throw up whatever he eats,* I thought. *Why did he oversleep?*

"Poor guy," Freddie said, still watching Bryan, the smile gone from his face. "Let's get going, guys."

We walked out as a group down to the field, which would turn out to be the last walking we did for the rest of that day. Ludwig barked at each team telling them where to go. We were up for conditioning first along with three or four other teams.

Bronson asked us all how we were doing, if we were settled in, told us we were all doing great, gave us a few inspirational quotes, and then commenced a death march.

"Great job everybody! Keep it up! Three more to go!" Coach Bronson yelled from the front of the line. He was leading us in what he called "five by fives", which basically meant a five-mile run. At each mile, we would stop and do some other form of exercise. It was clear the "five" was the miles, but none of us really understood why "by fives" was also included. I didn't have much free time to think about this more deeply, as we had just finished doing leg lifts for so long that my legs were already complaining. Martin was educating the back of the column in German curse words.

"Having fun yet?" Freddie asked me, shaking his legs out as we fell back into line and continued the run.

"Oh, you know it."

We resumed our pace, which was halfway between a jog and a steady run. Bronson was going for distance, not speed, but he was still going faster than my team back home when we did laps. Looping around the campus grounds, there were no aides with clipboards that we could see, so I think everyone was a bit more relaxed. If the coaches had been watching and noting who was leading the pack, there would've been people jockeying for the front.

We were running hard enough that keeping a steady conversation was hard but peppering in the occasional question wasn't impossible. All of Team Six—we had still yet to decide on a cooler name for ourselves—had started off together but mostly gotten split up over time. Freddie and I had stayed close to each other. I was okay with that—all the guys on the team seemed okay so far, but Freddie came off as the most down-to-earth.

Bronson, who seemingly was not even slightly out of breath, continued to yell out encouragement back down the line every quarter mile or so. I mostly focused on keeping my footing as we weaved between sidewalks and grassy fields and gravel.

"Going off-road! Watch your step!" he turned and led us between the rows of towering oaks along the edge of the practice fields. Half the camp was doing drills today, the other half conditioning. All of Team Six was on the run, with the lone exception of Mateo, who was with the other keepers, who evidently didn't need cardio. He clocked us running past and grinned, offering a mock-royal wave as we went past. Less flattering gestures were given back to him. The other teams on the field turned to watch us—some with pity, some with smirks.

The grass turned into pine straw, the pine straw into dirt, the dirt into thick gnarled roots and little branches. Everybody slowed a bit trying to keep their pace, and the uneven ground made my thighs and calves burn a bit more.

"You burn more calories on uneven ground," I huffed, high-kneeing over a fallen limb. "Fun fact for the day."

"Huh," Freddie said. "Guess that makes sense. This feels harder." He wiped some sweat off of his brow and glanced around the column a bit. We were solidly near the middle. "Biology class paying off, huh?"

"Yeah, yeah, whatever. I don't see any poetry to interpret out here, either."

"I'll let you make fun of English class if history stays off-limits." Freddie said, grinning.

"Alright, deal. What kind of history do you like the most, anyway?"

Bronson blew the whistle, which meant the pace picked up. Every few minutes we'd have to sprint for thirty seconds and then settle back into a normal pace. I ignored the lactic acid building up everywhere below my neck and hammered through until the next whistle blow.

"Where were we?" Freddie asked, huffing.

"What kind of history."

"Oh, right, right—uh, U.S. History. Probably 1800s. Old West and stuff."

"You want to be a cowboy?"

Freddie scrunched his face and looked around us at the huge line of players following Coach Bronson. "Hey, I'd say it beats being the cow right about now, huh?"

"Yeah, that's fair. Hopefully we don't get branded."

The next whistle blow was push-ups, which lanky Coach Bronson somehow churned out, with claps, faster than anybody else. "Great job, guys! Two more! This is going to make you guys dominate when you get back home to your teams!"

"He has to be on drugs," I heard Chandler say from somewhere behind us.

We hoisted ourselves up with aching arms and the run went on. Freddie and I swapped get-to-know-you facts. Freddie was from a military family going back to the Civil War. He talked his dad into soccer camp over some ROTC-esque boot camp. I was a sucker for old martial arts movies, none of which Freddie had seen. I was obligated to give him at least a dozen recommendations. Freddie had moved around a lot, courtesy of the military family. I'd stayed in the same place more-or-less my whole childhood (we'd moved when I was three years old, but that doesn't really count).

The last whistle came—a hundred-yard sprint back to the practice fields. I pulled back on the throttle just a hair to keep pace with Freddie. He was by no means a slowpoke, just not as fast as me. We slowed our momentum down to a jog and took in air, Freddie crossing his hands across the top of his head to fill his lungs faster.

"Wishing you'd gone to military camp yet?" I asked.

Freddie grinned.

"Loved the hustle out there, guys, great speed, great endurance," Bronson said, as though we'd, you know, had a choice between running fast and not running fast. "Let's go grab cleats, a quick sip of water, then meet back out here in ten minutes. Second half of the morning is scrimmages."

"Wait, aren't we swapping?" someone asked. Bronson shook his head. "Nope. They're running tomorrow. You guys are playing the teams who were practicing drills."

What? We were playing the guys who'd been doing nothing but light jogging and dribbling exercises?

In ten minutes?

Chapter Five

We sat, sliding in shin guards and lacing up cleats while Team Three stood across the field juggling balls and idly passing back and forth. I could feel the sun beating down on the back of my neck as I tightened mine and listened to Bronson.

"Listen, guys. There will be games where maybe you're a man down, or didn't rest well, or any number of things. This is practice for that. You get used to going uphill in practice, so it's second nature when you have to for a game. C'mon guys! You got this."

Nobody on our team said anything back to him. I could feel Chandler's whole body tensing from the exertion of biting his tongue.

"Now, before you all start getting upset—these aren't being factored into your tournament rankings. These are just casual scrimmages. Stand-out performances will be noted by the coaches, of course, but this isn't going to count against your team's standing."

"Who knows, maybe we'll go against a weak team." Freddie said.

Damian (who I'd finally figured out was the twin with the scar) raised an eyebrow. "Maybe Wilhelm will give us ice cream instead of suicides tomorrow too, Freddie."

Freddie shrugged.

From mid-field, Ludwig whistled, catching Bronson's attention.

"You'll do great," Bronson said, clapping his hands together. He had not once stopped smiling. "We'll start in five minutes, gentlemen."

"Okay, everyone!" Ludwig bellowed. *Wow, he has some lungs on him.* "We now split up for team scrimmages. This will be same rules as a standard game, except each half is only thirty-five minutes. Got it?"

The coaches were going to be refereeing. All the teams—those who had been conditioning and those who had been running drills—were centered around the practice field, and began getting split up to where they'd be playing. As if to prove my luck would not turn around anytime soon, we got Ludwig as ours. *Well, at least he's going to be super strict to both sides. God help the fool who Ludwig has to red card.*

"Okay, huddle up," Victor said. By this point I'd confirmed that he, Freddie, and the twins were all from the same high school. *We better hope it's the best high school team in the state,* I thought, trying to clock if anyone on the other team looked even moderately winded. "Everyone know their positions?"

"Hey, who made you captain?" Slick said.

"I did, nobody else was doing it. I'm captain back home, so..."

"I'm also captain back home too," Slick said.

"Yeah, me too," Miles said, grinning.

"I'm Spartacus."

"Chandler, I think me, you, and Kit are the only ones who've seen that," Victor said, in the same tone that your Mom says, *"Maybe that's not the outfit you want to wear to school today."*

You, Kit, and I, I thought, on reflex.

"We just got here, I would've said I was captain otherwise," Martin said.

"Pretty sure literacy's a requirement for being team captain," Chandler muttered under his breath.

"Whatever that was, Charles, don't want to hear it."

"That was Chandler, *I'm* Charles, why do people keep—"

"Hey, guys!" Freddie said, in the loudest and most authoritative tone I'd heard from him. He blinked after everybody actually stopped talking and turned to him, taking a second to find his voice again. "Uh, we already wasted a few minutes, and team Three already seems ready to go. Let's just let Victor do it this time and then we can figure things out for next time later."

There was a general chorus of mumbled agreements.

"We didn't even have captains last year," Mateo said to me as Victor helped hash out who was going where. There were a few disputes over who got to be striker, but Freddie seemed to be peacemaking well enough.

"Wait, really? I'd assumed we'd vote on them at some point or something."

"We don't need them."

I frowned. I'd already gotten dibs on left midfield, so I wasn't too concerned with everyone else's positions. "Hey, why didn't you just tell them that?"

Mateo grinned as he pulled on some keeper's gloves that may have cost more than the Beast did. "It was funny to watch."

Ludwig blew his whistle loud enough to give everyone early-onset tinnitus, and the game was on.

There was a definite lack of morale, something as visible to me as a storm cloud pouring down over just our half the field. We were slower jogging out to our positions, and the guys on the opposite side had an eager confidence, sizing us up and thoroughly enjoying the odds. I had a sudden pang of sympathy for being the slow zebra by the watering hole. *We need to play conservatively,* I thought, *but we wasted all our strategizing time bickering.*

I was a bit frustrated our first real, full scrimmage at Weltmeister was us fighting at such a disadvantage. That said, I'd played a man down before, or games on back-to-back days in the losers' bracket when everyone was still sore.

It was winnable.

Team Three got possession first, and their left striker (who must've been half-giraffe, the guy was at least 6'5) passed it back to their center. Our forwards—Victor and Slick—brought the pressure. The rest of Freddie's group who had come to camp together had opted to be defenders, both to make choosing positions go faster and to put their synergy to best use. Freddie had known better than to say it out loud, but our defense was going to be doing most of the work this game.

I followed them in, keeping a careful distance. My eyes flickered across the field. Their right striker was Oliver, who either hadn't seemed to notice me or hadn't cared. I moved in close enough to guard him if the ball came his way.

They were making crisp, smooth passes between each other, keeping the ball cautiously on their half of the field. Victor and Slick were pursuing but didn't have the gas tanks to hound them very aggressively. I watched their short passes, too precise and well-timed to be picked off easily. I couldn't shake the mental image of a cobra swaying back and forth, waiting, watching. The other midfielders and I pushed along behind them, trying to cut off their angles. I could see, just from the movements of our team, everyone had come to more-or-less the same conclusion I had. We didn't have the energy left to pressure them all game. We were going to have to be reactive, as frustrating as that was.

What are they waiting for? I wondered. We stole possession briefly, then a pass from Victor back to Martin was intercepted, and they kicked the ball back to an open player.

It was going to be at least four or five seconds before we could get anywhere within range to pressure them, and it clicked into my head a heartbeat too late.

While we were running, they'd been learning strategic field use and ball movement.

Their left fullback shouted something I couldn't quite make out, launched the ball as if his leg had been a howitzer, and their strikers took off at a dead sprint.

Victor and Slick turned as if they were in slow motion, but I was already running, backpedaling for half a second before my brain could clock the trajectory. I turned and sprinted, trying to force the dull ache out of my thighs and calves and move in.

I could hear the thundering of footsteps behind me, and Oliver's hand-painted cleats came into my peripheral vision.

I was coming close to where Freddie and our other defenders were positioned. They were moving in to where the ball was dropping, but Team Three's left striker was going to get there first. Too many of our defenders were going over to try to stop him: they'd made us overcommit, and none of our guys realized it.

Oliver caught up to me, swinging out far to the right side of the field.

He's wide open for the cross, I realized. *That pulled them left. We're clumping up like a bunch of toddlers who've never played before.*

I adjusted course and moved to cover Oliver, shouting for Charles to peel and cut off his angle. It felt like I was pushing harder than I had even in the column sprints, but after two seconds, maybe three, Oliver was pulling ahead of me.

"CHARLES!" I screamed.

Charles turned, but he wasn't going to be able to move over and cut Oliver off in time—and running my absolute hardest, I realized I wasn't going to be able to catch up either. It wouldn't matter if I could beat him in a 1 on 1. He'd have a shot on goal before I could get there to contest him.

I turned my focus off from where the ball was and the scramble to keep it from their striker. My mind was fixed entirely on beating Oliver to the goal. I could tell exactly what they'd done and what they were doing, where I needed to be to stop him from making any plays. I just couldn't get my legs there in time.

I thought about being late the first day, Mom speaking in German, Kyle leaving, Patrick snickering, every negative thing that had happened thus far, and tried to just pour it all on like gasoline into a fire. My legs were burning from the sprint, but the distance started to close, a few inches, then feet, then I was on Oliver's heels.

The ball came soaring in. The pass was surgical—it came down a half pace ahead of Oliver. It couldn't have been smoother if there'd been no defenders on the field and the other striker had a hundred tries to line it up.

Oliver tapped it with a single touch and sent it in the bottom right corner. Mateo hit the ground trying to stop it as the ball hit the net.

The most infuriating whistle blast of the summer cut through the air, and I slowed my pace to a stop.

Oliver turned, looking at me as if noticing me for the first time. "Slow, 64." He turned and jogged back to his side of the field, getting some high fives, which he didn't seem too enthused about. That severe cloud still hung about him. He settled back in his position and watched as Mateo hurled the ball over to the ref.

Alejandro let out a string of curses under his breath, which was the longest sentence I'd heard from him so far. Actually, it might've been the only words I'd heard from him so far. I wasn't paying attention. Freddie was telling everybody to shake it off and get back in position, but I wasn't listening to that, either. *Slow, 64.*

I should've gotten there ahead of him. I saw what they were doing, I'd just been too slow to react. I didn't move quickly enough, I didn't cut him off, I didn't even yell to Charles to do it in time. *I wanted to beat him, and I couldn't.*

"Hey, man," Freddie said. Some part of my brain recognized he was speaking to me. "It's all good, we got this."

We set up for kickoff, the whistle came, and the game resumed.

Our team shifted to being more cautious, leery of being overextended again. The consequence was—and whether they had planned it this way or it was just opportunism, I couldn't tell—they muscled ahead and took solid control of the midfield. I'm not sure we took the ball into their half of the field more than three or four times after that. When the whistle blew for halftime, they'd racked up another goal, and we had nothing to show.

Everyone needed time to suck down water and air before we could talk. I had figured people would start blaming each other. I'd figured correctly. I didn't join in because I had nobody to be pissed at but myself. Freddie and Miles tried to talk people down. Martin wanted to shift positions around entirely. Victor argued that we were starting to play better as the half went on so he should stay striker. Slick said we would be winning if the defense was doing their job. Charles replied with suggestions as to some courses of actions Slick could take in regard to his head and his rear end.

"You good?" Chandler asked. He was sipping water from a plastic cup, slowly, checking his shoelaces. He was on the opposite wing as I was, muddied from sliding for the ball on more than one occasion.

"No," I said. "I'm pretty angry."

Chandler shrugged. "Use it."

"Gee, thanks, coach." I took a deep breath and took another small sip of water. "What do you think we should do?"

Chandler shook his head. "It won't be popular."

"Humor me."

"Alright. We pull back two from the midfield—you and me—and put them on the defense. We run a diamond in front of the goal, put the two of us parallel to it, and the center midfielders maybe twenty feet in front of that. Forwards go where our midfielders are right now."

I envisioned it. I didn't need to be Sun Tzu to see the problems. "No offense whatsoever. No way for us to get to Slick and Victor. Not a winning play."

"Let's face it, this one's lost," he said, quietly. "We can't win, but we could probably hold them to two goals if we play it smart."

"Bronson said it wasn't going to count."

"Yeah, Bronson said that. But c'mon. If the coaches see us getting absolutely annihilated, even if they don't put any numbers down on their notes to officially reflect it, they're still going to look at us and think 'oh yeah, I saw those guys get beat 7-0 yesterday.' Everything we do here matters for recruiters, no matter what they're telling us or what they're putting in their notes."

I thought about it. There was a cold, triage logic to it. I didn't doubt that he was probably correct—across the field, the guys on Team Three's bench were standing up, juggling the ball, laughing, and we were sitting down, arguing and drinking as much water as we dared without risking cramps or vomiting. I'd been in games like this before, where there was that invisible momentum shift, and a sort of psychological pressure builds up over time. It would be hard to score three goals—or even to tie it up—and keep our defense tight enough to hold them at two. We weren't coordinated enough to make our current set-up work, but trying to change positions

Chapter Six

Freddie stirred at his cereal a bit, chewing on his lip. "Did a lot of people see?"

Martin snorted. "Everybody saw. I mean, I feel bad for the guy, you know, but—like, wow. It was wild."

"Explain to me," Mateo piped up, "Why he has the nickname, though? Am I missing something?" I was impressed by Mateo's confidence. His English was excellent—he'd apparently studied abroad in London where he'd met Miles—and despite being the smallest guy on the team, he didn't really back down from talking smack to anyone. The fact he could out-sprint all of us maybe contributed to that.

Martin waved his hand dismissively. "No, it's not a language thing. Mole Rat because when the other guy slide tackled him, his pants came off, like, completely, and there was no hair down there at all."

"And a single, very large mole," Chandler said, swooshing his hair back. "I honestly think he should see a doctor, I'm not even kidding."

There were some chuckles up and down the table. I didn't join in, and I noticed Freddie didn't either. All I could think was if that happened to me. I'd have to join witness protection or something because there was absolutely no chance I would ever let myself be seen in public again. Having to jog out onto the field with Freddie while the rest of the camp had already started practice had made my skin crawl. Just thinking about being out on the field, completely naked from the waist down, and then everyone laughing at you? I shuddered. I would rather miss every goal for the rest of the summer or get ranked as the absolute worst player than have to go through that.

"Aw man," Freddie said. "That's...that's rough."

"Quite unfortunate," Miles, said in agreement. He held his hands under his chin and surveyed the room. "What's his actual name? Mole Rat is hardly what I'd want to be called."

"No idea," Martin said. "I mean, I feel sorry for the guy, but...but it is funny."

Miles gave him a nod of admission, and a slight grin, but still winced. "Let's change the subject, shall we?"

"Who do you guys think is the best team?" Chandler asked.

"Obviously us, you guys have me," Freddie said, flexing his arms, which made everybody chuckle. Freddie wasn't bad by any means, it—it's hard to explain, I guess? He just had the energy of the table figured out. Like no one actually thought Freddie was bad, or that he thought he was a legend. It seemed to knead the tension of talking about the poor Mole Rat kid away. As well as the fact that some team would have to be ranked last at the end of all this, and, well. Nobody wanted to be Mole Rat, I suppose, in any capacity.

I felt awful. I didn't even know the guy's name and his whole summer was already ruined.

"I don't know if we've played enough to know," Charles said.

"I agree," I said. "I think we probably need a few scrimmages to really know." *Maybe we'll actually manage to win some of them, too.*

"Team Three has the one guy that hit the goal from half-field yesterday." Martin said. "That was crazy."

"He had lame cleats, though," Mateo said, as though this was a factor that would actually be included in the rankings.

"Oliver," I added. *Slow, 64.*

"Yeah, him." Martin nodded. "He may be the best so far, but the coaches haven't put rankings out yet."

"Best team won't be there until halfway through the summer," Chandler said.

"You mean there's more guys coming?" Charles said.

Chandler frowned. "No, not like that. I mean—look, right now, there's maybe a couple teams who just came with all the guys from their teams back home, and they're probably 'the best'," he put down the mug to do air quotes, "—but I don't think that necessarily means they're going to stay the best."

"I don't understand, if they're the best, they're the best." Martin said, cutting into his fifth pancake.

"I get it," I said.

"Then explain, Charles isn't making sense to me."

"I'm Chandler, *he's* Charles."

I saw Martin grinning, which made me realize he was screwing up their names on purpose. *How did he learn them so fast? It took me way longer.*

"Whatever, just—you talk, Kit."

I glanced over at Mateo, who nodded like he was already agreeing with me. "What he means is right now there's maybe a few teams that came with some synergy, or like ours, where Freddie and his guys have experience with each other but not the rest of us. Or maybe some teams have a guy like Oliver who's extremely good on his own, but probably not good enough to carry them to number one. So, what he's saying is who's best is going to come down to who figures out how to, you know—play well together."

"Careful, Kit, you're starting to sound like my guidance counselor." Freddie said.

I grinned, and he got a few laughs, but, again, they didn't feel malicious. I couldn't really put it into words.

"So, Kit," Mateo said, turning to talk to me as Chandler and Martin got into an argument over the ranking system. "These letters. Walk me through it. You sure you're not writing to a girl, man? You can just tell us. Unlike Martin, I don't think you'd be making it up." He nodded towards the letter writing stuff I had. I'd brought it and started writing before everybody else got here. Honestly, after the razzing the first morning, nobody really made a big deal out of it, and I was too tired at night to sit down and write. I normally despised getting up early, but getting to land the table closest to the French toast station so you could see when fresh ones came out made it worth it. Almost.

Plus it felt like Mateo was actually sorta interested and not just setting me up for a roast or something. I hoped.

"Nah," I said. "Writing to some of my friends."

"Friends plural," Mateo said. "Look at Mr. Popular."

"Yeah, I wish. Just my buddy Kyle, and a few of my friends at another camp."

"Why the letter writing at all, though?" Mateo frowned. "You don't just text him?"

"I don't have a phone. They said they weren't allowed."

Mateo gave me a sly grin. "Ah, Kit. I remember when I was just a young, naïve first-timer at Weltmeister, all innocent and clueless."

I was pretty sure his first summer was, you know, last year. "What are you talking about?"

Mateo raised an eyebrow at me. "You know like half the guys smuggle phones in, right?"

"Don't you get kicked out if they find you using one?"

"Yeah, so you just make sure they don't find one," Mateo said, as if explaining to a four-year-old. I think he realized it came off rude, so he followed it up fast. "But, uh, the letters are cool. Maybe I'll borrow one from you later? My girlfriend would like the old-fashioned romance." He glanced down at my stuff. "Might cross your name off the stationery first, though."

"Oh, totally, yeah." I shifted my stuff out of the way to make sure no coffee or cereal milk or anything got on it. Or maybe it was to give my burning face a second to return to a normal color. There was really no way of telling which of the two it was. "Of course, I can help you out. So, you've been here before?"

Mateo nodded. "Two years—well, I mean, this is my second year. I recognize a few kids from last year, but I think most people graduated, so I don't see a ton of familiar faces. They try to keep the teams together, mostly, but the only guys left from mine came from a school together, and I don't see them here." He shrugged. "Must've gone to a different camp or something."

"Anything crazy I should expect?"

"I hear they might make us start running one of these days," Chandler muttered into his plate.

I smirked, but Mateo didn't hear it.

"Eh, not really. It's pretty straightforward, for the most part."

I tried to think of any other questions somebody who had been here the year before might know. "Did anybody get sent home last year?"

Mateo frowned. "Not that I can remember...but there were enough people I couldn't fully tell. I mean, I remember people saying they knew of someone who got sent home, but never anybody who actually got sent home."

Chandler and I met eyes, both thinking for a minute.

"Well, as long as it's not me. I was wondering—"

My voice trailed off as I noticed Bryan walking by with a tray, hair wet. God, was this guy just always late?

I saw as he went by the table across the aisle from us, a few guys—they looked older, maybe seniors—glancing up at him and snickering not particularly subtly as he went past. Bryan walked faster, not making eye contact with me, and booked it around the corner.

"Poor guy," Miles muttered.

The people at the other table continued smirking until someone said something I couldn't hear that made a couple of them laugh out loud. It took a moment to click for me. *He's Mole Rat,* I realized.

I felt my stomach drop just as hard as it had when they told us were scrimmaging after a morning of running sprints. He was out of earshot, but it was clear he'd heard the snickering. I should've invited him to come sit with us, but he clearly thought I was a jackass now because he just walked on past. A part of me was telling me that I should go find Bryan so I could invite him to come sit with us anyway. I mean, his team definitely had to be icing him out at this point. It's what Kyle would've done, I thought. Kyle would not have cared if other people were laughing. Actually, he would've cared, but he would've been able to beat them up so it wouldn't have bothered him, per se.

That part of me was making noise inside my head, but I stayed seated. The guys at the other table were still laughing, craning their necks to try to get a look at him.

"Anyway, you were saying, Kit?"

"Yeah, I, uh—remind me what we were talking about?"

The conversation slowly resumed, but I didn't say too much more.

If I'd let him sit with us maybe the rest of the guys wouldn't have wanted to sit with me. I tried to tell myself it was because I needed to bond with my team, we needed to develop camaraderie and everything else coaches always said so we could perform for the scouts, but absolutely none of that made the somersaults stop. *I just didn't want to be a loser. Nice going, Kit.*

"I'm going to go back to the dorm and get ready for morning session," I said after a few more minutes. I got a few goodbyes from those not actively chattering and put my dishes away. I took one of Martin's several plates with me. My team felt right, already. Freddie and his guys were obviously more tightly knit than the rest of us, but the other Team Six guys all seemed friendly and warm. We had a few free agents like me, a few who had come as smaller parts of a bigger team, but nobody seemed like a total jerk.

I suppose maybe I did now. I just didn't want to screw up not having to be alone within the first week. I just hadn't expected it. It had been so sudden and I didn't really know what to do, if he came up again I would let him sit with me, but of course he wasn't about to come ask to sit with me again.

I was back at the dorm. I'd been replaying that stupid scene in my head the whole time and my legs went on autopilot. What if they were back at the table calling me out? Did anybody else care? I couldn't get that first day feeling, of showing up late and having to jog out in front of the entire camp, unprepared, looking like a freaking idiot, out of my head.

Freddie had stuck his neck out for me, though.

I'll find him and try to make it up to him, I told myself, which helped with the guilt. A bit. I felt like I'd already screwed up too majorly to do much about it.

Back in my dorm, I changed into all my gear (barring cleats—there was a zero percent chance I made it down the stairs in those without wiping out) and still had thirty minutes to kill.

I needed to do something that wasn't thinking about Mole Rat. About Bryan. That was his name, not freaking Mole Rat.

I figured I would work on finishing my letter. Writing had the added benefit of helping me not think about how sore my legs were. The coaches had told us to lie down with our legs propped up to help with soreness. *You know what also helps with soreness, Wilhelm? Not running.*

I scratched the pen on the packaging the letters had come in to get it running, then started to write.

Kyle,

How's it going? I think this is the first time I've written a letter since we had to do it in third grade, so apologies to you and Mrs. Evans if I mess something up. I also have no idea where the mailbox is on this campus, so there's a possibility you receive fifteen of these at the end of the summer. Or maybe the coaches read through and confiscate our mail the way prison wardens do.

I paused, blinking.

I guess that joke doesn't really work if you haven't met the coaches, but they're not the warm and fuzzy type. Also I'm probably the only person writing mail. Whatever, you know what I meant.

I was nailing this letter.

How's Colorado? I'm jealous if the temperature there is anything below what it is here.

Talking about the weather, Kit. Just because you're writing a letter doesn't mean you have to make small talk like you're ninety years old.

Anyways, I apologize for not being able to text you like a normal human, but no cell phones allowed (also I am currently grounded—wonder whose fault that was). Or, so they said—one of my teammates said some of the kids sneak them in, so maybe I'll give you a call later on if that's true (you should write back with your number though, because I 100% do not have it memorized). I'm having fun for the most part—at least, now I am. The first few days were a bit rough because I didn't know anybody, but things seem to have stabilized for the most part now but I finally got placed with a team and they're pretty good guys, both at soccer and in general. Guess you can relate to that.

Even if you tried to keep Mole Rat from sitting with you.

I shook my head and took a deep breath.

There is more running than you can imagine, but I can already feel like I'm learning a lot, and I'll be a lot better by summer's end than I would have just scrimmaging at home with my team a couple times a week for fun or something. I know the idea of getting better at a real sport is probably foreign to you, but rest assured it's a really satisfying feeling. The dorms themselves are pretty nice, though—

I stopped again. Something about trying to put into words that having to share the showers with everybody on the hall felt, you know, weird. I don't know. Like I was sitting in the room writing the letter naked or something. And even though I felt like I could tell Kyle pretty much anything, I couldn't shake the notion he might laugh. Or, I don't know. Tell someone else we both knew from back home.

He'd never done anything like that before (*or anything, like, say, telling a kid he can't sit with you because he's not cool enough*) but for some reason as the thought crossed my mind it seemed so suddenly possible, like it was such a massive risk to even hint at that to anyone. Even though the bathrooms at boarding schools everywhere probably sucked, so this wasn't even a really uncommon opinion to have. And who actually enjoyed hall showers? Aside from psychopaths or something.

I looked at the page for another minute.

Though the eggs are pretty terrible. I'm not sure how, because even I can make eggs, and the rest of the food is okay. The usual day is waking up, breakfast, morning drills (mostly the more boring stuff) then lunch, a bit of downtime for a nap, afternoon drills (we get to do more scrimmages here, so it's more fun), dinner, then we have an evening session which is usually watching tape of games or games to relax and stuff. Dodgeball, tug-of-war, that kind of thing. Mateo (went here last year, he's from Argentina, I think his family's loaded so I'm being nice to him)(I'm kidding)(well, I mean, I am being nice to him—you know what I mean) says they even will let us play manhunt later in the summer if we all hit certain benchmarks, which everyone's pretty hyped up for. The campus is super huge. It's like Hogwarts, but the only things that are trying to kill us are the breakfast bar and the coaches.

I glanced at the clock. I had ten minutes to get down to the field, and I'd been making sure I was there with at least five minutes to spare every day since my less than stellar first impression.

Anyways, I need to run (literally and figuratively) so I'll write later. Remember to put your number on the letter back. Also, send a letter back.

Sincerely,

Kit

P.S. When we watch tape of soccer games, nobody gets put to sleep. Has your baseball team ever managed to do that?

I smirked and tucked all the stuff inside my desk, which was completely empty aside from the letter writing supplies Mom had given me. It felt oddly sacrilegious to have a desk without anything for studying. Mine back home was usually stacked with books and sorted binders to keep everything for all of my classes straight. I wasn't the most organized person I knew, but not keeping track of everything was a quick way to fall behind in tough classes.

Which is all to say, I was enjoying not having any homework, but I did miss being challenged by it. Soccer had cerebral challenges to it for sure, but I missed the feeling of studying hard and acing a test.

I jogged down to the field and joined up with the rest of my team—Team Six, though we were feverishly debating cooler names than that—and before too much more time had passed, we were in the thick of it.

Once we'd been assigned teams, the drills started ratcheting up. In terms of conditioning, it stayed about as tough as it had been before, but the drills rapidly became more complex, and far more punishing. Playing against other teams, the nerves were always there. Coaches and aides were jotting down turnovers, goals scored, things like that. I don't know how robust of a system they had, but you couldn't shake the feeling every time you stumbled or missed a shot, it got logged down somewhere.

Beyond that, you were playing against people who felt the exact same way. Any time we came head-to-head with another team, things felt as intense as they normally did during post-season playoffs. And the actual camp tournament hadn't even started yet.

Morning drills became lunch. I kept an eye out for Bryan but wasn't able to see him. Lunch became a power nap (Richard snored). Power nap became Coach Bronson taking us on what had to be at least a ten-mile run, letting us know it was "just one more lap" around the campus each time. The run became showers (or waiting out everybody else for the showers in my case). Showers became dinner. Dinner became watching an old World Cup match and Wilhelm pointing out all the mistakes both teams made, all the excellent plays, all the moments and techniques he approved of. Tape became sleep.

I got to spend more time with Freddie, who was the guy on the team—hell, the whole camp—who was the easiest for me to talk to, even if it was tricky to get one-on-one time with him when his high school teammates were always hanging around. On one of those occasions, we'd gotten busy talking about how one of our games had gone before I realized he'd followed me into my dorm building.

"Hey, wait," I paused, the hamster too tired from Ludwig's drills to push the wheel in my brain any faster. "Are...we in the same dorm?"

It was Freddie's turn to arch an eyebrow, grinning a bit. "Uh, yeah. I noticed day one."

My cheeks burned. "Oh. Yeah. Duh." It had been a little over a week and I'm sure I had to have *noticed* Freddie coming to my dorm at some point, I just never processed it. Although he knew I was here too and hadn't brought it up. "Wait, why—why were you letting me walk back alone from dinner every night?"

Freddie's grin got wider and his eyes gleamed like he was about to ask me to be a part of the crew for a heist. "Dude, don't tell anybody, but if you wait until everyone clears out, you can just go ask the kitchen staff for extra cookies and they'll hook you up."

"They'll give you more than one just for asking nicely? Are you serious?"

Freddie nodded, the warmth melting. "But I'm serious, you tell anybody and I'll have to kill you. That's what a second, fresh-out-the-oven cookie is worth to me, Kit."

I laughed. It occurred to me that I hadn't mentioned the first day yet. It had been on the forefront of my mind when Freddie and I were first placed on a team together, but there had been so much going on between getting acclimated to the routine, nonstop drills, and—and, well, the stuff with Bryan—to bring it up. Besides, like I said, there wasn't much of a chance to talk one-on-one with him, and I didn't feel like hashing it out in front of anyone else on the team. I realized he had bothered to remember I'd taken Biology, which I'd just mentioned off the cuff early on.

I wanted to say thanks, not just for taking the hit with me the first day, but for...just being nice in general. There was something about Weltmeister that was fun, rewarding, challenging—but there was always the sense in every conversation of wondering who in the group had the higher ranking, who had the fastest mile time. I hadn't felt that in a single conversation Freddie had been a part of. Talking with him made all the stuff I'd worried about the whole ride up and all the weeks before coming to Weltmeister feel almost silly. He'd make sure to include me in the conversation when the guys from his high school were making some kind of inside joke or tell me when I played well (even when I, uh, maybe didn't). That was—that was genuinely cool of him, and I wanted to say that, and say thanks, but I couldn't really articulate it. It felt like telling Kyle about how weird the dorm showers were. It would have felt like coming wildly underdressed to a party or having to go jogging out in front of everyone again, so visibly late and unprepared.

But I guess now was as good a time as any. If I didn't say anything, it'd seem ungrateful, anyway. I had to say *something*.

"That was, uh, really cool of you to have done, by the way." I wiped some sweat away, my weight going from one foot then to the other. I noticed Freddie's brow starting to furrow a bit, and I could feel myself getting redder. *Is he—was that weird? Did I say something weird?*

After a moment it clicked. *He has no idea what you're talking about, genius.* "Oh, um, the first day. The first day, I mean. Sorry that was—yeah. You got the evil eye from the coaches for being late with me and you didn't even know me. Thanks, man." *Stuck the landing, Cook.*

Freddie smiled. "No worries, it, uh, it just felt like the right thing to do, you know? Don't mention it."

Something about his tone seemed evasive, as if he wanted to hurry past it as much as I did. Was he just humble, or was it something else? I tried to remember the details of that first afternoon, which hadn't even been two weeks ago, but already felt like years and years.

I wanted to give Freddie a hug, but before I could make my feet move some part of me thought it would be awkward or weird or something. For a minute all I could think about was the first time we'd done the zipline at Brightbirch and despite knowing the harness and safety lines and all were going to catch me, I was just looking over the ledge and thinking about how I'd turn into modern art if I jumped off. Before I could figure out why I was thinking that or remind myself it was completely normal, —or really figure out any of this and why it was weird—Freddie said, "Let's get ready. I think we'll do fine in scrimmages."

"Uh, yeah, we will for sure."

The next few days settled into a routine like that one, though the individual components varied. We had dodgeball one night instead of tape, lots of short sprints and scrimmages instead of distance on Wednesdays, and occasionally Richard snored on the Richter scale instead of at mere foghorn volume.

I got to know the other, less chatty guys on the team better. There was Victor, who kept attempting not-so-subtly to ask about my GPA after I made the mistake of mentioning I was taking all honors and AP classes next year. Alejandro continued to say very little, but what he did say was quite friendly. And Slick, whose continued commitment to the Elvis hair maintenance even in the Weltmeister summer heat never failed to amaze me. I don't think any of us had the heart to tell him he was the better part of a century behind on the haircut. Who knows? Maybe he'd be the one to bring it back around.

Also I couldn't throw stones when it came to haircuts. Maybe I should've asked him for advice.

Whenever we weren't playing or running—and you may have noticed but we were running a lot—we were usually having a dumb argument at meals (by we, I mean Martin and Chandler), where we all ate together more often than not. Usually, all eleven of us were there, with the occasional loss of someone who just wanted to eat quickly and catch up on sleep, or if someone had a friend they knew from the year before tag along.

I was surprised how little time it took to start to feel like I had gotten the swing of things. Not the soccer parts, I mean—those came naturally already. Those were familiar. The...social parts, I guess. I'd worried it'd be a summer of saying nothing and nodding, because the first time I mentioned I'd taken an AP class Mateo had outright booed and Martin had asked how often I actually *went* to the class. It turned out Chandler wasn't a stranger to all-nighters studying, and it was a reassurance to just have one other person have a foot in jock and nerd territory at once, I suppose. The team started coalescing. I wrote some letters home and to my Brightbirch buddies, but it didn't feel as much like I was writing to ask for money to spend at the jail commissary anymore. I had stories to tell them.

It was just shy of two weeks in that I learned the answer to one of my first questions at Weltmeister. We'd been speculating whether or not anyone actually went home early.

We found out, in a way.

Bryan had quit.

Chapter Seven

As the weeks went on, I started to understand Weltmeister, until all of a sudden I didn't.

It got tougher and tougher to tell you what happened on specific days. The routine started to make sense, and then it started to become second nature. My sense of time started shifting more to what I was feeling or doing rather than a calendar day or time. I could relate something specific to a really funny moment at lunch, or a particularly grueling set of sprints, or the tension of a viciously fought game. In a way, the routine started to feel good—I knew what was coming up, what to expect, what to do.

And then Weltmeister started making about as much sense as it had on the drive in. Frankly, most things stopped making sense. I suppose it's not fair to put the blame on Weltmeister.

There wasn't a ton of talking at the breakfast table the day after we got absolutely stomped by Team Three. Or lunch table, or dinner. There was mostly running, and fuming, and it was an even split whether someone was mad at themselves or somebody else on the team.

To be fair, we were all pretty pissed at Bronson and Ludwig. Freddie or Miles would chip in with an icebreaker. It'd hang in the silence for a few moments, the tension would thoroughly freeze back over, and then we'd move on to the next station.

Over the next few days we shook the bitterness off. With all the running, there wasn't enough energy to stay actively angry around the clock. Besides that, nothing helps you get over a loss like absolutely stomping some other team, and we managed that more than a few times. We scrimmaged every single day. Some were specifically designed like the one we'd gotten crushed in: there was some caveat or condition we needed to follow, or a new aspect of training the coaches wanted to see us implement more thoroughly. We had games where we had to pass the ball at least five times before each shot on goal, games where we had a maximum five touches on the ball before we had to pass, games where we had to play a man down.

Once we'd gotten clear of the first two weeks, things started cranking up. It felt like some great old slumbering bear had finished yawning and stretching after a long winter, and was very, very ready to eat. It was weird to imagine going back and telling me on the first day, cheeks flushed, doing more burpees than I'd thought the human body capable of that it hadn't really gotten tough yet, but that was the truth. The summer started to heat up. I mean that literally, not just figuratively: as we crept further along into June and closer to July, time in the air conditioning was almost better than winning.

We ran.

They shifted our long runs to the early morning hours before breakfast to knock out the worst of it while it was still (ostensibly) cool. Freddie and I got used to jogging together, discussing music, movies, books, school. We swapped fun soccer stories at first, takes on professional teams, and then got more into personal stuff as the miles went by. Did he actually enjoy moving around all that much for his dad or did he just pretend to? He didn't know. Did I really want to go to medical school one day, or was that just something I'd always felt I was supposed to do? I really didn't know.

Smart people became doctors after all, right? And who didn't love traveling to new places all the time? We told ourselves stuff like that.

"Holy crap," Freddie wheezed. "Slow down, dude, we've got like twelve more hours of running today."

"Sorry," I said, blinking as the sun jabbed right through the branches at the horizon and into our eyes. "Just trying to work on my cardio a bit." *Slow, 64.*

"You're working too hard, Good Lord. You can't run fast if your heart blows up in your chest."

"Yeah, that's how it works, for sure."

We ran, we ate.

We slowly started to work the kinks out as a team. Emphasis on slowly. We probably had some dumb argument or another at least once a day over positioning, someone being at fault, what we should've done instead of what we actually did. I couldn't identify anyone on our team as a weak link—it wasn't like there was one single person holding us back. And we weren't the worst team on the rankings, either. We weren't number one, but we weren't last. Martin kept insisting we throw everything at striker and mid, leave three back, and play more aggressively. Slick would agree enthusiastically, Alejandro would agree monosyllabically, and then Chandler and Mateo would start arguing against it. I could occasionally catch Alejandro's jaw tighten or him take deep breaths and massage at his temples as the arguing went on.

"You expect me to block every shot that gets past with three defenders, and the midfield off halfway to—"

"It will work, I'm telling you, we just keep the pressure on them, swing the midfield back if they get possession—"

"*If* they get possession?" Chandler said, sipping his coffee with forced stoicism. "You mean, like, *if* Bronson makes us run tomorrow? *If* the eggs still suck at breakf—"

"Yes, what Chandler's saying. I'm telling you right now, when they score a goal, everyone's going to be mad at me, not saying 'oh, wow, Martin's plans had some holes in it, huh'. And by everyone, I mean coaches and recruiters too, I'm not going to be able to flag them down and say, 'Hey, Mr. Wilhelm, that wasn't really my fault!' The way we've been playing has been working, why—"

"It's been working, but it could work better. We still haven't beaten Team One yet, or Team Three—" *Saying we haven't beaten Team Three is an understatement.*

"—and if we want to beat them, we need to shake things up."

"Or," Chandler said. "We shake things up and lose even harder."

"Ever the optimist, Chandler!" Miles said, a grin tugging at his lips.

"Bite me, Harry Potter."

"This is stupid," Victor said. "We could've just—"

"Passed the ball to you more?" Damian muttered under his breath, but I don't think Victor caught it.

Martin continued his conversation with the smoothness of a freight train going off a bridge. "I mean, point stands, let's not dress it up—"

"Guys!" Freddie said. I realized that he'd been talking for about thirty seconds now trying to get everyone's attention, and my brain just hadn't processed it. I'd been focused on eating. Well, I was eating, but I was off in my own head. We'd had a tough match yesterday, and the kick I'd almost missed had stayed stuck in my mind. What if I'd been a second slower? What if I'd lost us the game right there? I turned in time to notice one of the first scowls I'd seen on Freddie's face all summer starting to form. "Have any of these arguments ever, like, changed anything? I don't remember a single time you guys finished one of these agreeing the other side had a good point."

Chandler sipped with irritation. This manifested as very loud slurps.

"Why don't we just talk about something else and just see what happens in the moment or something? Or you guys just flip a coin, or we test the idea out in one of the non-tournament scrimmages that don't count?"

Freddie's brokered truce lasted a solid fifteen minutes, which a pretty remarkable record.

We ran, we ate, we played.

None of our arguments lasted more than a day because there was always something changing. New drills, new tactics, new challenges. We'd cycled through most of the teams by the end of the third week, even if we hadn't played them all yet in ranked matches (we played Team Three again in another scrimmage, but it wasn't a ranked one). One of the coaches would record the scrimmages once every few days and we'd spend two evening sessions a week going over the matches. Ludwig was a man of few words, but he squeezed a lot of mileage out of each one.

"This," he said, pausing. He shined the laser pointer at a game we'd played against Team Four. We won, but it was ugly. The red dot danced around the right half of the field, where we'd clumped two of our midfielders and two of our fullbacks in a frenzy against half their midfield trying to get the ball.

He circled the wide-open part of the field where the defenders should've been. I could feel Damian and Charles doing their best to melt down into their seats. "This was dumb." He un-paused the game and kept going.

"Tough break," I murmured, as loud as I dared. Unsurprisingly, Ludwig did not respond well to people talking during tape reviews.

"Thanks," Charles or Damian said. Even knowing about that scar, in the dark? From behind? It was a blind shot.

We cycled through tape, we identified problems, we focused on them. Incremental changes, the coaches insisted. "You're not Ronaldo by tomorrow," Wilhelm was fond of saying. He'd point out the tiniest of errors in the way Mateo guarded the near post, or what was making Freddie half a second slow to identify who to pass to. He would point out a million mistakes but give us each one specific thing to hone in on. "Next time we watch tape, I don't see that—" he said, jabbing a finger at me, frozen uncomfortably large on the screen. *At least my hair grew back some.* "I see an actual Cruyff turn, yes?"

My face burned in the dark of the auditorium room. I wasn't even mad at Wilhelm. He was 100% right. I was doing it wrong. *Slow, 64.* "Yes, sir." I felt a gentle squeeze on my shoulder and felt the burning fade from my cheeks as I glanced at Freddie next to me. At least somebody had my back.

"Good. Now, someone explain to me what game the next half was, because it was certainly not soccer..."

We ran, we ate, we played, we watched.

"He," Chandler said, knees up to his chin, eyes peering out from between his long dark hair, "is annoyingly good."

I watched Oliver's casual victory jog back from Team Nine's goal. He'd done that three or four times thus far. "Yeah. Preaching to the choir."

"Is he the top ranked one at the moment?" Miles asked, as casually as you'd ask about the weather.

"No," Martin said. "Top ten, not number one."

"Who's number one?"

"I think a fullback on Team Two."

"A fullback? Really?" Alejandro asked.

"Hey, what's that supposed to mean?" Charles said from somewhere behind me.

"I mean, I didn't know how they calculated it when you're not scoring any goals."

"It's probably all made up, what the coaches decide," Chandler said. He seemed oddly content not being in the top fifty. I was thrilled to be in the top fifty—not anywhere near number one, but top fifty felt really, really good. It sure wasn't bad for a sophomore. Dad was thrilled when I told him in a letter. Top fifty as a sophomore meant maybe top ten was a real possibility as a senior, barring me blowing out my knee or something.

They updated the ranks each week. Martin was top twenty-five, and Slick had landed top twenty. Quietly, we didn't think he was going to stay there—he'd had one insanely good game, but it had been Alejandro who set him up for four or five clear shots on goal. I wanted the best for him, but I didn't think he could replicate it.

Don't focus on them, focus on yourself, I could hear my Dad saying. Oddly, I agreed with him. I wasn't as bothered by not being ranked the best as I thought I would be at the start of camp. On the one hand, it was still relatively early in the summer. Beyond that, even with recruiters and scouts coming in once a week or so (the coaches tried to hide this from us, but it was pretty easy to clock the only people who weren't yelling in German accents), I had a few years before college. I just wanted to get better. Faster.

I listened to Chandler and Martin talk a bit more about strategy. We were taking shots on goal, and waiting in line was giving us a few seconds to talk as we rotated through the line.

"You good, dude?" I heard Freddie ask from beside me.

I blinked and turned, breaking my attention away from the game one field over. It wasn't like I needed to keep my eyes on them to tell you what was going to happen: Team Nine would turn over the ball within one minute of kickoff, then one of Team Three's strikers would kick the ball past Nine's goalie so fast it would put a hole in the net. None of Team Nine were looking in Wilhelm's direction. I couldn't blame them. "Yeah, yeah, just focused on them playing."

Freddie turned and observed the field for a moment, blue eyes blinking. It was odd how a pretty much identical color blue in Wilhelm's eyes could prompt bowel-emptying fear in most of us, but with Freddie it was calmer. More relaxing. Mischievous. "You focus on that Oliver guy a lot."

"Oh, uh, do I?" I said. The words came simultaneously too late and too fast to be natural.

Freddie grinned. He had a slight gap between his front teeth. He'd mentioned wanting to get braces. He chewed on his lip, thinking. "They were the ones we played in that first scrimmage."

"Yeah, he scored that first goal on me."

Freddie frowned. "You've had other goals scored on you since then, right?"

"Three times," I said, automatically. "The giraffe-looking guy,"

"He's so tall!" Slick said, as if we were unaware.

I took my shot and bent it too far out. Mateo didn't even have to dive. *Focus, Kit.*

I kept talking as we circled back into the back of the line. "...the guy from Nigeria, and that striker on Team Four."

"Both very good," Martin said. "I think those two are in the top twenty. But the giraffe kid, Kit, you see him coming from a mile away, I have no idea how he gets past you."

There were a few laughs, and I grinned.

"Still, I wouldn't let it get to you. 4 isn't bad."

"No, it's not." They'd been fast, though. Faster than me.

Freddie nodded, turning back to watch. "Okay, no worries, just wanted to be sure you weren't going psycho on us or anything."

"If you do go psycho," Chandler said, deadpan, "Try to limit your rampage to within the limits of a yellow card. I'm not playing another game a man down."

We ate, we ran, we played, we watched, we talked.

"I am saying," Chandler said, heat rising into his voice, "You're still super wrong."

"No, I'm saying, you're not letting me finish, let me finish!"

"Fine. Go ahead. Finish your wrong statement."

"If all three of them teamed up, and had time to plan, they could beat Superman. The time to plan is crucial!"

"Slick, you need to open a window when you spray your hair, man, you must be breathing in too many of whatever those chemicals are. There is ZERO chance. Not on their best day."

"I don't spray it, I use *product*, it's—"

I lagged behind the Iron Man/Spider-man/Green Lantern vs. Superman debate and swatted at mosquitoes. We'd been let out early from evening session (the projector had broken; Bronson decided it was wiser to dismiss us early than have us learn any more German profanity from Ludwig as he tried to fix it) and had a solid hour to kill before lights out. About two-thirds of the team had decided on a walk around the campus, since Martin mentioned we hadn't seen most of it at a speed slower than a Bronson run yet.

"Where do you fall on the debate?" Freddie asked.

I shrugged. "I don't really watch comic book movies or read them or anything."

"They're graphic novels!" Slick said.

Freddie nodded and lowered his voice to avoid Slick's notice. "Eh. Fair. I mean, Superman totally wins, but I'm not getting involved."

I glanced at the bickering ahead. "Ah, really? Why wouldn't you want to get involved in all that fun?"

Freddie grinned, but it was fleeting. "I mean, it's interesting to talk about, I guess, but not really worth it."

"Not worth it?"

Freddie shrugged. "If I start arguing in that sort of thing, Damian or Victor will come over and then they'll *have* to be right and I won't hear the end of it all summer. Heck, I'll be trying to study for midterms months from now and getting a dissertation from Victor where he cites every Superman comic ever to prove some point. It's easier to just avoid it."

I supposed he had a point, although it was not something I would've considered. Maybe it was just because I hadn't come here with anyone, so the thought of anything that happened here at Weltmeister following me home felt...odd. Like the whole idea of taking midterms. It felt like when you're having a dream and remember you have some assignment due the next day, but your brain can't figure out how that belongs or fits in at the moment.

Plus I didn't mind arguing with people.

I missed a step and stumbled. *Oh God, am I like Damian?*

"You good there?" Freddie asked.

"Yeah, thanks." I paused. "Well, if you ever feel like arguing with them I'll back you up."

"Appreciated," Freddie said, "But I will 100% not be taking you up on that offer. I'm rooming with Damian, after all."

I grinned. The sun was getting low over the horizon, and it was one of the prettier sunsets at Weltmeister. The clouds were stretched incredibly long and thin, there was orange and pink all over the tops of the trees, and just enough of a breeze that it felt pleasant to be outside.

Most of the buildings on the campus were built from bricks, tall and majestic. If my memory of the brochure I'd reread sitting alone was correct, it was first built in the 1870s. Ivy crept up the trees, a belltower would ring out periodically, and fountains and little gardens littered the grounds. Had Martin stayed quiet, it would've been calm, picturesque.

"How much trouble do you think we get in for going inside some of these?" Martin asked. He'd walked past some of the bushes and peered inside one of the windows, nose to the glass. "We could do a heist or something."

"I imagine you'll run until you're back in Germany, good friend," Miles said.

"That is quite far," Martin said. "Looks like just a classroom, anyway. Aren't these rich people schools supposed to have lounges and stuff?"

"I've never heard of a high school having a lounge," Victor said.

Martin turned towards me. "Kit, you should know."

"Huh? Why?"

"You have good grades, you're probably going to a fancy school or something. It makes sense, right? Where's the cool part?"

"Kit's only a sophomore, he's only been in high school a year," Chandler said.

Martin frowned. "What, you don't have better schools for the smart kids here? Like Gymnasium?"

"Every school has one of those," Damian said.

"No, dummy, he means like a magnet school or something," Chandler said.

Martin's frown deepened. "Magnet school? Like for engineering?"

"No, you—ugh. Never mind. Forget it."

Martin shrugged. "Well? I'm still wondering, here."

He was too much of an oaf to actively try to insult anybody, but something about the words had snapped my brain back to jogging out in front of the camp that first day or watching Mole Rat walk away. "Uh, I have no idea."

"Guys it doesn't matter what school you go to, obviously we're all getting drafted to *Real Madrid* straight out of Weltmeister." Freddie said.

He was met with a chorus of boos, laughs, and less-than-entirely-tactful opinions on Real Madrid. He did, however, briefly succeed in uniting Slick and Chandler against a common enemy.

The conversation settled back in as Martin jogged up ahead, examining a tree to see if it was possible to climb up, shimmy over a branch, and hop onto a second-floor balcony. Miles was struggling to dissuade him tactfully.

Chandler and Slick started talking more loudly, and Victor jogged on over. He tended to orbit little cliques in the team, in a way, and even though he'd come with Freddie and Charles and Damian he didn't seem particularly close to them. *Is that how I look back at home, now that Kyle's gone?*

"Thanks," I said quietly.

"Don't mention it," Freddie said. "Last thing I want to do is think about college applications anyways."

"We better start heading back," Miles said. "I need a shower."

"Same," Freddie said. "Kit, you coming?"

"Hm?" I turned. *I wonder how much longer the showers will be busy for.* "Yeah, sure, sure."

We walked for a bit. I intentionally walked slowly. I was in zero rush and honestly after all of Bronson's runs I made it a point to move at a tortoise pace whenever I got the chance. My quads thanked me.

"Worried about college applications?" I asked. I then thought about it for a second, which I figured I maybe should've done before I asked the question. "Wait, you just said you didn't want to think about it. My bad. Ignore me."

Freddie gave me a grin, but it was half-hearted. It came and went. "No, it's fine. I mean—it's different talking about it with you versus Victor or my dad or something. Victor's always wanting to compare exact test scores or talking about all the requirements to get into this school or that one, like it's some big game or competition."

A part of me felt like I shouldn't press. I was curious, though, and figured Freddie would tell me if he didn't want to talk about it. "And your dad?"

Freddie was longer to reply on that one as we opened the doors to the dorms, knocking the mud off our shoes as we went in. As he lifted his right leg up I saw him wobble for a second—Ludwig's squats that morning were particularly vicious—and I grabbed his shoulder to stabilize him. Freddie flashed me a grin, taking a second to find his train of thought again. "Yeah. He...I don't know. I think he thinks I'll go to West Point like him or something and that's not...really what I have in mind."

I grimaced. Yeah. Granted, I couldn't imagine training for the Army being harder than the stuff Wilhelm put us through, but the culture of it just didn't seem very Freddie. "Ah. Yeah that's...kinda tough."

Freddie shrugged. We walked up the stairs (my quads were no longer thanking me) and down the hall, where people were moving in and out of their rooms, trash talking after the day's scrimmages. "Yeah. I...I mean I don't know. It's good I can talk to you about this kind of stuff."

"Of course, man," I said, as we walked closer to my dorm. "It's what teammates are for."

Freddie slumped, just a bit, as if all the working out that day had caught up to him all at once. We stood outside my door for a second, and I tried to think of something to follow that up with, but nothing was coming to me. I realized how much it sucked to have Richard freaking Laskins, who had said a total of ten words to me all summer, as a roommate, instead of someone I could actually have a conversation with like Freddie. I rubbed at my neck and saw Freddie glance back the way we'd come then check his cleats again. He seemed...tense? What was I supposed to say to that? *I probably shouldn't have pressed about his dad,* I thought.

"Yeah, well, uh, night man. See you tomorrow. Get some rest."

"Yeah, you too."

There were games of kickball in evening sessions, a dodgeball match or two, and—because we were all able to hit a certain mile time—manhunt. Watching tape was educational, but I think the coaches figured having the occasional night where we didn't go to sleep replaying all our mistakes over and over was probably good to keep anybody from going postal.

Speaking of which, I got letters. Some came from Mom (she kept trying to slip German phrases for me to use in there), I got one from Dad (it had pictures of the dogs, advice on how to line up shots on goal, and a promise for ice cream upon return) and, maybe three weeks in, one from a Mrs. Vandenberg.

I did not know any Mrs. Vandenberg, but the mailing address was from Colorado.

The writing looked like it had been made with a hatchet dipped in ink. I had a suspicion Mrs. Vandenberg did not, perhaps, write this letter.

Dear Kit,

I am not actually Mrs. Vandenberg, this is Kyle. I initially forgot to put postage on the letter I sent you, because nobody sends letters anymore, dude, so it didn't go anywhere. I asked the mailman, he said I needed to go buy stamps, but the car is in the shop (the speed bumps out here are REALLY hard to see at night). So I get the idea to just put your little kid sport camp's address as the main address, then no return address, so the mail guy will just return it there for me. Genius, right? The mailman then knocks on our door the next day and he is NOT happy. It turns out that's apparently, technically illegal. I asked if I was going to go to mail prison, and it turns out that made him even more not happy. Crazy, right? He also stops to inform my parents. Which leads me to believe that if he ever winds up in mail prison with me, he's going to get the snitch treatment, and that's all I should say in a letter this guy may intercept anyway.

So anyways, thanks for getting me grounded for a week and/or sent to mailman jail. I think he could've just given me a stamp and the problem would've been solved. So now I'm definitely not trusting this guy to deliver my mail, even if I DO get the right stamps. I finally get stamps, and just send this from my neighbor's mailbox. She's really nice and I mow her lawn for some spending money once a week, so I don't think she's going to narc on me. If she does?? Good luck keeping the HOA off your lawn, Vandenberg.

ANYWAYS, good to hear from you dude. I'd wondered why you hadn't been responding to any of the videos I was sending you. I remembered you texted me about not having your phone right after I got your letter. Colorado is really fun—you need to come out and visit when you're done with camp. I'm able to go hiking a fair amount, which is pretty sweet, and all the mountains and all are really pretty. I've included some pictures.

There were three or four photographs of breathtaking forests, mountain ranges that stretched for miles, and then the final photo was of Kyle, bare ass exposed to the camera, next to a sign which read "BUTTE'S CANYON AHEAD".

"I swear to God, Kyle." I grinned, but I couldn't help thinking of Mole Rat, and I didn't want to look at it any more after that.

I paused for a moment.

"Wait, who took that picture?" I wondered. Huh. Question for the return letter.

HAH made ya look. But for real it's pretty fun, man. I definitely miss all of you guys back home, but I'm fitting in well here and making some friends. It took some time and the first couple of weeks definitely sucked. I was seriously considering trying to, I don't know, sneak on a train and come back like an old-timey hobo or something, but thankfully I decided to stick to mail crimes instead. All that to say it's good to hear from you, brother.

The guys on the baseball team are all pretty cool, which is something that happens when you play cool sports. Nerd. They all do dip, though, which is absolutely wild. They keep offering me some, and I don't want to be a jerk, so sometimes I'll take it and just spit it out when they're not looking, but holy crap. These guys are not going to have teeth by the time they're forty.

Conditioning sucks—

"Oh please," I muttered.

—but I think I'm impressing the coaches and while I don't think I'll get to be starting where I want to this year, I may get to start some, and can hopefully work my way up to first base. Which is the first time I've been trying this hard to get to first base since seventh grade. My folks are doing really well, aside from being pissed off about the car and me committing what is apparently a post office felony.

Hope you're doing well dude, glad you're having fun and learning a lot. I'll try (emphasis on try here) to write again soon. If you keep working hard you can go to a summer camp for a real sport next year.

Kyle

He included an address at the end with a caption that said: "address of nearest prison to write to in case Vandenberg goes to the cops."

I grinned, reread the letter, and started working on writing my own one back.

We ate, we ran, we played, we watched, we talked.

It had been a few days after getting the letter from Kyle, and things had seemed to more or less shake out. We had solidified into positions, with everyone figuring out where we clicked best. The bickering was more about pointless stuff rather than who was screwing up the games for us. We were winning more than we were losing, and we started to creep up in the rankings, both individually and as a team. It was a good routine. It was the routine of camp when camp made sense. I would think occasionally about Mole Rat, and how maybe if I'd just let him sit down at our table he wouldn't have quit early, or how something about the notion of Kyle, who I'd hung out with since second grade, sending me a picture of his naked butt was funny, but also kind of weird, but if I'd told him it was weird it just would've become even more weird, even though Kyle never got mad or freaked out when I told him weird stuff. Or some word other than weird. I knew words other than weird, in fact, a lot of words other than weird, but my brain wasn't seeming to want to focus on anything other than, well. How weird it was, I guess.

The last day Weltmeister made sense we were warming up for the morning run, gathered around the tree that had become our unofficial team meet-up spot. Mateo had come over to smirk at those of us who had to run miles every day, Martin pulled back his feet behind him to loosen quads that wouldn't have been out of place on a water buffalo, I double- and triple-checked my cleats.

We ate, we ran, we played, we watched, we talked, we stretched and as I helped lift Freddie's leg to stretch his hamstrings his shorts rode up, his boxers hitched, and I saw pretty much everything.

I felt my jaw drop and my eyes started blinking faster, like maybe if they did it enough when they opened again it would've just not happened or something.

The whistle blew, Bronson took off, and everyone scrambled up and took off at a jog, barring me, who was standing there still trying to process. Had anyone else noticed? Was he going to be the next Mole Rat? Was he going to quit if people said anything—was *I* supposed to say something? Was it—

"Dude, hurry up!" Freddie shouted, falling in beside Martin and Damian and turning around the bend.

My legs started going about a tenth the speed my brain was. My heartrate seemed like it was already on the fourth or fifth mile.

It was the last time that I believed I understood what was going on Weltmeister.

Chapter Eight

"Kit," Freddie said, his tone lower and harder than I'd ever heard from him. "You need to tell me what the hell is going on."

Around us there were distant shouts, somebody yelling, a guy laughing like a hyena. The top half of the teams got to play capture the flag tonight; the bottom half was watching tape of their losses, accompanied with gentle and ever-tactful commentary from Coach Ludwig. The sun was getting low, and mosquitoes kept nipping at my legs and the back of my neck no matter how many times I swatted, and I could feel the welts forming. I was supposed to be doing a real, real deep flank to get the enemy team's flag, but I'd gone the opposite way, because Freddie was supposed to be going that way, and I wanted some space. Evidently, he had other plans, which included predicting my fake-out and following me to the wrong side. There went another tally mark on the "Kit gets outmaneuvered" column so far this week.

And the whole time this was going on, the adrenaline in my brain decided that I was focusing on a lot of things like mosquito bites and noise in the background other than what was immediately in front of me.

"Um," I said.

---⚽---

We were doing our morning runs. I say we collectively. Everyone else was running; I kept tripping over my own feet. The whiplash had just been so freaking sudden. I'd seen—you know—and then I had to just go and immediately do conditioning. And it wasn't like I could flag the coaches down and ask for five minutes to process that. I wasn't going to say anything, not to anybody. The last thing I wanted was to cause another kid to leave the camp. And besides, that would've been, just, so not cool to do to a teammate. Or anybody. Or Freddie. Especially not Freddie.

"You're off in your own world today," Freddie said. "You even listening?"

"Huh?"

"I asked what you think about Martin's set-up he wants us to try."

"It's brilliant!" Martin shouted from a few yards ahead.

"Not you, dummy!"

"I still want to hear it," a guy from Team Twelve said from behind me, which garnered some laughs.

"Oh," I said. "I, uh—I don't really know, I just want to focus on running right now."

Freddie nodded, trying and failing to hide a frown. We had an unspoken agreement that chatting during the jogs helped to take our minds off what Bronson considered a light run and what the United Nations considered a violation of the Geneva Convention. "...yeah, sure thing dude. Did you not get enough sleep or something last night?"

"No—I mean, yeah. I didn't. I just need a second. It's fine."

"Uh, okay."

I jogged, keeping my eyes down on my shoes, which got muddier as the run went on.

⚽

All the teams had solidified their turf in the dining hall by this point in the summer. Unofficially, everyone had claimed certain tables, and then they'd unofficially claimed the seats at said tables. So, it wasn't like I could really sit somewhere else and not make it kind of a big deal, but at the same time, I didn't want to sit next to Freddie and have him ask me any more questions about what was going on. Or have someone else start to say something—I mean, if I'd been sitting somewhere else, and someone else had seen and asked me, I could tell them to keep quiet about it without Freddie finding out. I'd be mortified if that had happened to me. I'm already uncomfortable enough with the shower situation being younger and less developed than everyone here and it's not really a situation I ever had at home since I always went home to wash up after practice at school. I can't imagine being on display like that. Nothing Freddie had said or done implied that he realized what had happened. If he had, he should've been at a theater camp instead of Weltmeister, because it was Oscar-grade acting.

"Any idea who we're scrimmaging today?" Miles asked, sitting back down at the table. He'd grabbed a few extra glasses of water and passed them out to anyone who wanted them.

Technically, we didn't know who we were playing until the afternoon session started, but after three and a half weeks at Weltmeister we'd started to make some sense of the way everything worked. Well, the other guys had, at least. I thought I had. There was an almost-zero chance we'd play the same team twice in a row, and they tried to mix it up to have all the teams play each other more-or-less equally. If we ruled out the teams we'd played in the last three or four days, and tried to gauge which of the remaining teams hadn't played those guys either, we could usually get a pretty solid idea.

"Going to be Team Three, Thirteen, or Four," Victor said, crossing some names off a list on a napkin as Martin and Damian helped jog his memory about who we'd seen playing each other the day before. Victor wanted to be a lawyer, apparently, and this sort of problem-solving was a part of the LSAT, so he insisted he should try to guess the team we played every day for something approximating law school practice. I don't think you got to use a napkin for the LSAT, but at least he was trying.

"Four has a very good goalie," Mateo said with the same enthusiasm of a kid being told he's going to finish all the vegetables on his plate if he wants ice cream.

"And Thirteen has that fullback," Chandler said. We all knew the one he was talking about: the guy was easily the bulkiest player at the camp, and I'd spotted him occasionally doing squats with some of the shorter members on his team over his shoulders, fireman-style. He was maybe the only person at camp who did not need to be afraid of Coach Ludwig. "That guy might be able to score off a goal kick." Chandler paused, thinking. "From two fields away."

There was a general chorus of agreements, muffled through bites of food. It was quickly followed by other debates over who had better players and the best way to approach them.

No one's mentioned anything yet, I thought, my plate barely touched in front of me. *So they must not have seen, but Damian and Charles were standing right behind me, and I thought they were looking in my direction—*

"You worried about playing Team Three?" Freddie asked, making me flinch.

"No," I said. Freddie's expression flickered a bit—I hadn't meant for it to come off so snappy. "I mean, I'm not. It'll be fine." *If only I could get this image out of my head.*

Freddie nodded wordlessly and turned back to talking to Victor.

"C'mon, man," Freddie said, blinking sweat out of his blue eyes. There was a feverish shout from maybe forty yards right of us, where someone had snatched the flag and was sprinting as hard as they could to their side of the campus. We'd sprawled out across a huge chunk of the Academy grounds, so it wasn't all flat playing fields. We'd bunkered our flag up by the trees where Martin had contemplated a heist the week before. Freddie and I, though, stood a little way into the forest where we went running with Bronson every morning. My brain was thinking about the smell of pine needles, and how odd it was to see all the trees and trails standing still, and how I really should've just taken a different route and avoided this whole situation. Not the image of Freddie's goods being put on display. Definitely thinking about the pine needles. *Nobody has seen or he would've gotten the Mole Rat treatment by now,* I thought, which just made me think of how badly I screwed over Bryan all over again. *So why am I still so worried about this?* "This is—I mean this has been going on for days now. You've been super weird."

"I'm sorry," I said, the sound of it mechanical, like an automatic response when you're put on hold. What was the right way to say *Hey I saw your junk and now things are really weird* or anything even approximating that? If I'd had time to prepare, maybe I could've put together a halfway-intelligent way of expressing it, but the truth was with everything going on the last few days I was just sort of hoping all of it would go away on its own and I wouldn't have to stress about it. "It's not—it's not anything, I mean, I've just been off."

"You have been, both in games and...just in general," Freddie said, again with more force than I'd heard him use all summer. It stung a bit. I knew I'd slipped up—the backslide in the rankings showed it—but I didn't want to hear about it. It had sucked enough having to write back to Dad about it when he asked what my rank was this week. "It definitely seems like something's going on with me specifically. I mean—did I do something? Did I say something?"

I caught my gaze drifting downwards. I took a sharp breath, turning and looking at the trees around us. Those few seconds of the hamstring stretch just kept playing over in my head and all of Freddie's questions were just hammering it home even more. I didn't want anybody to come barging through thinking we were sneaking around for the flag or something. I mean, ostensibly that's what we were doing, but I didn't really care about capture the flag right now. "It's—it's not like that, or anything, I mean...I don't really want to get into it."

Freddie didn't really seem mad, just bummed. I could tell he knew what I was saying wasn't really the truth, but I didn't know how to get into the truth of it without making things even more awkward than they already were. If I'd been Mole Rat'd, I wouldn't have been able to look anyone in the whole camp in the eyes, and that was what had happened to Freddie, just with fewer witnesses. Just me, as far as I could tell. I mean, would that just torpedo the rest of the summer? What if it made things weirder than they already were? What if then I had to deal with thinking about all of *that* and had to deal with Freddie being pissed or not talking to me or whatever? And here, now, he was asking all these freaking questions, like he had been for the last few days, as if I didn't know things were weird, or that I was playing like absolute garbage, as if these were all brand new things I needed pointed out to me. And why can't I focus on literally anything else?

"If there's something going on," Freddie said, after taking a few seconds to chew on his lip, "—you can tell me. I'd want you to tell me because I don't like dealing with whatever this is. Even Chandler and Martin weren't ever this frosty to each other, man."

"I said I don't want to talk about it!"

"Kit," Alejandro said. His words were clipped and pointed. "You need to swap with Damian."

"What are you talking about?"

Alejandro grimaced. "You know what I'm talking about. Swap."

I could feel my cheeks turning red as I turned away. Alejandro says five words all summer, and they're to remind me how badly I'm sucking at soccer.

And he was right.

"Damian," I called out. He turned and clocked me over the sound of Freddie and Miles telling everyone it was still winnable. Team Thirteen was up 3-1, which most certainly was winnable.

Winnable if we didn't make any stupid mistakes, which was exclusively what I'd been doing so far. Their striker may as well have caught me with my pants literally down around my ankles (which just made me think about the whole thing with Freddie all over again) for all the reaction speed that I had when he blitzed past. To top getting smoked by him, I'd been too far out of position to stop him five seconds later when he took a ball lobbed right to him, set up, and crossed it to the other striker to score.

"Yeah?" Damian said, looking up at me. It's hard to explain sometimes how much emotion people can convey with just a single word. I mean there's a lot of different ways to say the word "yeah", but Damian found the most irritated one.

"Swap with me," I said, barely able to get my voice loud enough for him to hear. Stupid. Absolutely stupid of me. Two goals, both my fault, both within five minutes. If that. I normally got on the field and my brain just went into the flow of it. I was looking at positions, open space, angles. For whatever reason my muscle memory and game sense had just short-circuited completely. I was having to consciously think about what I wanted to do, and not just *do* what I wanted to do, and it was making me over-think every single decision. *Slow, 64.*

Damian did not offer even token reluctance. Since we had too many forwards and midfielders we rotated one of the fullback positions periodically. I had hit my quota for sucking at fullback for the game. He jogged back to swap with me and I moved up to midfield.

"You good, man?" Freddie asked as I jogged up. Victor and Alejandro were setting up for kickoff.

"I'm fine," I said. I scraped the mud off the side of one of my cleats with the other one, just for them to get exactly as muddy as they'd been before when I put my foot back down. *Stop being such an absolute moron.*

Freddie said a quick comment to Mateo, who nodded and shouted, "Diamond! Charles, sweeper."

Freddie jogged up to the front of the diamond and the wings pulled in a bit closer, leaving Charles to bring up the rear.

Freddie was watching me and gave me a small nod when he caught my eye. I looked away. I could appreciate him trying to be nice—not even trying, he just *was* being nice—but it was just hard to make eye contact or talk with him without picturing *it*, and he had no idea. I'd known secrets about people at school before and talked with them when they were unaware it was common knowledge, but that was different. At school, there wasn't anybody I was tight with. I'd hang out with people, sure, but it wasn't anything on the level of time around the clock, for weeks, with the guys on the team here. *God, I miss Brightbirch.*

Victor's pass got picked off, and their right midfielder turned and dropped the ball back to their fullback. It wouldn't be accurate to call him Team Thirteen's one-trick-pony; he was a one-trick-Clydesdale at the bare minimum. The ball rolled slowly to him. He timed it, reeled back, and rocketed the ball into low orbit with casual ease.

It was going to be coming down near us, and I could see their strikers and mid-fielders rushing up to grab it. Freddie was jogging backwards, trying to clock where it would land, but he wasn't going to be able to turn in time to match the guys sprinting right at him. I could.

"MINE!" I shouted before I was even totally sure where the hell it was going to come down. I wasn't going to screw up anything else this game. It wasn't even because the coaches were watching or jotting down rankings and stats. It was that I could feel that unspoken irritation from the team, the sort of situation when the air gets tight and stiff between you and someone else. And that was me and everyone else right now. I didn't want to be the one that screwed it up for the team and pulled us down to last place.

The ball came down and I forced myself to take a full second to calm down. I watched it, waiting, timing it—

"Kit!" somebody shouted. It wasn't needed; I could hear their strikers closing in, but I needed to get my timing right. I had a second and a half, maybe two, and that was all I needed.

The ball landed and I trapped it under my foot, bringing it to a complete stop.

Somebody was shouting my name in warning, but I wasn't focusing on that, just on the ball and what I had in mind.

Their striker ran in to swipe it. I rolled my left foot up onto the ball then snapped it to the left. Thirteen's player cursed as he realized what I'd done: as his momentum sent him running past me towards the bleachers, I pivoted and grabbed the ball before the next attacker could close in.

"*Ronaldinho!*" I heard Martin yell, laughing. I heard him, but I wasn't listening, if that makes sense. It was a detail my brain filtered out because it didn't matter right now. It was just me and the opposing player closest to me.

He was maybe a second away. Thirteen's left striker was on me more quickly than I'd anticipated. *Too slow, idiot, run faster.* His foot flicked out, contesting the ball, but he didn't have possession of it—not yet. I pulled back, stepping to the right and planting my left foot, reeling back with my right to knock the ball to kingdom come.

I let him shift his weight, for just a brief second.

I dropped my right foot and side-stepped over, cutting him off right as he tried to reverse course with the ball. Freddie and Miles were both two or three seconds away. They may as well have been back in the dorms. I'd have cleared it or Thirteen would've scored by then.

The striker pulled back, trying to wrest the ball back with him and get it to someone on the wings. It pulled him ever so slightly off-balance as he tried to reposition.

I lunged in and tapped the ball through his legs, sending it wide, towards where Damian should be. If their left midfielder had been sharper, he may have intercepted it—but Damian got there first. He took a heartbeat to gauge the field and sent a low crisp pass up to Slick.

"Nutmeg!" Martin yelled, to which Chandler told him to shut up before he got us in trouble with the coaches. Chandler was still grinning, though.

Mateo was not grinning. "Where was that ten minutes ago?" Mateo said.

I didn't have anything to say back to Mateo. *Stay focused. Don't be slow again.* I jogged back up into position, trying to keep my eyes on our drive up the field and not the fact Freddie was now a few yards from me, trying to give me encouragement the entire rest of the game.

"Come here," Wilhelm said. I think he meant it calmly and conversation-ally, but it still came out as a drill sergeant's bark. Or an attack dog's. Take your pick.

I blinked, looking around the rest of the team. We were inhaling cups of water and letting our legs rest. We were probably done with the hard work for the day, but this was Weltmeister, after all.

I may as well have had the plague. Everyone, with varying degrees of subtlety, stepped out of the blast radius that came with a Wilhelm chew-ing-out, clearing out plenty of space for me.

"Talking to you," he said, jabbing his clipboard at me.

I swallowed my water, contemplated what an underwhelming last meal it was, and jogged over to Wilhelm. He started moving away from the teams at the water coolers to the quiet side of the field.

He studied me for a moment as he walked. This close, I could see his mustache quivered a bit while he talked and coupled with the belly peeking out from his shirt, I could not shake the image of a walrus from my head. Unfortunately, this was the least opportune moment to contemplate Wilhelm's similarities to half-ton mammals. I kept my face neutral.

"Why do you make mistakes this game?" Wilhelm asked.

I waited for a second, unsure if it was a rhetorical question or not. He gave me a prompting grunt and I fumbled for the words.

"I, uh—I didn't—I just wasn't thinking. And the second one I was still rattled from the first mistake, I guess."

I knew I'd screwed up, but not so severely that it warranted a 1-on-1 with Wilhelm. We'd wound up tying, too, which was one hell of a turnaround considering my early-game performance.

Wilhelm nodded on this for a moment and scratched at his chin, think-ing. It was the longest I had seen him contemplate on his words. He wasn't a stupid man—all the coaches knew their soccer—but he normally came off decisively. He snapped out where we were running, how we were splitting up, what went wrong.

"You're in the top fifty."

Barely. I wasn't sure if it was a question or a statement. "Um, yes sir."

"You play like that more, you're in the bottom five."

I looked down at my cleats, which were nearly covered in mud as Wilhelm paced the edge of the field. "...yes, sir."

"But my point is, three or four days ago, they look at the numbers. They think you're better than most of the camp." He drummed his knuckles against the clipboard. "So, in the last three or four days, did you get injured?"

"No, sir."

"Hm. Did you suddenly forget how to play soccer?"

I took a deep breath. "...no, sir."

"The same play that got past you on the first drive—I've seen you do it twice. Once to Team Nine, once to Team Two."

I blinked. Wilhelm wasn't consistently with our team. None of the coaches were, bar Bronson for morning runs. They rotated in and out. He must've seen the better part of a hundred players at work every day and remembered those specific games. "Yes, sir."

"And when you do it then, you do it naturally. Practiced. Perfected. You *know* that trick. I don't even think it mattered. Because he would have gone past you if he had one leg the way you started this game. So, the only explanation is that you lost focus. How else do you lose to the kind of maneuver I have seen you pull off before?" He let it sink for a moment. The noise of my team was getting a bit louder again as we started slowly making our way back around the field. "You want to know the truth?"

I nodded.

"Sure, you can look at the numbers, and the numbers say the worst kid and the best kid here have a big difference in what they can squat or how fast they can run. But the truth is you all still have so much to learn before you're really, truly good at soccer. That difference in those numbers doesn't mean as much as you all think. You all fixate on them. The most useful thing the rankings tell me is who gets scared when they get bad news and who gets determined."

I didn't have much to say to that.

We'd done a lap of the field. Wilhelm gave me a stern look. "Don't make the same stupid mistake again. Don't turn off your brain. Focus matters more than any of those other statistics. You're younger than most of the other players. They're older, stronger, taller. Longer legs, bigger stride, more experienced. Some have been here two years in a row now. Unless you plan on growing twenty centimeters taller by the last week of the summer, those are not things you can change by the tournament. Identify your problems. Identify your solutions. Every year, I see the same thing. Some kid is half a minute slower on a run and thinks he will get a scholarship if he wears himself out sprinting every morning keeping up with Bronson. Then, he is so tired the rest of the day, his team loses all their matches. He does not identify what his problem is, and how he can change, and so he loses. If he wants to be fastest at camp, and wants to change, he should've started running every day a year ago."

He took a finger and pointed it directly at my head.

"*That* can change. You are maybe a little faster, maybe a little better at soccer than you were last week when you dribbled past someone. This week, how did you get beat if you're still the same? Or even a little better? If being ranked the fastest is all that wins you games, why did you, faster this week, make a mistake you never would have made two weeks ago when you were a little slower, a little weaker? What changed? Can you run a five-minute mile now? Can you beat anyone in the camp in a one-on-one that you could not before? Or did you just get distracted?"

I nodded. He'd made his point. It stung, but nothing he'd said was wrong. "...I understand. Thank you, sir."

"When he dribbled past you, I bet anything that you thought you weren't fast enough, or you weren't good enough. You sprinted as hard as you could the rest of the match, I was watching. You played well. But you didn't play well because you started running faster, you played well because you started thinking and paying attention. You played better because you stopped screwing around. You could have beaten him on any of those plays running half as hard if you'd been thinking twice as much. We do not make you run so you become fast. We make you run so that when you need to be fast, you can think about soccer, and not about your legs hurting."

I nodded. There wasn't much to say.

He levelled the clipboard at me and gave me a stern look. "Bronson will make you faster whether you want it or not. Ludwig will make you stronger whether you want it or not. You are the only one who decides if you want to improve mentally, or not."

"Yes, sir. Thank you, sir."

Wilhelm grunted and walked away.

Freddie took a step back. "...alright, fine, man. Be a jackass."

"*I'm* being a jackass?" I said, taking a step closer. "You've been asking me questions non-stop for days. I tell you 'hey, I'm cool' and you follow it up with a hundred more questions an hour later. And I'm the one being unreasonable?"

Freddie scratched at his chin and turned away for a moment. I could feel that heart-hammering you get when you're in an argument. Some small quiet part of the back of my brain was saying that shouting and yelling at him was not the best idea, and that this wasn't helping, but the bigger, louder part of my brain was tired of dealing with all of this. I mean, I hadn't gotten a minute alone to even begin to process what happened.

"Fine. Fine." Freddie turned and jogged back off into the woods, muttering under his breath.

I wanted to shout something at him as he went but I couldn't really bring myself to say anything. Nothing sounded sharp in my head until after he had vanished through the trees.

Good job, Kit, you pissed off the only guy you can talk with. AND the guy who brought half the team with him. Great work as always. I rubbed at my temples with my hands, trying to take some deep breaths. Shouting at him had just happened. It happened fast. I wasn't the kind of person who shouted at people. I didn't even remember the last time I'd gotten into an argument with somebody, and I'd only ever been in a fight or two in, like, elementary school.

I leaned back against a tree, listening to a small group rush past with the flag, a dozen guys hot on their heels. I kneeled and tried to breathe until I felt relatively calm again.

"Okay, Kit," I said to myself, after making sure nobody was around to see me talking to myself. I didn't think my rankings would improve if I got put in a padded room. "Not...not a great situation."

I tried to think of what advice people would give me. Kyle probably would've laughed and said Freddie was being annoying. I mean, that—that wasn't entirely wrong, but it also didn't really feel that helpful. I couldn't shake the feeling I'd screwed this up and caused this, and I needed to apologize or find a way to make it right. But there wasn't a way to do that without explaining to Freddie, "hey, man, things are weird now because I saw your family jewels" and as tense and uncomfortable as things were now, I didn't see how telling him that was going to make it better.

Dad would've said focus on soccer and it would just shake out.

"Yeah, haven't tried that before," I muttered.

Mom would've given me a hug which—I don't know. I felt like I could probably use at the moment.

My friends at school—well, with Kyle gone I didn't really have any, to be honest. There were kids in study groups, and there were teammates, but I hadn't stayed on the freshman team long enough to be tight with any of them, and the JV team already had cliques by the time they pulled me up. So, that was useless.

My friends at Brightbirch, I figured, would probably have just told me stuff like this didn't happen at Brightbirch.

I sat against the tree and had to admit they were pretty much right.

Chapter Nine

The shouts and laughs and post-game trash talk of capture the flag all got quieter as I walked. In turn, the crickets got louder and the mosquitoes more aggressive.

That about sums up the last few days.

I wasn't fully sure where I was going. The nagging voice in the back of my head—the one that's always convinced you forgot one of your binders or shin guards or something right after you walk out the front door—kept telling me how pissed the coaches would be if I got caught wandering around the grounds unsupervised after dark. The nagging voice, in this instance, was very much correct, but the rest of me didn't care.

I kicked a few pinecones and stomped on sticks. Unsurprisingly, acting like a four-year-old did not make me feel better. Up ahead I knew there was a fence around the edge of the school grounds, and probably cameras or something set up, so I turned back before I went too much farther and started wandering back.

"Stupid," I muttered to myself. "Absolutely stupid." I'd barely managed to make friends here, and as soon as I had, I dropped bombs on all the bridges I'd made. The irony of me essentially Mole Rat'ing myself in an attempt to keep the same from happening to Freddie was not lost on me but didn't make me feel much better about things.

There was one huge chorus of shouts and screams in the distance. Some-body had won at capture the flag a few minutes ago was my guess. That meant they'd probably be wrapping up and being sent inside in around fifteen minutes. I would've stayed out walking around until midnight if I could have, but I did not think I would survive two chewings-out from Wilhelm.

As the sun started creeping lower and lower (it remained just as hot outside; Weltmeister was unfair) I heard grunting, the smack of a ball, and footsteps.

Anything other than my current situation was worth focusing on. I crunched over the pine needles until the sound of someone drilling shot after shot in a row became clearer. There would be four or five kicks, then jogging, then kicks again.

I broke the tree line and had to squint in the evening light to make out who it was. A player—not a coach, as I'd figured—had found the batting cages for the baseball team over on this side of campus. He'd absconded with five or six soccer balls, lined them up, and hit practice shots in rapid succession. The balls curved surgically to the right with the first volley, left with the second. He dropped and did push-ups, a few squats, held a plank for a half minute. Then he jogged and set them back up.

My legs were taking me closer before I fully processed what was going on. I was maybe twenty yards away when I clocked it was Oliver.

Oliver finished lining the balls up, fidgeting with one of them for five or six seconds to get it positioned exactly on the line he'd set up. He turned and looked up at me. His features were difficult to make out at dusk, but I certainly didn't see a smile there. *You and everyone else.*

He paused. I wasn't sure if he was trying to remember me, or just making it look like he was trying to remember me. "64," he said.

Slow. "Yeah. Team Six. Or, you know. Kit."

Oliver shrugged, backed up, and fired off a few shots again. He studied where they'd hit the net after he was done. I could see he was soaked through in sweat, and he repeated his routine. He stayed quiet.

"I take it you're not a fan of capture the flag," I said after he gathered the soccer balls and lined them back up.

Oliver didn't find it amusing. His hand twitched as he was positioning the ball, and I could hear that nostril-flare-exhalation you probably saw your mom do when you spilled something all over the carpet. "No."

What a conversationalist.

"Bending it?"

Oliver took another breath, somehow curtly. "Yes." He fired off his shots again, then paused, looking.

This close, I had a better view of what he'd been doing. His left-footed shots were just a bit sloppier than his right, but—well, saying sloppier wasn't really accurate. It was like saying that a 99 on a test was sloppier than a 100. Technically correct, but not how any reasonable human would describe it.

I watched him for a minute more, enjoying something that wasn't related to accidentally seeing a teammate's crotch and/or having said teammate be mad at me and/or ruining the summer.

"You want lessons or something?" Oliver finally said.

Jackass. "No. How kind of you. I was just clearing my head."

Oliver turned away and resumed his routine.

Message received.

I considered saying something to try to mess with him, or some little jab, but nothing was coming to me. I had enough crap on my own to deal with that making more enemies at camp hardly seemed like a smart decision. Beyond that, there was something different to Oliver hitting his shots then falling down to machine-pump pushups and crunches and leg lifts.

He was stopping to think after every round of volleys, studying where the shots had landed and adjusting his stance ever so slightly for the next go.

I considered what Wilhelm had said.

I turned and walked off from the lonely baseball practice fields. Distantly, I heard Oliver say, "Damnit!" after another volley of shots, then heard him set them back up, rinse, and repeat.

My feet were carrying me to the noise, closer to the heart of campus where the dorms were. By now, Freddie had probably told Victor or Charles or Damian, or maybe all of them what a jerk I've been. Damian for sure—they were rooming together. What was I supposed to say when they got on me for that? By the time we sat down for breakfast tomorrow morning I'd have close to half the team pissed, and it wasn't like the rest were feeling warm and cuddly after how close I'd come to losing the game against Team Thirteen.

I tried to brainstorm solutions, letting my pace slow even more.

My first, and most ambitious ploy: I could fake my own death. I was pretty sure that Ludwig had connections in hell, though, so he seemed like he'd be able to figure out I hadn't actually passed onto the afterlife.

More realistically I could apologize. Thinking about that made my stomach roll over a bit—apologizing is probably what I should've done. If it hadn't been—you know—if I'd slipped up and said something dumb or screwed him over with a bad pass or something, I'd be fine to apologize. Lord knows I'd tried apologizing to Mateo for that game. But if I tried to fix things, he was going to want to know what was going on in the first place, and there was no way things were going to go back to normal once that cat was out of the bag. It was going to be weird.

I shook my head, trying to focus on something else other than the thought of it. That left...just...doing nothing. I mean, it wasn't that bad of an idea, I figured. At least a dozen times Kyle and I had gotten mad at each other, not talked for a day or two, and gone right back to how things were the next time we hung out. Maybe this would all blow over after a night or two and things would settle on down. I could just work on my poker face.

Maybe.

I crossed past a few of the maintenance buildings, walking through the trees that circled Weltmeister until it got too dark to walk in the woods. I came back to the edge of the soccer practice fields and spotted the coaches herding everyone who'd been allowed to play capture the flag back to the dorms. The others were walking over from one of the bigger classrooms where they showed the game tape.

I chewed on my lip. Perhaps I'd walked a bit too slow. There was no way to walk across the practice fields without being noticed. Wouldn't that be a lovely repeat of Day One all over again—and Freddie probably wasn't feeling inclined to stick his neck out for me this time.

We had been told very specifically not to wander off on our own the way I just did. I'd seen Ludwig nearly blow out one of the veins on his forehead when he caught a guy on Team Five doing pretty much what I'd been doing the second week. We got a bit of leeway for capture the flag (though we were nominally supposed to stay in duos) or if we were in groups during free time, but a few portions of the campus were off-limits, and I'd almost certainly meandered through them. Oliver seemed to have taken up residence in said portions, but that was a him problem and not a me problem.

Well, Oliver as a whole was most certainly a me problem knowing I would have to play against him again, but not an immediate one. More pressing was not getting kicked out of camp by being found wandering off, and then not getting kicked out of the team by pissing off everyone's favorite member, and *then* I could deal with not getting kicked out of the top fifty.

The whistles blew, hurrying everyone along and back to the dorms. It started to sink in how dumb wandering this far off was. I didn't have any plausible excuse for this. If Wilhelm caught me, maybe—*maybe*—I could say I was trying to clear my head like he'd told me.

And maybe he'd take me for ice cream and poetry recitals after.

"Think, dummy," I told myself. Going across the field was a no-go, I would've been spotted, and we weren't supposed to have split off on our own during capture the flag anyhow. I could try to loop all the way back around the practice fields, maybe, and pop out closer to the dorms from the far side. The issue there was that it would take me right past where the coaches stayed (we know where the coaches stayed because Martin had proposed sneaking into their rooms and messing with the rankings; it took two hours to fully convince him why that would not work).

I tried to envision the campus from the top-down. The dorms were in a quad, basically, centered around a small common area with some benches and stuff. You walked for a few minutes west and you got to the practice fields, and on the far side of those was where I currently stood, watching the players slowly disappear around corners and into buildings. Oliver had been practicing over to the southern side of the campus, where the baseball facilities were set up, and very markedly past the boundaries.

My mental image of the campus came to me pretty easily, even the parts I hadn't personally walked through. I suppose rereading that brochure the first day was worth something after all. I was pretty sure I could loop back past Oliver and cut past a few of the academic buildings. There wasn't another camp on the school grounds currently, and I could just come up on the far side of the quad and slip into the dorms from behind.

I chewed on it for a bit. I didn't think anybody would be over there. I could just slip through a door after the coaches went to sleep or something.

It could maybe work, whereas I would for sure get chewed out if I tried to pop out of the woods and play it cool now.

I started heading back the way I'd just come through. I paused for a moment to watch Oliver continue drilling shots, setting up, calisthenics, drilling again.

He'd skipped capture-the-flag. So he'd probably been out here all of evening session. And didn't look to be slowing down.

I shook my head, reminded myself of the current hierarchy of my problems, and kept walking.

The far side of the campus didn't have all of the lights turned on at night—I suppose even rich kid schools have hefty power bills—which made it easier to keep from anyone seeing, but also...you know. It was pretty spooky. I mean, best case scenario, I ran into the Dead Poets Society. Worst case scenario? If there were going to be ghosts on a campus, it would be St. Michael's.

The southern academics building was equal parts really old bricks and really fresh ivy. I walked quickly but quietly, keeping my ears open, head on a swivel (for all fifteen feet away I could see in the dark). The ambient chatter from the fields, loud enough to be heard this far away during the daytime had died down fully. I figured everyone had been corralled inside to bed or to shower for the time being.

And yet there was noise up ahead.

I blinked for a moment, then hunched down. I was still in the middle of the sidewalk. I scrambled over to one of the doorways. Bricks poked into my back and my hip as I tried to squeeze up close without jostling the doorknob. I figured they probably didn't have alarms on these buildings, but with my overall luck at this point in the summer, it felt like an unnecessary risk.

I waited, trying to listen through the crickets and not squirm as mosquitoes nibbled at my legs. It.... was definitely not English.

But it also wasn't German. I didn't recognize one of the coaches' voices. Hm.

I peeked my head out around and saw somebody pacing around one of the trees about twenty or thirty yards away. It was starting to get truly dark now—stars out and everything—so I couldn't tell for sure, but it was too small to be a coach. I could tell it wasn't Ludwig or Wilhelm, because it didn't look like one of the trees was walking around another tree.

I squinted for a minute more. I'm aware the smart thing would've been to just keep going and not press my luck, but I—well. Whatever this was, it wasn't all the other crap I had to deal with.

I leaned closer. The voice was familiar.

"Mateo?" I said.

The figure stopped talking and whipped around, visibly jumping up.

"Who's that?"

"Kit."

"Kit? What?"

I jogged out from the doorway. Mateo had a cell phone in his hand, and I could distantly hear a girl's voice coming through the end.

I smirked at him.

Mateo put the phone back up to his ear, started speaking sweet-nothings in Spanish, and flipped me off with his free hand.

I grinned and kept walking. Mateo's finger followed.

I hadn't spent too much time on this part of the grounds, and as Mateo's voice grew more distant, all the rest of it came creeping back. It was like a cycle, or my brain running on a hamster wheel, or trying to swim out of a riptide or something. I just kept circling back on how much I'd screwed things up, the hamstring stretch, yelling at Freddie.

I stopped to massage my face and temples for a minute. "Just focus on getting back." I took a deep breath and got to the corner of the next building over, where a few waist-high hedges were bordering the doors. I'd gotten to the far side of the dorm quad. I felt pretty stupid crouching down and peeking over, but I would've felt much more stupid getting caught.

Nobody was around. This part of campus was quiet. Well, not really—there was rustling from the trees in the wind and birds that kept making noise nearby, but there weren't people. I took a moment to think and map out the best way up, then crouch-walked as quick as I could over to the next building. I hunched and waited, listening, peeking around.

I could hear voices, again, and this time in English.

I leaned around the next corner as far as I dared. As best I could tell, I had looped back around close-ish to where I needed to be. I was basically opposite where the entrance to my half of the dorms was. I just needed to figure out a way to physically get back in the building from behind without anybody—in particular whoever's voice I was now hearing—noticing. Someone was walking along the sidewalk, coming in my direction, talking on their phone. *Mateo wasn't kidding about everyone sneaking those things in.*

I listened for a moment. No, the figure was too tall to be a player. It was Bronson.

Shoot.

Of the coaches to run into, Bronson was far and away going to be the most merciful, but he also was still a coach. I turned and crouch-walked back, trying to glance around. There wasn't a ton on this side of the dorm nearby to cover me up if he continued walking this way unless I went back over to the hedges.

I hugged the building and went around the corner. Bronson's voice was getting louder, if only by a touch.

I took a deep breath. I probably wouldn't get kicked out of Weltmeister if I got caught. Probably. And it was dark enough that I could more than likely hide and avoid this problem to begin with. I looked around and just saw the periodic bushes adjacent to the first-story windows of this dorm. There weren't any big trees or anything like that to scuttle behind. My best bet was going to be to just hunker down behind the bushes and hope he went the other way.

I didn't have any better ideas. For a brief second, I considered sprinting to go try to warn Mateo, but I thought better. There was a decent chance Bronson would hear the running. Besides that, Mateo was speaking quietly enough—and Bronson loudly enough—that I think he'd notice in time.

It did leave me to wonder how Mateo was going to get back in the dorms with Bronson walking around here.

Which...I probably could've just waited and trailed Mateo back in, now that I was thinking about it. I mean...he clearly had been doing this without getting caught. For two summers now. And I just walked past him to find my own way in.

I knelt behind the bush, already sore legs burning, and could almost hear the sound of Kyle roasting me.

I'd always heard people say good grades didn't necessarily mean you were smart, but that was the first time I really believed them.

Bronson's voice was getting more distinct. As best I could tell, he was probably about parallel to where I was on the other side of the dorms. If he kept going on the sidewalk, he'd stay about ten or fifteen yards away from where I was. At the edge of his vision, crouched down behind a bush, I thought I had okay odds of not getting spotted.

I turned around, trying to see if there was anything I had missed before he got there.

And I got my lucky break.

One of the ground level dorm windows was cracked open.

I ran it through in my head, trying to think. I probably had a good ten or eleven seconds before Bronson turned the corner, since he seemed for once to be moving at a leisurely pace.

I scrambled over and pushed up on the window. It resisted for a moment, then slid up wide enough for me to squeeze through. I pulled myself in and fumbled over in a decidedly not-cool manner. I pushed myself up against the wall and grabbed hold of the blinds to keep them from rattling and shaking and making it obvious somebody had just passed through.

I waited.

Bronson turned the corner and came around, laughing. He was talking about family stuff, it sounded like. Talking to his mom or dad, maybe? It felt wrong to be listening in on that, but it also wasn't like I had asked for that to happen. Or for really most of the last few days to happen.

Bronson meandered around for a bit. He walked through the little open area behind the dorms, coming pretty much right next to the bush I'd been at. I flattened myself up against the wall, trying to hold really, really still. If he came and closed the window, he was going to see exactly where I was.

I waited, doing my best to stay still, not breathe. My nose itched tremendously.

Bronson asked about his dogs, laughed at whatever the person on the other end said, and started slowly walking away.

Once his voice had gotten out of earshot, I let myself slump off from where I'd pressed against the wall and take a deep breath. It wasn't that late, objectively speaking—it was probably 10 p.m. at the absolute latest—but it felt like the witching hour.

I sat up and glanced around at the dorm room in what little ambient light got through. It looked more or less identical to the one I was in, just the chairs folded up on the desks and everything as it was when the last occupants checked out. I was pretty sure that the dorms here would connect to our dorms. They had all of Weltmeister in two different dorm buildings—there was the one that Freddie and Victor and I were in, and the one Chandler was in. But we didn't actually take up every hall of those buildings—they'd locked off some of the other halls to keep us from snooping around and going where we weren't supposed to.

Which...well. It was pretty reasonable to think, given where I was.

But, point being—I was pretty sure I could get back into my hall from this building, as long as at least one of the connecting dorm doors didn't lock from this side. If nothing else, it gave me someplace to wander around and not have to worry about talking to anybody for a bit. I wouldn't have to deal with Freddie talking to Damian and Charles and Victor and them all being pissed at me until the morning, if I was lucky.

A part of me knew Freddie wasn't the type of guy to talk behind people's backs, but I just didn't know how else this was going to play out. Surely at some point one of those guys would ask, and Freddie would vent. Or maybe he was pissed off enough that he would start talking trash. Either way, same result.

I stood up and walked to the dorm door, opening it up. They automatically locked when shut from the outside, so I grabbed one of the desk chairs and used it to just barely prop the door open in case I needed to get back out through the window.

Sadly, there wasn't anything game-changing in the rest of the halls. It looked pretty much exactly like our dorms, just empty and dark and with less of a smell of soccer socks. My mind immediately wandered to how old this campus was, and what kind of ghost stories the kids who stayed here year-round probably told. The looming brick buildings and all probably made this place awesome come Halloween. The old campus made me think of history. History made me think of Freddie.

I massaged at my face again. I just needed to clear my head. Sleeping on things would probably give me some kind of an answer. Or just put me in a better mood. Or at least my quads wouldn't be as sore.

What I needed more than anything was—

I stopped massaging, face scrunched.

Wait.

I jogged down the hall, being sure to glance out the windows for any flashlights or cell phone lights or anything. Coast was clear.

I opened the door about mid-way down the hallway and checked all around it. There was no way turning the lights on inside would be visible from the windows down at either side of the hallway.

As long as nobody came by and closed that one window, I had easy access to my own private showers. Hell, my own private *dorm*.

The fact I didn't have a towel or change of clothes with me did not slow me down.

I took my first shower in weeks without a swimsuit on. It was at least thirty minutes. I looked like a prune when I was done. It was the first good thing to happen in days.

Chapter Ten

The beep sounded and everyone's feet thundered across the field.

It wasn't fully clear exactly how the coaches ranked everyone—obviously, winning games mattered, as did doing well in drills, but no one had offered a theory that really seemed to make complete sense to me on which drills mattered and which ones didn't. Some of them were just meant to hammer on one or two specific skills; I couldn't see the coaches seriously considering who won the juggling contest as a major factor in the rankings.

That said, some of them were obvious. Like the beep test.

The beep test was, as with all of Weltmeister's finer pleasures, pretty straightforward. Everyone in the camp lined up across the practice fields and sprinted to the other side. The machine beeped, and then we did it again.

If you were thinking that the practice fields must've gotten pretty crowded in doing this, you would be correct, but only for the first few levels. The beeps kept getting faster and faster and if you didn't make it across before the next beep you got eliminated. Rinse and repeat.

Normally I would view getting to run fewer sprints as a blessing, but this was one of the rare times I wanted to go until my knees blew out. Bronson was observing everyone with his clipboard behind his back, maybe just looking at form and technique. I couldn't tell you anything about proper running form; it wasn't exactly the reason I loved soccer.

A few of the others were just jotting down numbers. Everyone who didn't make it across the line before the beep jogged to the side and fumed.

I crossed the line and slowed to a stop a few seconds before the whistle. I turned and went back to the line, trying to take as much air in as I could.

Most of the team had been near me, but in the stampede we'd gotten split up and spread out. Slick absentmindedly brushed a hand through his hair and Mateo wiped away at some sweat on his forehead.

"Man, the whole point of playing keeper is that I don't have to—"

BEEP. We took off.

They'd probably culled about a quarter of the herd at this point. I wasn't immediately worried about not making it this round or the next. I didn't think I was the fastest player at Weltmeister—well, I mean, I *knew* I wasn't the fastest player at Weltmeister—but I wasn't going to get cut early. I just wasn't going to let myself. I glanced over and saw Wilhelm talking with a few of the aides on one of the other fields. This was about endurance. Mental fortitude. It felt like the column runs on the first day all over again.

We hit the far side and turned back around. Barring the morning run and some drills, it hadn't been a particularly heavy morning. Most of us still had plenty of gas in the tank. Those who didn't were on the sidelines.

Freddie jogged up to the line beside me, red-faced. I wasn't even sure he'd noticed me—he seemed tunnel visioned on the sprints ahead of us. Couldn't blame him. Part of me wanted to tell him good job or something, but I didn't want to rattle him right before we—

BEEP. We ran. By the time we cleared the eighth level I was starting to breathe harder. Another fifteen or twenty got cut.

"Martin, shut up and save your breath, for the love of God, I—"

"What, Chandler, you tired already?"

I grinned and turned back.

The beeps continued. With fewer people on the field, it was getting easier to run to some degree. I didn't have to worry about crashing into anybody or getting tangled up.

I didn't bother tuning in to this hour's re-run of Martin v. Chandler. I gave the sidelines a quick scan.

Slow 64.

A sprint, and then another. The rest periods, which had been pretty short to begin with, were cut tighter and tighter. After the eleventh level, there had to have been less than a quarter of the camp left. I dug my cleats into the sideline in preparation and tried to do the numbers in my head in the two seconds I had before starting up again. If I couldn't make it this round, what sort of ranking did they put me at? I didn't even know what metric they'd used to determine how fast I was before.

"Alright boys," Bronson said. For such a skinny dude, he could make his voice boom when he had to. "Keep up the good work. We're getting to the fun part now!"

Lovely. The beep came and we went. I think at that point most of Team Six had gotten knocked out, but I'd been keeping my eyes on my own two feet and not any of the rest of the field.

Slow, 64.

It must've been the hardest that I ran in my life. They snatched someone up for not making it fully to the far white line before turning around, so I made sure to run visibly past before digging my cleats in, turning, and coming back. It was the sort of running where your brain can't focus on too much else, just on trying to egg your legs on faster, on trying to ignore the fact you can hear your heart pounding in your everything.

Everything below my neck was on fire by the time I heard Ludwig call out my name. I'd say I finished out my sprint to the far line, but by that point my best sprint was pretty much just a normal run. I walked over to the rest of the team and just focused on catching my breath back.

"Nice job," Alejandro said. He'd been the last one before me to get knocked out. Mateo might've been the quickest in a forty-yard-dash, but Alejandro could go all day. I gave him a wordless nod back, huffing too hard to say much more.

I didn't watch the last few get whistled out one by one. I knew Oliver had still been on the field when I went off, but I don't think he outlasted everyone. Little victories.

"Good work everyone," Bronson bellowed again, smiling wide. It was a sharp contrast to the permanent scowls that littered the other coaches' faces around him. "Quick five for water and then we start rotations."

I grabbed my little cone cup and sat on the ground, taking my time to get my wind back. Everyone was chatting for the most part. I caught Freddie sitting a bit to himself, nursing a cup of water like I was. He seemed to be lost in thought. He crossed his legs and shifted his blue shorts down a bit, wiping some of the grass off his calves.

I twisted my cleats into the ground as I sat, legs rocking a bit. I didn't see any particular need to go bother him. We hadn't really had a one-on-one talk since—you know. He hadn't been hostile or talked trash as far as I could tell. Damian, Charles, and Victor had all treated me more or less the same as well. I'd just been taking Bronson's morning runs in silence.

I crumpled the empty cup in my hand, thinking. Damian went over and said something to Freddie I couldn't make out, and Freddie gave him a smile that looked pretty forced. He blinked and started to catch me watching the two of them, so I turned my focus back to my feet.

Things weren't as weird as I had thought they would be. But it still kinda sucked being icy like that.

The next round of whistles came and I pulled myself up for drills.

The rankings were only updated every few days, which gave me time to put on a good showing. I was pretty sure I'd run hard enough to avoid backsliding at least by the physicality standards. I'd played better since nearly throwing the game to Team Thirteen. I could at least hold where I was, and hopefully climb up a few spots.

As much as I was able, I tried to put all the stuff with Freddie out of my head and focus on just playing. On doing my best. And, honestly, as dumb as it may sound, having my own showers was...amazing. I guess I hadn't noticed that I had spent the last few weeks surrounded by other people around the clock. Maybe it doesn't really make sense that I wished I had more friends and people I could really connect with at Weltmeister and simultaneously loved having my own space.

The rest of the morning was filled with hard drills. We did box runs, a bunch of ab work, and even the runs where they strap a parachute on your back for resistance and make you go across the field as if anyone had any gas left after the beep test. I didn't think I would ever feel as stupid as I did on the first day jogging out late in front of everyone but putting on a parachute while standing in the middle of a practice field was a pretty close second.

"Careful, Mateo," Chandler said. I unbuckled the belt, legs aching a bit, and handed it to the keeper.

Mateo raised an eyebrow as he wrapped it around his waist, making sure it wasn't all tangled. "What? You think I can't outrun you?"

"No, I think you're so skinny you might just fly off once you build up a little speed on that thing."

There were a few chuckles (promptly cut short by Ludwig asking why it was necessary to laugh to put on a parachute. Always the life of the party, that one) and Mateo gave Chandler a grin before cinching it tight. I smiled, looking around.

Everybody had laughed, or at least smiled or something. Freddie, on the other hand, looked more like he'd gotten hit in the gut by a soccer ball and knocked the wind out of him. He was up a minute or two later, taking a minute to fumble with the belt before heading off on his run.

Slick waited until Ludwig had gone to interrogate Team Eight, standing next to us. He looked me in the eyes and said, "We run too damn much at this camp, you know that?"

———— ⚽ ————

Lunch was eaten mostly in silence. Even the normally talkative ones—Chandler, Martin, Miles—were pretty hushed up. I think everybody was just too winded. I was shoveling down two sandwiches and then taking a nap as soon as I was able. I was also trying not to think about the fact there were a great number of stairs between me and my bed. If it wasn't so hellishly hot outside I would've just found a bench under a tree and conked out, but I was pretty sure if I tried to sleep outside at Weltmeister this time of day I would've woken up as a puddle with a heat stroke. And then gotten a lecture from Wilhelm telling me my form could be improved.

I thought about that, and the ever-middling array of lunch options, but none of it really distracted from the fact Freddie should've been sitting in the spot next to me, and he wasn't there for some reason. Nobody had mentioned it, so I didn't want to dig into it. Right? That would've been weird. Maybe. Or did it look ruder to not say anything? Ugh.

The afternoon (why are naps always too short?) was two scrimmages, mercifully neither for tournament rankings. A win and a draw. Not bad. I wasn't playing as well as I wanted to, but I didn't identify any times that I completely whiffed a play or gave a goal away or anything like that. I made some solid passes. Avoided any stupid screw ups. Wilhelm didn't feel the need to pull me aside.

It didn't feel as gratifying as it should have.

We ate dinner with only a moderately higher energy level than we did lunch. It had been one of the longer, more grueling days at Weltmeister. Fortunately, the evening session was just tape, no tug-of-war or anything like that. As hard as the coaches worked us, they did seem to have a good gauge for when was too far. Like, medically too far. It was already well over the line of what anyone would consider a fun summer activity.

I gave myself a moment of being wistful for Brightbirch and then got my focus back onto where I was at. Occasionally, I'd stop and wonder what the guys there were doing as I was hammering out push-ups or wheezing my way through the fifteenth lap of a box run, but I'd had those moments less and less as the summer went on. I wasn't sure how I felt about that.

They divided us into a few larger groups and crammed us into a few of the lecture rooms, where they started putting tape up on the projectors for us to look at. Ludwig was our designated commentator. Every time he paused the tape to give insight into someone's mistake or point out bad positioning, he did so with the tact of a water buffalo.

I should've been paying attention and trying to learn from all the mistakes Ludwig was pointing out—my own and everyone else's. But honestly, my legs were so tired that most of what I could think about was how good it felt to lean back in the seat and prop them up on the bottom of the chair in front of me. It was like someone had poured lead into the entire lower half of my body. I could hear Dad and Wilhelm in the back of my head telling me to stop slacking off. My quads were louder.

I scanned the room as Ludwig took two full minutes to explain how bad this Team Two player's throw-in was. I'm not disputing it was a trash throw-in, but it felt like a bit of overkill. I could see the player in question up near the front of the room slowly withering down in his seat the longer Ludwig talked. Poor guy.

Team Six was clumped together across three different rows. We'd fallen more-or-less into our usual positions, with one exception. Freddie was posted up near the back of the room, still looking...off.

I turned back, Ludwig's voice droning on in the background. I'd thought things were going to be catastrophic, you know? I figured Freddie would've said he and I argued the night of capture the flag and then either the guys he brought with him would flip out on me, or things would be weird, or...I don't know. But instead, things just seemed almost normal, but not quite, and that was stranger than if we were just actively mad at each other.

"Alright!" Ludwig said. This man had no indoor voice. Half the room flinched. The other half developed tinnitus. "Five minutes, get water, stretch. Come back and we talk about why you do not try to cross the ball in front of three defenders, Team One."

Ludwig's comment was met by a smattering of sheepish mumbles, and we got up for a minute. We probably had another hour of this before we went back and settled in for the night.

I watched the rest of Team Six get up and chat. It wasn't like I wasn't friends with any of the guys—I could hold a conversation with any of them. I think they liked me (barring when I screwed up royally on the field) but it also wasn't like any of them, when we had free time, were coming to talk to me first.

Damnit.

It wasn't really the best timing, but I also didn't want to wait any longer. I was pretty sure if I sat back down and waited for another hour, I'd talk myself out of it.

Another hour.

An idea came to me.

It wasn't that long after dinner, was it?

I drummed my tired feet on the ground, trying to think things through.

"Five minutes! Go, water, break, come back! We are starting back in four minutes, thirty-five seconds, players!"

I was not back in four minutes and thirty-five seconds. I was out of the building.

I tried to tell myself that the classroom was dark, and not all the way full. So one person missing wouldn't be super noticeable to Ludwig or any of the assistant coaches (as luck would have it, the one who'd been sitting in the back of the room had only been paying attention at the start, then he was on his phone). Plus, Ludwig had already covered the game we were in, so he wouldn't have had a reason to call me out by name and notice I wasn't there. Right?

I stood outside the classroom across the walkway, tucked back where I could see people coming in and out but not be immediately visible if Wilhelm or Bronson came outside or something.

I was really starting to make a habit of being a delinquent. I knew Kyle would have approved, which is how I knew it was a habit I needed to kick as quickly as possible.

I waited a bit, surprise in hand, held gingerly inside my pocket. I had it wrapped up as best I could manage. After a bit, I started to hear movement and noise from inside the building, and I saw people start pouring out, heading from the classrooms up to the dorms. I squinted and tried to make out who all it was. Looked like Teams Eight, Eleven, and Thirteen. I waited some more, feeling profoundly stupid as I stood next to a bush. I'd started out crouching, which I knew was stealthier, but—look, my legs were *really* tired, okay?

After another few minutes of waiting (read: mosquito swatting) I heard Martin laughing. A few seconds later, I could hear everyone else. I slipped out trying to tell myself that my idea wasn't stupid, and stuff would work out. Right? Right.

There was a mass of players walking out and I had a good moment where none of the coaches had a clear line of sight at where I was. I stepped out from the other academic building and joined back up with Team Six.

Damian's eyes narrowed. "Hey, where'd you come from?"

"Wait, that was optional? We could've just left?"

"No, I just, uh—" *think of a good excuse, something believable* "—I, uh, really had to poop."

"Wait, the whole time?"

"Do you need a doctor?"

"Dude, that's not normal."

I nodded and offered some half-decent explanations and gathered Ludwig had not clocked my disappearance. I walked for a minute, not seeing Freddie, and moved back through the crowd to notice him. He must've hung back to grab water or something after they excused everybody for the brief down time before bed, since he wasn't up with the rest of the team.

I saw him coming out of the building, lagging behind the rest of the players. He still looked...drained. I mean physically he looked normal, maybe slouching a bit, but he just didn't seem to have the same energy to him. Freddie had been the one, barring maybe Miles, who'd stayed pretty even-keeled so far in the summer.

A part of me felt stupid doing this. I considered just committing to the IBS alibi and moving off before Freddie saw me and not saying anything, not risking rocking the boat any worse. Things were kinda almost normal. I mean, we weren't actively hostile. It just wasn't—

Stop fretting and just go apologize, Kit.

I took a deep breath and walked over. Freddie and I were at that distance where we were far enough apart that we couldn't start talking to each other yet, but we both saw each other, so there was this weird quiet period where we were both just walking before we were close enough to say anything. I could hear the voice in the back of my head telling me we were off to a great start already. I told the voice to shut up.

"Uh, hey," Freddie said, blinking a bit. "Wait, why are you coming from that direction?"

"I—uh—" I turned, and saw the coaches were coming up behind us. Shoot. I hadn't really considered that. I mean, duh, they were going to come and make sure everybody went back to the dorms and stuff, but I just needed like five minutes to clear the air. "Just walk with me a sec?"

"Oookay," Freddie said. I didn't really wait for a response, I just turned and started going. I could hear him coming up behind me, and when we turned the corner, I stepped back against the building. There was a bit of an opening between two of the academic buildings, a little walkway under a covered arch, and none of the lights were on in this half of the academic wing. If we didn't make any noise and none of the coaches stopped to turn and look to their right, we wouldn't be noticed.

My heart was pounding about as fast as it had when I'd been doing all those stupid sprints that morning. I was trying to think of a halfway-believable excuse for why I was doing this if Wilhelm turned the corner, but none were coming to my mind.

"Dude, what—"

"Just come over here!" I whispered.

Freddie hesitated, looking back the way he'd come, and I reached out and yanked him over to where I was, pulling back against the wall. It was a bit of a tight squeeze between the arch columns, but Freddie committed, not wanting to get caught. Three or four seconds later the coaches turned the corner, talking to each other in German.

One second went by, then two.

It suddenly occurred to me that they might have remembered seeing us ten or eleven seconds ahead of them, and then notice we were suddenly not there when they came around the corner. *Brilliant, Kit, brilliant.*

As luck would have it, though, I saw Ludwig was on the far side of the two coaches walking past, and the assistant with him was still on his phone. He must've had the brightness cranked up to near-blinding levels. He didn't look up, and probably couldn't see ten feet in front of him in the dark as it was.

They walked past, Ludwig's voice loud enough to cover the sound of our mildly terrified breathing, and once they were gone, I gave it a ten count before talking. My hand was still grasping at his upper arm so I could pull him back if the coaches came back by again. I could feel him shaking, just slightly, and the muscles in his bicep tensing under my grip.

"What's going on? We could've gotten in, like, a ton of trouble!"

"I'm sorry," I said, then realizing I was about to apologize again for the whole...everything, and that I was going to sound like a broken record. I just forced myself to take a deep breath and barrel on forward. There was no real way to apologize to somebody without sounding stupid, I figured. "Look, I—I know stuff's been really weird, so I just wanted to apologize and make it up to you, but I didn't think they were going to be there, and I just needed, like, two seconds to say that, and so I just came over here without really thinking."

Freddie was still pressed up against the wall beside me, blue eyes barely visible in what little light had made it from the far buildings into the little overhang.

"Oh," Freddie said, blinking. He was blinking a lot. Like more than was needed. Was I blinking too much? Was I talking too fast? Why was—"I, uh, thanks, man. I didn't—"

"And you just seemed, you know, bummed out today, and I thought—well I didn't think it was because of me like that sounds really arrogant, you know, but just, I felt bad that you were like my closest friend here and I just made stuff really weird so I wanted to try to make things cool again so I—" I had to stop and take a breath, which gave me the chance to fumble in my pocket and pull out the surprise I'd gone hunting for halfway through reviewing tape.

It was wrapped in cafeteria napkins, hopefully enough of them that the cookie inside was still edible and not sweaty or weird or anything. "I, uh, it was supposed to still be warm."

I looked down at Freddie unwrapping the cookie. His blonde hair was especially messy after a long day of sprinting entirely too much. I should've gotten him a better cookie, now that I was looking at this one again it wasn't the best I could've done.

"But I didn't really think that through, or, um, any of this through, so sorry, I just wanted stuff between us to be—"

His eyes bored into mine. I could see the twinkling reflection of a nearby lamppost and watched the gears turning behind them reminding me of the look he had the first time I saw him.

"I, uh, anyways, I just don't want stuff to be weird, so I'm sorry, and I was hoping—"

Suddenly his face was close to mine, his everything was close to mine (there were freckles and his nose). I could feel his breath (on mine some-how). I didn't get to say more.

Freddie leaned in and kissed me.

Chapter Eleven

I pulled away. Or fell back. Or stepped back. Or—or something. I did something, I think. I know I hit my head on the brick wall behind me.

I said ow. I mean, I heard someone say ow and they said it in my voice and I felt my lips moving, so I was pretty sure it was me, but it still was taking a second to register. Everything seemed like it was happening very slowly but also like it had already happened hours ago and I was trying desperately to catch up. Freddie looked at me and I could see his eyes widening—they were already wide, but they were changing, like before they were maybe wide from excitement and now it was like wide from concern.

"Did I—oh, I'm so, holy crap, I'm sorry, I didn't—"

"Uh, no, no—I hit my head on the wall, you didn't—"

Freddie and I were both talking but I couldn't have told you any of what either of us said. I was trying to—I was trying to just grasp what had happened. My heart was shaking like I was having a seizure and my legs were tense and tight and I couldn't catch my breath and I was definitely breathing too loud and too often. I could feel my hands shaking, and they felt both clammy and sweaty and way too warm all at once, and there was a sort of jolt that kept lighting up the sides of my face and all the way down to my chest where it felt like my stomach had slowly winched its way to the top of the first rollercoaster drop only to go screaming all the way down.

The only thing that I could think of to compare it to—and I was thinking of this in the moment, Freddie's voice and my voice both floating interminably through my brain as I kept thinking of other stuff—was competing in the championship game for my spring season club team a few weeks before, where all the nerves had been there for everyone. Well, for me. Everyone else wasn't super worried because it was just a club team invitational. But if I whiffed this, well, there was always a chance Weltmeister would've rescinded the invitation, and it might've been too late to get in at Brightbirch again, and it would've been too late for any other soccer camps or anything like that. I'd already told people I was going to Weltmeister, and there was going to be nothing worse than saying "hey, not only did I suck too hard to go play soccer, I also sucked too hard to hang out with my other friends, so I'm back here doing nothing all summer."

"Kit," Freddie said, and I tried to swallow and get my throat to be less dry. Why was my mouth dry but everything else so freaking sweaty? "Kit—I, are you...are you okay? I'm sorry, I didn't—"

This wasn't a championship game. My brain was somewhere else and right there beside that archway at the same time. I couldn't really figure out exactly why that was the first thing my brain had decided to leap onto as a reference point. I—he had kissed me. Like, with his mouth. I mean, obviously with his mouth, but—I...I just hadn't expected that. Or at all. Or really known anything about what I was expecting. What had I been expecting?

I looked back at Freddie realizing that I had been so lost inside my own head. Thoughts were bouncing around like someone had thrown a bunch of marbles into the dryer and put it on tumble. I hadn't really paid attention to him. He had shrunk, almost. Just barely, almost imperceptibly, in the matter of a few seconds. The back of my head still ached. I could see his shoulders had sagged, and there was something like doubt flickering in his eyes and making his mouth open and close without any sound coming out, like he was looking for words and couldn't quite coax them out.

"I shouldn't—"

I realized he thought I was pulling away because I didn't—because I didn't want that (did I?), and not just because I was surprised, and it caught me off-guard. It was my first kiss. Ever. I don't know how I'd anticipated it happening but not like that.

In that second all the marbles in the dryer stopped bouncing around. The adrenaline that was pumping into my brain slowed things down and I took a minute to not think about how I shouldn't have yanked back or why I was sweating so much or why my body felt weird or any of that, I just tried to think.

Freddie had kissed me.

And right now, Freddie looked wounded, worse than he had before. I'd just screwed things up and made them even worse. There was something about him that was just soft, the curl of his hair that drooped down over his forehead right over his eyes, the hunch of his shoulders, the—

The way his lips felt.

His lips. Freddie is a boy. A boy just kissed me.

In the brief little nanosecond that my brain remembered it was useful for productive, helpful thoughts, I realized that I'd hurt Freddie by recoiling and I hadn't meant to, I didn't want to hurt him, and I wasn't going to be able to convince him I hadn't meant to with words because I sucked with words, and I'd just been caught off-guard by the whole thing, it wasn't even that I hadn't enjoyed it, in fact, I'd—

I'd liked it, it felt right, it felt—

"Kit, I, God, I—I didn't mean—"

Before I lost my nerve or let myself overthink things too much I leaned back in and put my hands on either side of Freddie's face and kissed him.

I think I messed up and did it too hard. I'd never kissed anybody before, barring about ten seconds before. I clonked our foreheads together because

I got the angle wrong in the dark. Now both sides of my head were hurting. Granted, the stuff in-between them didn't seem to be doing too much for me, so maybe it wasn't that big of a loss.

It was Freddie's turn to step back, laughing a bit and rubbing at his forehead. "Ow, hey, dude, I take back the apology if you're gonna act like that about it."

I laughed a little and rubbed at my own forehead, wondering briefly if we'd have corresponding bruises in the morning and what excuse would possibly explain that. For a second my brain started winding up, thinking about one of the coaches looping back to grab a forgotten clipboard or phone and walking right into us, or the team, this somehow making things on the team weird.

Instead, I just tried to take a deep breath and looked back at Freddie. He was smiling, now.

"Can we, uh, be cool now?" I said.

Freddie smirked. "Yeah, I, uh, I'm...I'm cool with this. If...if you are, I mean."

I blinked, wondering how my throat and my mouth were so dry but I felt like my palms were soaking wet. "I—I, yeah. Yeah. I—I think so. Um—"

Freddie arched an eyebrow up at me.

"Do—would...would you want to go hang out for a while?"

I felt like I'd been saying the stupidest possible things with Freddie for—days, really, but tonight especially. That seemed to undo some of it. Whatever invisible knot or tension had been there before, all the confusing awkwardness...well, it still felt overwhelming. And confusing. And a little awkward. But now it didn't feel bad. It was maybe even good.

"I would like that," Freddie said, nodding. He was nodding a lot and shifting his weight back and forth from foot to foot and rubbing at his sleeves and his hair, fidgeting and fidgeting. "I don't know where we could go, though. It's going to be lights out in like half an hour and also we're going to have a pretty tough time explaining why we were so late to the coaches at the door."

"I got it covered," I said. "I found—well, it's probably easier to just show you. If you're cool with a bit of running around after-hours and risking getting murdered by Ludwig and Wilhelm."

"Well," Freddie said, brushing his hair back into place, "I figured we were going to die doing sprints one of these days anyway. This seems more fun."

"Low bar to clear, but I'll take it. This way."

I nodded and stepped past him to the threshold of the archway, where I kneeled and peeked out. I looked over the small shrubs that adorned the sidewalks, ready to fall flat if someone was coming back this way. I couldn't hear or see anyone. "Okay, follow me," I whispered. Without thinking about it, I stuck a hand back for Freddie and after a half-second pause, before I had time to wonder if that was weird or if that's what I was supposed to do or not, I felt his hand close around it.

"Sorry, I'm sweaty—"

"It's 200 degrees outside man. I'd think you were an alien or something if you weren't sweating."

I snorted and pulled him out, crouch-walking as quick as I could over to the next spot of cover. There was a walkway that had some brick columns supporting the roof above it alongside the sciences building, and we ducked from column to column, pausing to listen for footsteps or watch for lights turning on, but nothing came. I felt a bit silly, like maybe we were little kids playing at secret agent or something, but there was also the very real risk of getting found and chewed out by Ludwig.

Also, it was fun.

We crept back to the side of the dorms where I'd found the open window. I'd pulled it back as close to being shut as I dared to make sure no passing maintenance guy or anything spotted it. I glanced again, waiting and watching. Maybe Bronson had another phone call.

"Okay, all clear," I said.

"What are you talking about?"

"I found this the other night when I—" I realized it was the night Freddie and I had gotten into an argument. Shoot, was I supposed to not talk about that? "—I was walking around." I grunted and wrested the window open. I nodded and gave Freddie a boost as he clambered in, then I came in after him. The height of the window and the position of the desk right under it meant there was pretty much no graceful or cool-looking way to climb in. Fortunately, Freddie didn't seem to mind. I pulled the window almost-shut behind me and turned.

"Whoa," Freddie said, looking around. "I mean, it's just like our dorms, but—still. Is the whole building unlocked?"

"From the inside, yep," I said. "The best part is it lines up to ours, so—"

"—so we can just slip right back in," Freddie murmured. "Is there anything cool here?"

"I mean, there's me."

Freddie rolled his eyes.

"Hey, I can keep the secret dorms to myself if you don't think I'm cool enough."

"You haven't told anybody else about these?"

I shook my head.

Freddie nodded, chewing on his lip. "Do the lights and stuff work?"

"Don't!" I said.

"Oh, no, I wasn't going to turn them on, I was just wondering if—like utilities and stuff. Water, lights, all that."

"Yeah, I've been—I've been showering here, actually."

Freddie turned and clocked his head sideways a minute. "I...I guess I hadn't noticed you taking any showers the last few days now that I think about it. And it doesn't make sense they'd cut power to half the building."

I didn't say anything in response to that, and Freddie let it hang in the air a minute, but I think we were both thinking that he'd said he noticed when I was in the showers.

The buzzing feeling ran down along my ribcage and out to my arms and legs again. My brain and my eyes and my feet assured me that I was kneeling on the floor of a St. Michael's dorm, but there was something else that was entirely convinced I was swimming, half-weightless, and just being pulled this way and that. "I, yeah. Here, let's get away from the window in case someone walks by. Bronson likes to talk on the phone out here at night."

"Anything juicy?"

"No, he just misses his dogs."

"Oh. Me too, honestly."

I gently pushed open the door into the dorm hallway and eased it shut behind me, triple-checking it wasn't locked behind me.

"Have you already explored the whole place?"

"I mean, not really. I just hang out in the showers and sometimes just read or write letters in here a bit when I need a minute to get away from everything."

Freddie paused, thinking. "Let's go all the way upstairs."

"Why?"

"Just wondering about something."

He had a bit of a glint in his eyes.

Freddie took the lead and we walked down the hallway, crouching when we got near the big open windows about halfway down and standing back up when we were in the clear. We got to the stairs at the end of the building and made our way up and up and up.

In all the chaos, I'd forgotten just how much running we'd done earlier that day, but the third and fourth flight of stairs were all too happy to remind me. I mean I was—I had a lot to think about, I guess, or maybe a lot to not think about—but all I was focusing on for about thirty seconds was just how bad my thighs hurt getting to the top of the stairwell.

We got to the top floor and my brain started to pick up where Freddie was going. Periodically during the summer, they'd come through and do maintenance of the different buildings—ours included. Obviously, they couldn't do a lot while we were all living in there, but I guess St. Michael's was a pretty old school so they had to do renovations and stuff a lot. They were doing renovations on this half of the building while we were in the other half, and I suppose next summer they'd flip the two, or something like that.

Where Freddie's brain had gone was that on top of the dorms, there was a—not quite a clock tower. It didn't have a clock. It wasn't even a full tower, really, just kind of this top part that jutted out over the roof. I didn't know enough about architecture to describe it correctly, and to be honest, I had way more to focus on than what the thing was supposed to be called.

The door from our side was locked shut—at least half the guys in our building had tried to open it at some point or another, and there had been a short-lived contest to see if you could kick a ball from the top of the stairwell hard enough to get it all the way to the bottom. I wouldn't have been surprised if they'd welded that door shut just to be on the safe side from lawsuits.

I mean, after all, at some point, some troublemakers would've had the bright idea to go sneaking around and try to get up there, right?

The door on our side, however, was open. There were a few boxes of tools and supplies and some half-empty water bottles lying around. The renovation guys had been doing work up here and on this half of the building throughout the summer—they'd just left the doors open and figured they were fine if the exterior ones were locked.

Freddie and I shared a glance and a grin and kept going.

We stepped over some of those big plastic sheets they lay down when they're tearing up buildings and renovating and tried to make sure we didn't step on anything important. There was a ton of dust in the attic of the dorms, and for a moment I was worried we were going to leave footprints. But to be honest there were like fifteen thousand footprints on those plastic sheets already, and I wanted to be on top of the building with Freddie more than I wanted to not get caught in that moment.

There were a few places where we had to duck or even crawl under some thick ventilation pipes, and a few spots where giant fans whirled and groaned and rattled. Freddie and I fumbled against the walls until we found a light switch. We turned it on—there weren't any windows to give us away.

We squeezed around some folding chairs and pages with notes and measurements and other stuff that neither Freddie nor I really cared about. In the center of the dark, cramped room was the one spot where the ceiling reached up over five feet: there was a metal spiral staircase going up.

"You wanna go for it?" Freddie asked me.

"Hell yes."

Freddie grinned at me, eyes alight, and headed up the stairs. I was right behind him and caught myself worrying that he might slip and I'd need to catch him before I had time to really wonder why that was a thing I was worrying about.

Freddie came to the top of the steps and tested the doorknob, which opened. "Dude," he said, turning and looking back at me.

I nodded. I had figured at least one of the doors would've been locked, but we'd gotten lucky. Or more realistically the maintenance guys got really careless.

He eased it open gently but quickly, and we both came outside before the light inside could get spotted. I checked to be sure it wouldn't lock shut behind us and eased it back closed.

I realized we didn't have anything to be worried about the light being spotted from the ground, given the angle we were at when I looked around. We were in a small little nook, and the stairs kept going up maybe eight or nine more feet to the roof itself. We crept on up, feeling the breeze come through. I could distantly hear cars driving.

Up top, a walkway stretched from one end of the building to the other, where the stairwells that led up and down either half of the dorms were. There was no way to access those stairwells from here—we were a whole floor on top of them, in fact—but if we clambered down out of the tower we could've walked along the top of the roof. I stood next to Freddie on the railing, glancing around at the campus.

I'd been telling myself as we crept up that I would check for anybody walking around campus, or make sure we weren't silhouetted against the night sky too badly, or all kinds of practical, smart things. But the truth was just that I got up there and leaned against the railing, legs aching, heart still going really fast, and looked out at the campus.

There were the baseball fields, the spot I'd seen Oliver drilling shots into the batting cages, the practice fields, every loop and turn and curve of Bronson's running trails, the academic buildings where we watched tape, the field where we'd jogged out for conditioning on the first day, the winding road that led right back out of campus...

"This is awesome," Freddie said, his voice barely above a whisper. He turned and looked at me. "Thanks for showing me."

"It was your idea," I said.

He started to say something, then had a better idea.

The third time we kissed there weren't any hiccups like the first two. His lips were soft, and I didn't concuss him, and it must've lasted for a minute before we pulled away, but it wasn't a bad kind of pulling away, it just happened, as if we'd both rehearsed and timed it.

"This is..." Freddie squinted, looking out over the distance. He leaned against my shoulder, and I could feel his warmth against me. It was, even with the breeze, still a hellishly warm Weltmeister evening, but the warmth felt good. Safe. "This is *not* how I expected this day to go."

"Yeah," I said. I arched my neck, looking all around. "Yeah, I—I mean I don't have anything to follow that up with. I was just hoping you'd like the cookie."

Freddie snickered and fumbled in his back pocket, pulling it out. We took turns pulling off pieces, looking out at the campus.

"So," Freddie said, licking a bit of chocolate off his thumb. "Not to, uh, ruin what's been pretty much the best night of camp—"

"What, you think this is better than dodgeball?"

Freddie grinned but kept going, "I mean beating Team Three did kick ass, true—but...I...I gotta know why you were being so weird, dude. I mean was it just...you know." He motioned between us. "Was it when I walked you back to your dorm that night? I didn't mean to make you—I mean, there were people around and stuff, so I figured maybe you just..." he paused, thinking. "I guess I figured I was misreading it. But, you were cool after that for a while and then got...the way things have been. So I don't know. I thought you figured things out and just weren't interested or...something weird. I don't want things to be weird. I want things to be like this."

I took a deep breath. For starters, I hadn't even considered—I mean I had thought that night was a little awkward but I hadn't really thought about it all that much since then. But apparently Freddie had? I'd been more focused on the—well, the whole incident. But of course Freddie wasn't thinking about that, because he had no clue about that. I guess I hadn't stopped to think about what Freddie had been focusing on this whole time.

In my defense the last fifteen minutes hadn't left me a lot of time to think.

Which I think I was okay with. I took a deep breath. Somehow, it still felt like it might be weird to say, like it might jinx things. It honestly felt like we were juggling a soccer ball back and forth, but the ball was made of glass, and we were standing on concrete, and if I said or did one really stupid thing or missed a single step that was all it would take to screw it up. "...if you tell me why you were all bummed today, I'll tell you," I said.

I don't really know if that was fair or right of me or not. I just felt like I didn't want to be the only one who had to say something weird. I felt like—maybe if we both had to say something like that, neither one would be as bad, or it would even out, or something.

But beyond that, I didn't want to see Freddie as melancholy as he'd been today.

Freddie didn't quite physically flinch or rock back, but something in his expression did, like he'd swum through a cold patch in a lake. "I...okay. If..." he paused. I didn't press him. It stayed quiet between us for a minute or two before he found his words and started to talk again. His side was pressed against mine, but he didn't make eye contact with me, he just looked over at the practice fields and talked in a soft steady voice like he was afraid if he stopped he'd lose the nerve to keep going again.

"I just...I don't know, man. Everybody else on the team is ripped. You and Alejandro almost won the beep test and Martin can bench like a stupid amount and even Chandler is rail thin, which is nuts, because I don't think that guy leaves the basement when he's not playing soccer."

I tried not to laugh because I didn't want to make it seem like I was laughing at Freddie. But I still laughed.

"Sorry, I think that was mean. Anyways, I mean, it just—it was doing those sprints and being last on the team, and the parachute belt, and not even being ranked, and—"

His voice started to trail. I gave him a minute to see if he was going to say anything else. "The parachute belt?" I asked. I thought back, trying to remember that morning. It felt as far away and as different a place as my first morning at Brightbirch had been. "...you fumbled with the belt for a second, but I don't remember anything else. You ran fine."

"I was the only one that had to notch the belt up a size," Freddie said, looking out, again not meeting my eyes. "It just...I don't know. It's stupid. And going and taking showers and stuff feels like one of those nightmares where you show up to school naked, I mean it—I don't know. I don't know."

"It's not stupid," I said, trying to think on what Freddie had said. I mean, Freddie wasn't built like an Olympian, but neither were half the guys at camp. Neither were most of the guys who were ranked. And it wasn't like that mattered, because the guys who could outrun Freddie in a dead sprint stopped giving it their all long before Freddie ever did. There was something nagging at me, too, something I hadn't caught onto, something—

"You skipped lunch today," I said, feeling it click.

Freddie said nothing to that.

"You're..." I paused, not wanting my words to come out wrong, but not wanting the pause to sound bad either. I didn't know how to say Freddie was fine without just saying, "you're fine," but that sounded like what Mom told me after that stupid haircut. So that would've been a terrible pick for several reasons. Nothing else was coming to me, and I felt like I needed to say something, so I just went for the first thing I thought of looking at Freddie there on top of the not-tower. "...cute. Don't worry about it." Did I just call him cute?

Freddie didn't say anything for a moment, and I realized he'd sniffled once or twice. I pretended not to hear. I wasn't sure what I was supposed to say, and tried to think of what would be right. I leaned over and gave him a small kiss on the cheek, because I didn't know if you were supposed to kiss when somebody was sad or not but I didn't want to do nothing. Before I could think about it anymore or say anything Freddie started talking again..

"Thanks," he said, shifting his weight back and forth a bit, but giving me a small smile. *Well I guess it was okay.* "Your turn."

I exhaled slowly. "Um. Well." It was my turn to look down over the railing while I could feel Freddie's eyes studying me. "Okay. So, uh. I guess first, if you feel, you know. You can use my showers if you want. I've been doing it, I don't like showering in front of a bunch of strangers. It's weird. Even showering in front of the team still feels weird."

"Really?" Freddie said, the shakiness melting out of his voice.

"Yeah, of course, I mean—there's like fifty empty showers on this half of the building. Go wild."

"Thanks," Freddie said. "But that wasn't the thing that had you acting weird."

"Yeah," I said, clasping my hands together, then unclasping them and putting them on the railing because that felt weird. Freddie put one of his over mine. "So, um, you remember when—it was last week, I was helping you with the hamstring stretch, and I basically got a view of the. Uh. You know. Jewel chest."

"Jewel chest?"

I could feel my face burning. "Um. Yeah. Like—like your family jewels."

"No—I understand what you meant, just—why would you say it like that?"

"Yeah that—sorry. That wasn't the best way to break that news, probably."

"Definitely not." I felt Freddie's hand on mine tremble slightly.

I took a deep breath and tried to keep going. "I just...I was worried that if I said anything it might wind up like a Mole Rat situation...not that you would be made fun of or anything, just that I thought maybe other people saw at first, and if some Mole Rat situation happened and you left that would've sucked because you're the person I'm closest with here at camp, and then I couldn't...I couldn't figure out why I kept thinking about it, and whenever you tried to talk I just...I kept picturing it and worrying about it. I was freaking out that I'd do something dumb and screw up the best friendship I'd made here and then...I...well. Did something dumb and screwed up the best friendship I'd made here, I guess."

Freddie didn't say anything for a minute, but he didn't take his hand off mine.

"Thanks for telling me, I know that was probably tough."

"I mean," I said, turning to look at him. "I guess less tough than it would've been a couple hours ago. I feel kinda silly about it now."

Freddie gave me a wide smile. "Well, that's...I mean, I was worried I'd done or said something. So I guess that's better. Sorry for making you uncomfortable. I wasn't trying to."

"No, don't—don't apologize. It's fine, man." I smiled. "More than fine."

"Yeah," Freddie said. "I think so, too."

We finished the rest of the cookie and stayed up talking until the last lights on at Weltmeister all went out.

Chapter Twelve

Breakfast the next morning was the first time I ate Weltmeister scrambled eggs without once stopping to think about how terrible they were.

I was sitting almost alone in the dining hall. A few early birds had trickled in shortly after me, but I'd literally been the first one to swipe through. The bulk of the camp was either going to take a shower or trying to eke out another quarter hour of sleep before the fear of Wilhelm put them in line for breakfast.

Team Six's table was empty, which gave me room to spread out my cups and plates. I didn't even really need the space. In fact, I wasn't even really that hungry. I just hadn't slept much—maybe not a surprise—and felt like my body should probably make up for lack of energy in one category with more energy elsewhere. I don't know if that was how it worked, metabolically—in fact, I'm almost certain it wasn't—but it felt like I needed to at least attempt to mitigate the issue. In true Chandler fashion, I'd adopted a mug of coffee, then had to go back up and dump stuff in it until the coffee became legally classifiable as a dairy product.

At some point today, I was sure the two and a half hours of sleep were going to catch up to me, but at the moment, I'd woken up wired and stayed that way. I figured the coffee would delay that crash. Maybe somebody here had smuggled in energy drinks or knew if there was a vending machine that sold them. I normally would've just accepted I was going to have an off day, but today was the most important day of the camp thus far.

The tournament was starting today.

That should've had me more nervous, or anxious, or—something. It wasn't like I wasn't excited about the tournament. I'd managed to keep my rank from plummeting into triple digits and held right near the edge of the top fifty. We'd all gotten better—noticeably better—and there was something exhilarating about finally getting to see if all those wind sprints were going to pay off. Sink or swim. Climbing up the wall without a rope.

And yet my primary thought was not any of that, or my coffee-flavored-creamer, or the leftover Goodyear tires they painted yellow and served as eggs.

I was eating, staring at the napkin holder in front of me, ignoring the half-started letter to Kyle beside me, trying to figure out if I was gay. I mean Freddie was gay, Freddie knew he was gay. He'd said he was not really out. I think only one or two of his close friends knew, tops. Not even his team knew. I didn't know what his high school or hometown or even his family was like, and even knowing what he shared, I didn't know what that made me.

I felt dumb for even wondering. It was the sort of question that, had I vocalized to Kyle, he would've laughed until something ruptured—not that any internal organs are necessary to play baseball, granted. It wasn't like Kyle didn't like gay people or anything, he just would've found it hilarious that I'd, you know, kissed a guy, and then woken up early the next day and sat around wondering if I was gay or not.

Which, I mean. I guess maybe he had a point there. The annoying thing about Kyle is that he was usually sixty percent right on stuff.

Yet at the same time, I wasn't really sure how that stuff was supposed to work. I mean, there had been a gay guy on my junior varsity team who was far and away the most popular member of the team. I mean, I certainly wasn't competition in that regard; I was either practicing, studying, or sleeping. But he'd go to parties and routinely make out with girls just because, apparently, he could? And it wasn't like anybody ever saw him do that and thought, "Hey, I guess Mason's straight now."

I swallowed the eggs. A minute of chewing had not meaningfully altered their consistency.

A part of me was almost annoyed at Freddie for having done this right before the tournament started. That part of me wasn't really whining that enthusiastically, however. For starters, the immediate follow-up was: if he hadn't made a move yesterday, when would he have done it? The last day of camp? Then what? I mean, he said he was and he'd thought I was cute from day one. Freddie had apparently been worried I figured it out and just wasn't into him, and he was freaking out about me being distant and cold until I gave him the cookie. Which, I mean. I just thought Freddie was really nice.

I scratched at the side of my head. *I don't think I'm very good at this yet.* I realized something. *If Patrick ever hears about how bad I am at flirting and figuring this stuff out he's never going to let me hear the end of this.*

But beyond the possibility of being roasted by my brother for the rest of my life, it wasn't even like I was worried, or freaking out. I mean, I was being in my head about it, and overthinking it, but I did that standing in line to buy a burger, let alone figure out...this. Which is good because Freddie had said he wasn't expecting anything right away and hadn't said anything about wanting me to say I was gay or that we were a couple or...or anything, really. He was just good with whatever it was.

I don't think I have a problem with being gay, I thought, pretending to enjoy my coffee. I could again distinctly hear Kyle laughing at that, telling me that was probably a good thing given recent events.

That made me smirk. Which probably made me look crazy, sitting by myself, eating two IHOP's worth of breakfasts, and just laughing at nothing, but whatever. Maybe it would scare the competition.

I guess what I found so freaking weird about it was that it didn't feel weird. I mean, I'd spent like a week freaking out over having seen Freddie partially naked, and then trying to deal with all the icy awkwardness that had been there afterwards. So why wasn't I worrying about this more?

I stared at my now nearly-finished coffee. I was not any closer to figuring any of this out than I had been at the start of the mug.

Helps you focus, my ass.

I leaned back and ran a hand through my hair, trying to think. I didn't think I had a problem with being gay. I just didn't think I was anything before, honestly.

I knew a fair number of other guys my age had already gone on dates and made out and stuff—a few had gone further than that—but none of it had really seemed to click for me. I figured it would happen in another year or two, and I'd been too busy to give it much more time than that. It was the same way I felt about getting married and having kids one day: it was probably going to happen at some point, sure, but I have two games and a midterm this week to worry about.

And besides, I knew plenty of guys my age who hadn't done any of that. Even, you know, guys who could have gone on dates but were choosing not to. Not just guys who weren't getting dates because they didn't shower or talked about anime too much or something. I guess that was a distinction worth noting.

If I was gay, did that rock the boat at all? I mean I hadn't thought anything of having Mason on the team in high school, but I suppose if I was also gay, that didn't really make me an objective voice to weigh in on the issue. I didn't think Kyle would care at all. I guess beyond that I didn't have a ton of guy friends. The guys at Brightbirch wouldn't mind, and I could keep it from them even if I thought they would—

Wait, was this the sort of thing I was going to have to tell people? Or make public?

At that I could feel the flicker of something twisting in my gut, the spiraling you get before a huge game or exam or something. Almost like stage fright. No, I mean—I didn't think Freddie would go around telling anybody, and if—

"Morning," Freddie said behind me.

I flinched and yelped in a really masculine and tough way before turning around. Freddie was grinning, hair wet from a shower—a private shower, one might've guessed—and he gave me a knuckle bump on the shoulder. It felt a bit off. I mean, it was just how I would've greeted a friend, you know, but was I supposed to do anything more than that, or say something? I'd always figured when I was eventually in a relationship, I could just get all the pointers on this stuff from Kyle.

"I said 'morning'," Freddie said again.

"Sorry, I'm totally out of it. Morning. Good shower?"

"Amazing shower," Freddie said, stretching. "Zoning out on tournament day?"

"Yeah, I, uh, might not have gotten a ton of sleep last night."

Freddie's eyes were a mischievous blue twinkle at that. I was distinctly reminded, for some reason I couldn't quite place, of when we'd snuck out of the cabins at Brightbirch to raid the kitchens for s'mores supplies. "Funny how that works. I'm going to grab some food. You need anything?"

"No, I honestly can't even eat all of this."

"I don't even think Martin could eat all of that, man."

I grinned and Freddie moseyed off, stopping to talk to somebody he recognized for a brief second and then heading on to one of the breakfast stations.

Man, when had he had time to make friends *outside* the team? I still couldn't even tell Damian and Charles apart one hundred percent of the time.

Freddie came back and sat down a few minutes later, and I gave up on forcing myself to eat more. We talked for a minute about the tournament, the opposition, the last few games. At once, it felt like there was an elephant in the room and nothing had changed at all. The longer we talked, the less it felt like I needed to pull out a notebook and outline what had happened, or what we were supposed to do, or how we were supposed to act, or any of that.

It just felt normal.

The rest of the team came trickling in shortly thereafter, but it had given Freddie and me maybe five undisturbed minutes to just chat about nothing. As everybody else settled in, the table filled up with noise. I hadn't gotten the opportunity to sit and dissect things, but as Freddie turned and chatted with Damian (who was initially trying to quiz Freddie on why he was out so late before Freddie deflected to talking about some really annoying guy from their high school) and Mateo asked his half of the table to analyze a cryptic text his girlfriend had sent him, I realized I...didn't really need to dissect things. Right?

I mean, even though it had only been twelve hours or so, I hadn't stopped and laid out a roadmap or guidelines or anything. It was just going without any kind of rigorous analysis.

I flipped the eggs around on my fork.

...maybe I'd just try to keep it that way for a while. Would be a pretty big first for Kit Cook—*among a few other recent big firsts*, I thought, feeling a sudden rush of jitters—but they were always telling us to challenge ourselves at Weltmeister. Not sure it's quite what Wilhelm had intended, but oh well.

Talk shifted quickly to tournament tactics, who we'd be up against, things we should do differently. There was a fair amount of trash talk, the spectrum of which almost perfectly matched the length of the table, with the quality of roasts of other teams getting progressively weaker the farther down from Chandler and Martin you got.

"So," Mateo said, tucking his phone away hurriedly and not at all smoothly as Wilhelm and Bronson walked by. Bronson looked like he'd just gotten back from a run.

Wait, did he go take a run *before* leading our runs each day?

I zoned out of what Mateo was saying for a moment to process that degree of masochism.

"—now, we're seeded seventh—"

A round of condemnations for the ranking systems, whoever decided team placements, and Ludwig for good measure went around the table.

"—so we're up against Team Four first. They're sixth." Mateo grabbed a pen from Chandler, who usually brought a notepad and pen with him to breakfast while he drank coffee (I feel obligated to mention Chandler never actually wrote anything with them, he just put them there next to his mug). He sketched out a bracket and jotted down the placements, Miles and Charles chiming in to help him remember a few of the other seeds.

"Hey, you guys want to put money on this?" Martin asked.

"No one trusts you to be bookie, Martin, let me finish. Now, Tournament days are—well, not easy, but easier. Runs a bit shorter, Ludwig won't make anybody do a thousand push-ups, nothing like that." He paused, looking at the paper. "Maybe just five hundred or so. Anyway, normal tournament rules. There's the group stage and then the winner's bracket and a loser's bracket. Basically like the World Cup except even if we lose, we still have a chance at winning, or at least to keep playing for second." Mateo flipped the paper out and jotted out what could loosely be described as a calendar.

"Reason you're not going to art camp, huh?" Martin said.

Mateo said something in German which made him snort with laughter, but I wasn't able to catch it. Just speculation, but I'm guessing the moral character of Martin's mother was brought into question.

"Anyways, tournament's the rest of camp. We still do morning drills, light afternoon drills, but they're not bad. Mostly to keep you warmed up."

"What," Charles said, "is the gameplan for playing Team Four?"

"Oh, are we working with gameplans now?" Victor asked.

Charles rolled his eyes.

Four's striker had scored on me, earlier in the summer. In my head, I ran through the shortlist of people who had beaten me in a one-on-one and gone on to score.

I looked at the sketched-out tournament brackets, noting the team placements. Seeing the team numbers jotted down in Mateo's lazy, loopy handwriting brought back replays of the times I'd been beaten over the summer. It lasted for a moment, then I blinked and turned my focus back to what we were talking about. *Don't dwell on screw-ups, just focus on being better.*

We talked shop and strategy until it started to get close to time to get ready. I put away my things and started walking back to my dorm to change.

I was just on the cusp of realizing that I hadn't—for what felt like the first time in months, even though I knew that wasn't true—worried about Freddie at all that morning. Well, okay. I was still worrying. But it wasn't like the end-of-the-world, can't-stop-thinking-about-it-type worrying I'd had after I accidentally saw Freddie's junk. It was different worrying. I'm not sure I was capable of not worrying, I just suppose...there hadn't been any freaking out or anything. Things were just normal.

I had just started to process that when I felt a hand clap me on the back.

"Hey, Kit," Damian said. "Can I talk to you real quick, man?"

"Yeah, of course. You want to swap positions?"

"No, no, you're killing it where you're at. Listen, uh, do you—do you know if Freddie's, like...okay?"

I blinked. A lot. Possibly a conspicuous amount. I was perhaps not the best at keeping my expressions neutral. It occurred to me, admittedly way later than it should have, that there was *maybe* a connection between this fact and the fact I had lost every game of poker I'd ever played with Kyle and his buddies. Food for later thought. "Uh, as far as I know, yeah. Why? Is something up?"

Damian scratched at the back of his head, turning and glancing around to see who was near us before continuing. "It's probably nothing, it's just he was acting all mopey yesterday and then didn't get in until, like, super late. He woke me up. I mean—I don't care, I just went right back to sleep, but like just making sure, you know. If he's out wandering around or something."

"Oh," I said. I mean, it didn't sound like Damian was insinuating anything, which immediately wonder if it was a bad thing if he insinuated something, and why was I worried? I mean, I didn't want it to be a thing people talked about—not that it would be like the Mole Rat incident, but I suppose some part of me wondered if—

Kit say something you're just walking lost in thought like an idiot.

"No, I mean—he seemed like he was having an off day yesterday but I don't think there was anything worse than that. If so, I don't know about it."

"Gotcha," Damian said, nodding as he walked. "Okay, I just figured I'd ask you."

I felt like it may have been less-than-helpful towards the goal of not bringing attention to whatever it was that Freddie and I were, but curiosity got the better of me. "What do you mean?"

"Oh, you guys just seem tight is all." Damian said. "I figured you might know. I asked Charles and Victor but they didn't have any idea."

"Gotcha," I said. I wasn't totally sure how I felt about that. Some part of me was annoyed he even went to Charles or Victor. I mean, they went to high school with Freddie and were around him all year. So he should've gone to them first, they knew him better. That made sense.

Right?

"Okay, let me change and I'll catch you on the field. If Mateo's right, it'll be a light run."

"God willing."

I bid Damian farewell and chewed on what he said until I jogged back out to the field. Everybody was stretching and limbering up, and I caught out of the corner of my eye Freddie go down as if to do a hamstring stretch, stop, and suppress a grin before shifting to stretch his own leg in a different way.

I did my best to hide a smile too. I hadn't ever been a part of a secret. Kyle always screwed up keeping a secret pretty fast and Patrick would always just tell somebody anyway, so I'd never really kept like a serious secret. Which I guess this was? Though it didn't feel like a secret. I think if I'd had a few days of not having anything else going on—no tournament, no burpees, no Richard snoring like a Yeti in an iron lung—I probably could've made heads or tails of this sort of thing. My brain kept wandering off and trying to make sense of things, and then remembering I didn't necessarily have to.

Which was odd. It wasn't the way I did things. I knew I wanted to play on varsity, and wanted to start as soon as I could. That meant working hard to get off the freshman team and onto JV my first year. That meant running extra after practice, watching tape, going to camps like this one. Same with school stuff—I knew the grades I wanted to get, how much I wanted to study, so on and so forth. There were other things I had nebulous plans for: at some point I'd need to figure out getting into a good college, and I guess I was supposed to go to prom at some point, but things like that or a first kiss weren't events I'd thought about as much.

Was your first kiss supposed to be like that?

I wanted to bounce it off someone and just get confirmation that I was either crazy or completely normal. Either one at least would've settled the matter and I could've focused on playing. But at the same time, I had a feeling asking the guys on the team what their first kiss was like would've resulted in some of the longest-lasting and most thorough roasting of my life. And, honestly? Would've had it coming for that one.

"Ready?" Freddie asked me.

I realized we'd get to talk again while we ran today. I caught myself smiling before I tried to shake it off and not make it seem like a whole big thing—but Freddie started to grin, too.

"Yeah, let's go."

"Only three miles today, boys, nice and easy!" Bronson bellowed from the front of the column, and we took off at a steady jog.

"So," Freddie said about a quarter mile in, once we'd gotten our rhythm and pacing down. Behind me I could hear Chandler and Slick talking about some movie series, but one of the Team Eight guys running behind *them* kept snapping at them to not spoil anything. "What's on your mind?"

I kept my eyes on my feet so if my face got any redder it wouldn't be as noticeable. "Oh," I said, trying to think of something witty. "...Modern History."

Freddie smirked. "Glad to see I won you over to the stuff that's actually fun to study in class."

"Nerds!" Martin shouted from in front of us.

Well. He wasn't wrong.

"Well, what kind of history should you teach me?" I asked Freddie. I clocked a root up ahead of me that I jumped over. A moment or two later I heard Chandler curse and stumble for a bit.

"Hmm," Freddie said, feigning deep, ponderous thought. "What kind are you curious about? What's on your mind?"

"What about nerd history?" Martin said.

I ignored him. "Well, mostly running is on my mind." I felt a sudden rush like I'd gotten deciding to slip out and grab the cookie, and before I could feel it go away I added, "Mostly."

It was hard to tell with his face starting to redden from the running, but I thought I saw the hint of a blush on Freddie's face. "Of course," he said, ever-so-slightly tripping over the words. "Well, let me think. The best runners in history—"

"Me!" Martin shouted.

"Martin, I'm amazed you can talk and run at the same time," Chandler shouted back.

"...were maybe...well, let me think," Freddie said. "The original marathon guy, maybe—"

"Huh?" I asked.

"Yeah, the first marathon guy. I think there was some important news he needed to carry—the Greeks won a battle, I'm pretty sure—so he ran twenty-six straight miles to deliver it and then immediately dropped dead."

I glanced up at Bronson at the front of the column. "How relatable."

"But you could also talk Mongols, if you throw in horses running, too."

"They're talking horses, Martin, you going to let them diss your Mom like that?"

I did my best to ignore them and listen to Freddie even as the pace picked up. "Tell me about them," I said.

"Well, no real shocker here, but they were maybe the best horse riders, ever."

"Aside from Martin's dad!"

Freddie had to pause to wait for the noise to die down before I could hear him again. I rolled my eyes and he gave me a wink.

"But, anyway, they did crazy stuff. They had figured out that they could cut their horses, just a tiny bit, and it wouldn't hurt the horses but they could drink their blood to sustain them and give them energy on long hauls."

I blinked. "Wow, really?" I wasn't sure I'd ever been thirsty enough to drink horse blood. Actually, I was sure. I had definitely never been thirsty enough to drink horse blood.

"Yeah that's actually nuts," Chandler said. "You think that's how Bronson has so much energy? I bet that guy has like three or four Clydesdales hidden somewhere."

I thought I saw the beginnings of a scowl when Chandler spoke up, but admittedly everybody scowls eventually on a Bronson run. Even the allegedly easy ones.

"Horses are lame," Martin said. "Do military history. I want to hear about stuff blowing up."

I didn't imagine it this time, I definitely saw something turn tense on Freddie's face there. *Oh.* "Actually, no, I want to hear more about the Mongols."

"Me too," Chandler said, "Go away, Martin."

"Oh, yeah, um, so they would also—" Freddie continued, and I let the impromptu lecture take my mind off the run.

When we were done we had a quick minute to breathe, get water, and reset. The rest of the morning stations were light enough—cone drills, ball control, juggling, very technical aspects. Even in the late July heat, nobody was sweating terribly bad.

Or, I suppose, if they were, it was from nerves and not from heat.

Everybody on the team kept trying to crack jokes and mention other stuff, but it seemed like every conversation seemed to swirl back around and around to the tournament throughout the day, no matter where we were or what we were doing.

"Team Four's got a really good striker, but who else?" Slick would say during our few minutes of rest between drills, interrupting Damian and Charles talking about how they could each take one half of the summer reading when they got back to save time. "And he's not even that good. I mean, I've scored like twice as much as he has—"

"—their keeper's nice enough," Miles said, with the slightest flicker of a pointed look to Martin "—but I don't think he's the best at Weltmeister by any means. Frankly, I think defense is the weakest aspect of their game. What do you think, Chandler?"

"I think you're being way too polite, their keeper looks like one of those inflatable air guys outside a car dealership when he goes for saves, the only question is if their striker can carry them, but—"

We finished drills, we finished lunch. "What do you guys think? How far are we getting?" Charles asked to Damian, Victor, Alejandro and myself, walking back from lunch.

"I think we'll make it pretty far," Freddie said. "We've really improved a ton. I mean, I think first week of the summer, I would've said we'd be lucky to win anything, but honestly, we're way better."

Alejandro, true to form, said nothing, but nodded.

"Only question is," Victor said, "Did everyone else improve more than we improved?"

Freddie looked like he was trying to remain optimistic but answered that with a shrug. I suppose you can only try to out-talk pessimism for so long before it just comes off like an after-school special.

What he said was right though. We had gotten a lot better.

And yet I was still thinking more about Victor said than what Freddie had said when I laid down for an extremely needed nap after lunch.

When I woke up, it was time for the tournament. Everyone trying their hardest. The final opportunity to fight for the number next to your name on the leaderboards.

I laced up my cleats and told myself my hands were definitely not shaking a bit.

Chapter Thirteen

"So," Chandler said, in what I'm pretty sure was the driest tone I'd ever heard someone use in my life, "you're suggesting that Freddie is staying out late because of drugs?"

Damian shrugged. I caught the slightest hint of his face reddening. He scratched at the back of his head and became quite interested in his cleats. "Well, I mean, no, just that his behavior's been off lately, he's out at weird times—"

"Freddie," Chandler continued, unabated, "Who once apologized to me six times for accidentally taking a sip from my water cup instead of his during halftime?"

"Okay, so maybe not drugs, that was dumb, yes, but something—"

"You actually thought Freddie was involved with drugs. Who is his dealer? Mr. Rogers? The Pope?"

"Alright, alright, point taken, I'm just saying something weird is all—"

"Hey," I said, my voice coming out snappier and sterner than I meant. Chandler and Damian both did a reflexive half-flinch, as if their brains processed the tone of voice and instinctively expected Ludwig, before realizing I was forty years too young and significantly less German. *Pavlov would've made a great soccer coach.* "Uh, sorry, that came out little stronger than I meant it. But can we focus? We're up in a sec."

Chandler shrugged, rolling a ball over with the underside of his cleat as he watched the assistant coaches jog across the field and get everything set up. His cleats were fairly worn, but it looked like he'd painted them himself at some point—and then painted over his first attempt when he changed his mind. He hadn't done the best job of covering up his rough draft, but they still looked pretty cool.

I looked down at mine. They had mud on them.

A whistle blew a few times and Wilhelm cleared the field—a few guys had set up a casual scrimmage as they waited for the real tournament games to start. It had been a mix of most of the teams, but I hadn't been interested. For one, I wanted to save my energy for the actual game. And two, it didn't really look that casual or fun. It was hard to just turn your brain off and not take things seriously when you were going to have to be on your A-game in fifteen minutes.

"Kit, you got any more thoughts?" Damian asked.

I felt the muscles around my jaw tighten. "I don't, not since you asked earlier."

"Alright, sorry, just wondering. It's weird—"

The rest of Team Six started jogging up into view, coming through the trees and looping around where a few of the coaches were dragging the goal back into place.

"Later," I said, and Damian took the hint. Why was he nosy? Was he just looking out for Freddie? That was nice and all, but I can't imagine Freddie hadn't told him everything was good already. What made him keep poking around?

I studied Damian for a moment as he looked out over the field. His scar gave him a bit of a rugged look, but I didn't think Damian was actually a badass or anything. I wouldn't have been surprised to hear he'd never been in a fight—I couldn't imagine Freddie's high school friends were routinely punching people in the parking lot after class. He had lean muscle, sure, but—

Kit, focus.

I took a deep breath and looked at the field, bouncing my weight from foot to foot to stay warm and burn off some of the jitters. The team assembled and shared a few quick words, but for the most part nobody was in a particularly joking mood. I mean, Martin was spouting off stupid one-liners like he was getting paid by the word, but that was just Martin.

"We all ready?" Miles said. It was odd to see him not smiling.

"Oh yeah," Slick said, untying and retying his cleats. He did this before every game, fretting that they had been tied slightly off and it would restrict his blood flow or something like that. After the fourth or fifth time we'd just stopped trying to point out he was retying it the exact same way as he'd had them before. "My objective for this game is to make their goalie cry."

Chandler smirked. "Feels mildly unethical, Ye-Joon, but I like the spirit of it."

There was another whistle blast and we all hushed up. Wilhelm walked over, clipboard tucked under one arm as always, and waved a meaty hand at Team Four to come closer. We gathered within earshot and he idly knocked his knuckles on the clipboard.

"Okay, first tournament game. You all know the rules, we've already explained it. Some of you, this is your first year at Weltmeister. Some of you have played in the tournament before, so this will be a reminder. I will be watching you all like a hawk. No funny business, no fouls, nothing like that. We've got extra eyes on the field for these games. I know there's pressure, take it seriously, play your hardest, but play clean. Understood? Any questions?"

Someone who was either exceptionally brave or exceptionally stupid asked, without raising their hand, "Are there recruiters here today?"

Wilhelm's nostrils flared. "Do not worry about recruiters. Worry about how you play."

"Any other questions?" Wilhelm asked.

Everyone else had a sense of self-preservation.

"Good. We start soon. Good luck."

Play clean, Wilhelm had said.

There were probably people here who *would* go for a foul if it meant they stood a better chance of a full ride somewhere.

We jogged out onto the field.I kept bouncing my weight from foot to foot, watching. I glanced around the field, looking at all of the Team Four players, then all of ours.

Victor mirrored Four's striker, standing taller and straighter than he normally did, foot resting on the ball for kickoff like an arrow notched and ready.

Alejandro stood beside him, swaying a bit like I was. His fingers were dancing at his sides, and he gave Victor a small nod and muttered something I couldn't quite make out.

Chandler stood on the left flank, face stoic, body posture relaxed—but his fists were clenched at his sides like he was going into a middleweight bout and not a soccer match.

Martin was next to me in the middle, creeping up closer to Alejandro and Victor, then pulling himself back. He was the only one smiling on the field, pulling back one foot for a last-minute quad stretch, then the other.

Slick was on the right wing as I turned in that direction, looking to be doing mostly the same thing as me. I watched him turn his focus to each player on Four's team, mouth moving soundlessly as he planned something in his head.

I arched my neck around. Mateo stood at the front of the goal box, fastening the straps of one of his gloves with his teeth and then the other, looking small in front of the wide net behind him.

Charles was closest to Mateo, head half-craned back to ask Mateo a question, gesturing out to something on Chandler's side of the field.

Damian was more-or-less directly behind me. We made eye contact, and he gave me a curt nod, followed by a half-tilt of his head to the side, brows furrowing up, and starting to open up his mouth to say something then thinking better of it.

Miles was opposite him, giving me a thumbs up.

Freddie stood in the center of the defense. I hadn't thought I could feel more jitters than I already was, but my adrenal glands eked out a few more. He swooshed his hair out of his face and gave me a smile, then nodded his head to the center of the field. I returned it and turned my focus to the kickoff.

Wilhelm blew the whistle, and it began.

Alejandro tapped the ball back to Martin and Four's strikers closed in like hungry dogs pulling free from their leashes. Slick bolted down the field, halfway-turned to keep the ball in his peripheral vision. Martin studied the field, pointed downfield twenty yards ahead of Slick, reeled back as far as he could to kick—and then gave it a light tap over to me.

Just as we'd practiced. I caught it on my right foot, bringing the ball to a halt, and took a half a heartbeat to study where everyone had moved. Four's left striker—their best player—hadn't taken the bait and was going to be on me in a second. He was moving fast.

Slow, 64

I spotted an opening in the frenzy of their strikers and our midfield. Before their left striker could block my angles, I kicked it low between two of their centers at Chandler's feet. He'd clocked what I was going to do and took off running up the left wing, driving the ball downfield. Alejandro and Victor were bolting towards Team Four's goal box. Their defense scrambled—they were running a 4-4-2, much like we were, but we had our fullbacks in a diamond, and theirs were spread out enough that they couldn't congregate on any one of our players quickly. Whoever Chandler sent it to would have a one-on-one before being open to the goal, and it did not look like Team Four's players had faith in their odds of winning those match-ups.

Chandler slowed, scanning the field.

"They're on you!" Miles shouted downfield. Four's midfielders were repositioning to contest the ball, and Chandler was angled away from them.

As they were nearly on top of him, Chandler rolled the ball back, as casually as he'd done a few minutes ago while waiting to play and sent the first midfielder barreling straight past. The other hadn't taken the bait; he slowed down as he honed in. It cut off any shot Chandler had on goal or any kind of clear pass to the midfielders beside him or strikers up ahead. Chandler attempted to fake left then cut back right. Four's midfielder stayed right on top of him, kicking and scrapping for the ball. *If he doesn't hurry, the other one will get back in position and overwhelm him.* I saw the briefest flicker of panic on Chandler's face, then saw focus overtake it just as quickly. He shouted, "Miles!" and leaned forward for just a moment before kicking it back behind him.

Four's midfielder was a half-second too slow. Miles snagged the ball as Chandler ran downfield. Miles hit the ball with the kind of precision you normally see in neurosurgery. He hit it with just enough spin and arc to get it up over the incoming attacker and dropped it ten or fifteen feet ahead of where Chandler had been when he passed it back—or, in other words, right where Chandler was running to. Chandler grabbed the ball, assessed the scene, and prepared to kick. The first midfielder was sprinting for him once again, but not with such reckless abandon this time. He took one more patient moment, studying the field, then he sent the ball in a looping cross up and over to Slick on the right wing. Slick slid around the defender, positioning himself for the cross. The defender covering him turned, but even the single moment that took was too long. Slick shifted his weight and fired a crisp volley, low across the ground to the bottom left of the goal.

Their keeper dove. I don't think he hit it intentionally—it looked, as best I could see, like he tried to catch it and accidentally smacked it out of the way instead.

"Idiot," I heard Four's striker near me mutter under his breath.

I didn't say anything back. I took a long slow breath.

It rolled helplessly towards the goal line, where the midfielder who'd overshot Chandler managed to stop it just before it earned us a corner.

It took me a moment to realize I had a huge grin on my face. We hadn't scored, granted, but we had absolutely smoked them. It was the sort of intangible feeling that's hard to really quantify to someone who hasn't played a sport—or baseball. It was a momentum shift. You could see Four's midfielders and fullbacks glancing between each other, hesitation flickering across their faces.

The midfielder who'd recovered it passed it to their right fullback as we reset. Our midfielders were pressing enough to threaten a long shot on goal or pass it to the strikers if we intercepted anything, but not so far up we'd be out of position if they cleared it down field. They passed it back and forth a few times, Victor and Alejandro moving like knights across a chessboard, cutting off their angles for passes and keeping the pressure on them. What Four was doing wasn't inherently a terrible idea—it was buying time for their midfield to get back in position. But even if on paper it was a sound enough move, it didn't come across that way seeing it play out. It seemed more like they were playing hot potato, not wanting to be the one to try to make a play and risk getting the responsibility for the screw-up.

"Great play, Chandler!" I heard Freddie shout from somewhere behind me.

I moved closer to the mid-line. Chandler shot a quick thanks without looking. *Hey, I got you the set-up there*, I thought, but now hardly seemed like the time to direct that at either of them. *Don't be a diva. Eyes on their striker.*

The game shifted to something rapid-fire. It felt like we were in the final minutes of a tied game even though it was barely the first half—we were in position to threaten a shot on goal nearly the entire time. Four's left striker was never too far from me, and I heard him drop four-letter-words at roughly the same rate their right fullback was dropping passes. We hadn't scored—yet—but we were keeping the ball solidly in their half of the field. Chandler would pass to Victor, Victor back to me, me to Slick. We were probing their defenses, looking for the opening.

Slick took a shot from outside the goal box, looking to catch their keeper off-guard. Their goalie caught it, dodging the pressure from Victor before punting it back to the center of the field.

The ball was coming down. Martin waved me back, catching it on his chest, dropping it to his feet—and Four's right striker sprinted in and knocked it clear.

The ball ricocheted off Martin's foot and went spiraling back behind us. I turned, keeping an eye on its movement as I tried to track where Four's left striker was behind me. Miles ran up, catching it and passing it over to Freddie, who turned, looking for a clear angle to get it away from the goal box.

"On you!" I shouted. Four's left striker was coming up on my left and I altered course to wall him off from Freddie.

Freddie nodded and sent a pass back out to Miles. I pulled a one-eighty and started moving back up the field. "Open!" I shouted.

Miles pulled back to kick, but Four's right striker was fast. Faster than I would've guessed. *Maybe he's the one we should've been watching.* Miles attempted to dance the ball around him, but the striker kicked wildly again. There was no way he was going to retain possession—or even realistically get a good shot on goal—but I got the feeling he was pissed off enough he didn't particularly care.

The ball rocketed back into the center, where Freddie caught it on his chest and dropped it low. Mateo shuffled to the side, knees bent and eyes on Freddie. Four's left striker was on him, now, and I was too far away to come in and help out.

"Freddie!" I shouted.

Freddie didn't acknowledge it, his face tight. Four's left striker closed in. He pulled the ball back as the striker lashed out with his left leg, barely jostling it past him. Freddie pivoted, blocking the striker for a split second before taking his right foot and kicking it back through the striker's legs over to Damian.

Four's striker turned, fuming, but Damian had two or three seconds before he could reposition and contest again. Damian passed the ball up to me and I turned, big stupid grin back on my face, and sent a through ball downfield to Slick.

Slick tapped the ball, delicate as a ballerina, past Four's right back, clocked the keeper's position, and fired a shot on goal fast enough to make the sound barrier nervous. The goalie dove—and hit the ground about a second after the shot had stretched the back of the net out as far as it would go.

Scoring a goal was the only occasion at Weltmeister that I was pleased to hear Wilhelm's whistle. Victor clapped Slick on the back, who I noted shot a quick glance back at Four's keeper's face.

"Great play there," I said to Freddie, jogging back into place.

"Thanks," he said, grinning wide. "Learned that one from you, what can I say."

"For real," Damian said, giving Freddie a quick one-armed hug. Well, quick—it felt like it lasted a little too long. "That was your best play of the summer, man."

Freddie laughed, clapping Damian's back as he returned the hug. His eyes glanced over in my direction and then back to the center of the field as both team's strikers set up for kickoff again. "Let's get ready," he said, decoupling from Damian and backpedaling away.

The whistle blew again. There was still a game to play—and win. Damian's stupid stuff—this and the weird hug—was making me lose focus. *Concentrate, Kit.*

Wilhelm tossed the ball to Four's strikers in a looping, underhanded pass and jogged back to the edge of the field. I spotted aides jotting down numbers, a few of the teams who weren't immediately playing in the stands watching as closely as they were. They were still taking notes, I was sure, just not literally. It's what I would've been doing.

As the two strikers set up for the kickoff I took a deep breath, trying to channel the dancing feeling in my gut and sudden, very persuasive urge to smack Damian into something I could use. *Focus on the game, then solve...whatever that is.*

I watched their strikers get ready, bouncing my weight from one muddy cleat to the other.

Chapter Fourteen

"Well," Freddie said, scratching at the side of his chin. He had the barest hint of peach fuzz coming in. He must've forgotten to shave that morning.

"Yeah," I said back. There wasn't a ton more to say.

We sat on the roof of the dorms. I kept letting my eyes glance up to the sky. It was drizzling, and there was distant thunder rumbling—the heavy low rumble of summer storms—but we hadn't seen any lightning yet, so I figured we were relatively safe for now.

I mean, I know it's risky, but I wanted to feel the breeze. I guess I wanted to do something a little risky, and I couldn't really explain why.

I pulled my shoes off, letting my legs hang over the balcony and feel the breeze. Just barely, rain got splashed against them, and I saw Freddie move to do the same. It would probably have been visible if it had been a clear night, but I didn't think anyone was walking out in the rain and staring straight up at the sky. The cool water felt good on my feet after how damn hard I'd run that day.

"So, uh, what do we do now?" I said.

Freddie leaned his weight forward on the bars of the railing, resting his head on the wet metal. It made his hair rumple against his forehead. He was looking off somewhere. *A thousand yard stare,* I thought. A term Freddie had told me came from World War I in one of our runs.

"I don't know," Freddie said. "I've got to deal with this mess somehow. I mean, this is—this could be really bad, right? And if it's—if it's like—"

he took another deep breath, massaging at the sides of his temples. I didn't know if I was supposed to lean in and hug him or try to hold his hand or anything. I could almost hear Kyle laughing at how little game I had, but I pushed the thought away.

Freddie seemed so shaky in the rain, like he was one of the branches on the huge St. Michael's oak trees getting pulled back and forth by the wind. He stayed sitting like that for a minute, thinking. "I have no idea what to do here."

I exhaled slowly. The rain clinked against the metal awning over our heads. "I don't know either," I said, trying to put more confidence and calm into my voice than I felt, "but we can just sit here and be clueless together."

"Excellent showing, gentlemen," Miles said, his voice overly posh. His grin, however, was very genuine. Mateo made some British joke I only caught the tail end of and Miles and Martin and Alejandro belly-laughed (well, I mean, Alejandro cracked a grin).

"I really do think so," Slick said, carving at his stack of pancakes. The cafeteria knives were so dull they may as well have been spoons. "I'm pretty sure I saw him cry as we walked off the field."

"You saw him *sweat*," Chandler said. "He might cry once their striker gets ahold of him, because that guy was definitely looking like he was trying to think of spots to hide a dead body, but I didn't see him cry."

"Chandler. You ruin everything. I saw him cry, I'm telling you. You would've cried too if you'd played against me then. Why do you never want me to follow my dreams?"

Chandler arched a single eyebrow to heights that must've cramped the muscles in his face.

"Everyone played super well," Freddie said, sliding in the conversation to prevent the umpteenth Chandler debate of the week. "I mean, I figured we were going to win, but I was kinda surprised at just how well we did."

Charles nodded. "Yeah. 3-0's not bad."

"Very not bad," Damian added. "Where does that put us on the rankings?"

Someone dug out the very wrinkled, folded-and-then-refolded piece of paper Mateo had originally sketched out the tournament details on since we were apparently collectively too lazy to just draw another one. They passed it over to Victor who started marking it up.

As he did, I felt a hand slip over mine under the table. I almost flinched and knocked my glass over, but fortunately I played it moderately cool for once and no one caught it. *See, I get lucky breaks sometimes.*

I squeezed Freddie's hand back, the tournament talk pulling my focus back after a moment or two.

"Team One lost to Eleven," Martin added, going off something Victor had said I hadn't listened to.

"No, Team Eleven won," Chandler said.

"Yeah, that's what I said," Martin said, committing to the bluff.

Chandler sighed.

"I can't remember all of the points scored," Victor said, twirling the pen in his hand for a moment as he jotted over the next games. "Our next game is against Team Nine, and last of the group stage is Team Three."

"They won," I said. Oliver had scored twice; two of their midfielders had each scored once.

There was a bit of an awkward pause. It was tricky for morale to hype ourselves up over how awesome a 3-0 win while the competition had just won 4-0.

Under the table, Freddie's hand squeezed mine again before pulling away, his fingers tracing my forearm as he pulled his hand up to get a sip of water.

"Anyways," Victor said. "Nine's our next game."

"If we kick Nine's ass, we don't even need to win against Team Three?" Martin said.

"I think," Victor said, chewing on a fingernail as he did some math on Chandler's notebook, "...I think that's right, but we'd have to win today by a pretty sizable margin. And Team Three would have to lose."

"We just focus on winning today," Miles said. "If we win today, it'll be almost impossible for us to not make to the next stage."

"And even if we lose," Freddie added, as if he sensed my next thought before it could materialize in my head, "We can still tie or win against Team Three and make it."

"Probably," Chandler added, sipping at his coffee.

Someone was drumming their fingers on the table. After a moment or two I realized it was me. "Winnable. We'll get to the quarterfinals."

"Three will be a tough game," Chandler said.

"Yes, but winnable."

"Every game is winnable," Miles said.

"And losable," Chandler added.

"Chandler, I swear to God," I said, rubbing my forehead.

The uneasy tension held for a moment, then two, then conversation trickled back in.

Nine hours to go.

I knew objectively, in the part of my brain that could remember all the formulas I'd needed in geometry and algebra II and chemistry, that the thoughts running through my head did not make any sense.

That said, the thoughts were running a lot faster than that part of my brain was. That part of my brain hadn't laced its cleats up yet.

Just chatting about nothing with Freddie on runs was easily one of the better parts of the day. Of the summer, for that matter. For starters, it made me not think about the actual running, which is something you can't put a price on. On top of that, I'd just gotten back to being able to just talk with Freddie after the weird phase we'd had. All the guys on the team were cool. I would've hung out with any one of them outside of camp. That said—Freddie and maybe Chandler—were the only ones that I could talk about deeper stuff with. Like if I told Mateo I'd read something cool in one of the books I'd brought with me, he would've probably said I needed to read less and go on more dates.

Which, you know. Now that I was thinking about it, my bookmark hadn't really moved in the last day or so. I'd spent my last two nights sneaking around the empty dorm with Freddie, whispering on the roof and watching for one of the coaches' flashlights, or heading over to the woods and walking through the trails they had set up there.

Kit blowing off reading for romance. Who would've thought.

Regardless, the point is I was jogging a solid seven or eight feet behind Damian and Freddie, in-between Charles and Victor, and very decidedly *not* talking. I got maybe an hour or two to actually talk one-on-one with Freddie every night, and here one of the few times during the day we got to chat, just the two of us, Damian had to come along and be Damian as obnoxiously as possible.

We—Team Six, that is—were in our usual little group in the column, somewhere closer to the rear. We'd all agreed there was no sense in trying to stand out by crossing the finish line first or impressing Bronson on tournament days. The recruiters were not waking up early enough to come observe us doing our morning jog.

"C'mon, man," Damian said. He was keeping his voice hushed enough that most of the others couldn't hear. With the sound of everyone running and other conversations, he was mostly successful, but occasionally someone else from the team would cock their head back, trying to pick up a word or two. I could feel my shoulders tensing back each time, and I'd try to ask them some stupid question and deflect. The last thing I wanted was half the team hounding Freddie about everything.

"Leave it alone, dude, you're—you're being weird about this."

"Alright, alright, I'm just saying, *something* is going on, not my business what..."

Freddie let out a sigh. I let out a long, slow exhale through notably flared nostrils.

We continued going in circles.

The storm had shaken the mugginess out the air. It was one of the few times I could remember feeling something approximating a cool breeze at Weltmeister.

"I don't know," Freddie said again. It felt like most of what we were saying.

I started to reach my hand over, but my arm wasn't taking orders. There was a sudden lump in my throat and the notion of moving my hand five inches over onto his was suddenly just as impossible as reaching across the field to do the same.

Just do it, Kit. Why are you nervous? I reached over and grabbed his hand before I had time to think on it anymore.

I felt a small squeeze back, Freddie absentmindedly rubbing his thumb against the inside of my palm as he looked out at the dark buildings and swaying trees.

"What's, I mean...best- and worst-case scenario?" That was what my mom had always told me to do when I was facing some big problem or uncertainty or something. Just try to map it out or put some kind of framework on it so you could at least try to do something.

Freddie leaned his head back and broke his hand free for a moment—*nice going you screwed it up*—to brush his hair back into place before putting his hand back where it had been. "I'm—I mean, best case scenario is nothing really changes, or nobody else figures out. Worst case scenario is..." Freddie's voice got lost somewhere in his throat.

"...the team falls apart a bit, or fights, or...something," I finished.

Freddie grimaced. "No, honestly, I hadn't even thought of that. Worst case is what happens after I go back home." He swallowed and looked down at our entwined hands. "This follows me home now."

"The devil," Chandler said, "Must be out buying mittens."

Ludwig blew the whistle again, as if to jolt everybody who was standing there trying to make sure they'd heard correctly.

Drills cut short? Rest of the morning off?

If I had thought it was possible to press down far enough through his forearm muscle to get to his veins, I would've checked his pulse to see if he was having a stroke or something.

"Go!" Ludwig said, somehow managing to make telling us to go relax threatening. "Go and rest up now! Tournament game later today, you need your strength!"

We split and meandered our way across the field, snagging a spot under one of the shadier trees to cool down.

"How long until lunch?" Martin said.

Charles glanced down at his wrist, looking at his watch. "We got like an hour."

"Then two hours after that until gametime," Victor added.

Mateo leaned back against the tree, grabbing the drawstring bag he'd taken with him onto the field with his gloves in them. "Martin, Kit, come over here for a second."

Martin and I shared a glance then stepped over as he wanted.

"Like two steps to your right."

"No. It's already like forty degrees outside I'm not standing in the sun for no reason."

I chewed on the numbers for a moment. "Uh, Martin, forty degrees Celsius feels a *little* high, but I also don't want to just stand still in the sunshine, Mateo. What's up?"

"Just do it for like five seconds, dude, I need to text my girlfriend and don't want Ludwig to see."

Martin snorted but obliged, making a show of stretching wide and trying to block Mateo from view from the rest of the field as much as possible.

I rolled my eyes but did the same. Let it not be said Kit Cook didn't help his teammates. "Amazed you brought that on the field, man."

"Yeah," Slick said, juggling the ball a few feet from the rest of the group, not looking up to talk. "If you get caught with that and screw us over for the game today I'm going to kill you."

"Your concern is appreciated," Mateo said, thick eyebrows furrowing as he hammered out a message a solid five or six times faster than I could've. "And yes, I know, bad idea, we've just been having a—it's been weird, I didn't want to wait until like nine o'clock to message her back. By the time I can message her she's usually asleep because it's a couple of hours later there."

Damian must've sniffed drama, because he wandered over from standing at the periphery of the conversation between Charles and Victor to Mateo's outer orbit.

"Lady problems," Martin said, yawning. "Can't relate."

"Shut up, Martin," Mateo said, starting to say another comeback but then losing his train of thought. He was one of those people who had to mouth the words of whatever he was reading. Though it was all in Spanish, so I couldn't understand any of it, it didn't seem like Mateo and his girlfriend were doing particularly well.

My first thought was *is this going to throw him off for the game?*

Then my second thought was that the first thought was a terrible way to react to a teammate maybe having a breakup.

"It'll be okay, man," I said, squinting at the glare. *It was wrong of me to think that, but also Mateo could've stood on the other side of the tree to do this.*

Freddie was off to the side, chatting with Alejandro. Talking to Alejandro was usually more of a "give" than a "take", but whatever Freddie had said to him made Alejandro grin and swoosh his hair back behind his ears. Alejandro murmured something back and Freddie nodded, asking him something about his hometown. He had his legs crossed—rather well-positioned to avoid anyone getting a glimpse again, one could note—and was resting his chin on folded arms, blinking the sweat away.

"How often are you texting this girl?" Damian said, stretching one hamstring and then another.

"'This girl'," Mateo said, his syllables clipped, "Is my girlfriend, and every day. After lights-out I sneak out the window and call her most nights, but the last few she's been all pissed off so I—"

I don't remember the rest of that sentence, and I imagine that Damian didn't either.

What I do remember is Damian's head coming up in a half-tilt, stretch forgotten. His mouth started to open to say something, and I saw him lose himself in thought for a moment.

Then he glanced from Mateo to Freddie and back to Mateo.

I turned away before he caught me watching and finished putting the rest of the pieces together.

After lunch, we were too wired to go lie down and take naps like we usually did. We'd had nerves before the first tournament game, but somehow winning had made us *more* nervous. The possibility of making it to the final round seemed far more likely, now, and something about that made our match against Team Four feel like a warm-up scrimmage.

We opted for a walk around campus, sticking to the shadier areas. I'd contemplated trying to see if I could slip Freddie away with a claim we were going to practice or something, but I didn't think there was any believable excuse I could've given that would've both kept anyone from being suspicious and kept anyone from wanting to tag along. I settled for walking close by him and trying to brush my hand against his whenever

I could. There were still little rushes and jitters, and I could catch his lips twitch in a suppressed smile in reply.

It was one of those brutally hot summer days where you just started sweating the second you went outside. The sky was completely clear of any clouds, too, which was just your usual Weltmeister luck for you.

We were far enough apart that each mini-group could have its own conversation of sorts. Ahead of me, Alejandro was responding to Victor's rant about some movie adaptation of a book with strictly neutral nods. Slick and Miles were discussing the upcoming game, strategies, and the weak links on Team Three.

After Damian caught up to the group, I had to pull away. My hands stayed firmly in my pockets. Freddie, whenever I spared a glance, looked like he was a hostage having to read a message off in front of the camera. Damian was beside him, the smirk that had been on his face only growing wider.

"Okay," Damian said, keeping his voice quiet enough that we couldn't hear. Or, at least, I guess that's what he thought. "You gotta at least tell me who it is."

If you say anything to him or try to interrupt, it'll just become super obvious, I told myself. I tried to listen to Victor's irritation at how they'd changed the costume of his favorite superhero, but it just turned to white noise.

"I don't—it's—I don't want to talk about it, man," Freddie said.

"It's cool, dude, I'm not judging or anything, I think it's great and all, I just…like I would not have guessed you were the sneak out and mess around type."

"I'm not messing around, it's not—"

Messing around? How did he mean that? Like making out, or messing around like something you didn't really care about?

"Hm. Okay. Is it..." Damian paused, and I could almost hear him chewing on his thoughts, turning the gears in his head. "Let's see. It's...well, you do make friends with everybody, I guess, so maybe it's not somebody on our team...but what're the odds there, you know? How much time could you have spent with another team? You're not a pick-up artist, I mean no offense, so it's gotta be—"

"Damian, can we just not talk about this?"

"Aw c'mon man, I tell you everything, this isn't—"

"Hey, Kit," Slick said, snapping my eyes to the conversation ahead of me. We turned by the dorms where the barely-cracked-open window was, and I felt a sudden compulsion to keep everyone moving past it and not let anyone notice. My hands balled up into fists in my pockets before I made myself take a deep breath and loosen up. *Nobody but you has spotted it all summer. It's fine. You're just on edge.*

"Hm? Yeah?"

"What do you think of Three's defense?"

"Oh, I—"

Behind me, I could hear Damian start to rattle off names. Chandler, Slick, Alejandro...

Why was Damian going straight to them? For the first time I thought about whether or not they were, perhaps, more dateable than me. *I'm smarter than they are,* I thought, glancing over Slick and Alejandro. *And I think I'm in better shape, I mean—*

"Kit?" Miles said, turning back to glance at me.

"Oh, sorry, lost in—yeah, I mean, their defense is solid, I guess. Middle of the road. Not as bad as, uh—" I blanked, completely unable to remember the team we'd played yesterday for a second. "—Four's, not as bad as Team Four's, but not awesome. I think their midfield makes up for it."

Slick nodded, running a hand through his hair.

"Their goalie is quite skilled," Miles said.

"He is a drama queen," Slick said. "He dives for everything when he doesn't have to. If we just make some low shots early, he'll tire out fast I bet."

"Slick, I don't mean to be rude, but I believe our plan was already to take shots on goal as much as possible."

"You know what I meant, don't—"

That conversation, and Victor's ahead of them, faded to radio static.

Damian had gone to the other guys before me when Freddie was out late in the first place, and then hadn't even considered me as a candidate for somebody Freddie might want to—be with. Date? Were we dating? I didn't know. This whole thing was just supposed to be its own thing, nothing I had to put labels on or worry about or overthink.

And yet for the first time all summer there was someone on the team wondering about how Freddie felt more than me.

"You think it'll interrupt the game?" Charles asked, looking up at the sky. There were some dark clouds on the horizon, but where we were standing was bright and sunny.

"It better not," Martin said, looking across the field. It was the most serious I'd seen him all summer. "I'm ready."

We checked cleats, shin guards, laces, took little sips of water, stretched, shook legs loose.

The breeze picked up, just barely, and I glanced around at the horizon. *Are those clouds getting closer, or farther away?* If there wasn't lightning, we were playing through it. *Will the rain help us more than them?*

Across the field, Team Nine was doing much of the same.

I checked my cleats again, making sure they were tight. Slick had rubbed off on me. *Slow, 64.*

"We lost the toss," Victor said, jogging back.

"They took the west side."

I let out a slow breath but tried to keep my face steady. We'd be playing into the sun first half, and by the time we swapped, I had a suspicion it would be pouring rain. "Doesn't matter. We're ready," I said, taking a deep breath. I looked over at Freddie, who gave me a nod and a quiet, tight-lipped grin.

Ludwig blew his whistle, and we went to play Team Nine.

It was like it had been when Freddie talked to me during the capture-the-flag game, or right after he'd kissed me, or when I'd fumbled trying to pull the cookie out of my pocket and tried to apologize—everything in my chest was tight and my gut was rolling. Not even just physically, I mean, like my gut instincts didn't know what to do or what I was supposed to be taking away from that.

"What, um, what do you mean by that?" I said.

Freddie took another deep breath and closed his eyes, head resting on the metal. "I mean...I didn't think about or plan anything here, okay, and I didn't think that people might find out—people I have to go back home with, who might tell people on the rest of the team, or the rest of the high school, or—" his eyes opened and widened for a moment, the realization snowballing and gaining momentum, "—or, God, my parents. Ugh. And I mean..."

He stopped, glancing at me and then glancing away. His hand felt limp in mine. Clammy.

I wanted to say it would all work out, but Freddie was right. There was a lot more risk to him than me here. It would've felt hollow.

"Yeah, I mean, I don't—" Freddie closed his eyes again. "I didn't, like—I haven't thought about what happens—"

There still weren't any words coming to me. I reached over and brushed the rain-soaked hair stuck to his forehead back into place, making him look uncannily like Slick for a brief moment. I tried my best to keep a straight face—it was, you know, a serious moment and everything and I didn't want him to think I was laughing at him. I did not succeed.

He must've been able to guess how silly he looked or seen it on my face, because he grinned.

It seemed to untie the knot in Freddie's shoulders that was keeping all the muscles down his arms and back tense. He slouched a bit, just thinking quietly. I didn't want to bother him, but the waiting felt long, like when you see a teammate go down after a slide tackle and there's a few infinite seconds where you're not sure if they're really hurt or just jostled, or when you're at the top of the Brightbirch zipline and step off the ledge and contemplate the structural integrity of your harness for one eternal second before the line catches you.

He took a long breath and nodded, blinking a bit. "...thanks."

"It's alright." I said. "I mean—I don't want to brush you off, it's just...we'll figure it out. We've survived five weeks of Ludwig's drills, you know? This is nothing."

Freddie smiled and turned, and I found myself leaning in to kiss him before I had time to stop and think about it or wonder anything more. We stayed there for a minute before pulling away. It was soft, and warm. Not warm like the oppressive summer heat we suffered daily at Weltmeister. Warm like stolen cookies fresh out of the oven. I wondered when the feeling I got when we kissed, that someone had hooked me up to a live wire, would go away.

"Thanks for being cool about everything," he said. "I don't think I could take any more craziness today."

"Don't worry about Damian," I said. "We'll figure it out. He'll be cool about it."

Freddie gave me a weary smile. "And to think losing to freaking Team Nine wasn't even the worst thing about today."

Chapter Fifteen

It had rained so hard the day we lost to Team Nine that there were still a few patches of marshy, soggy field holding on for dear life against the Weltmeister sun when we played Team Three two days later.

The whistle blew. We stopped. Of everyone on Team Six, Mateo was maybe the only one not breathing hard, face flushed from sprinting and sprinting and sprinting. Everyone on their team looked the same, barring Oliver. Run ragged, out of breath, and trying to keep a stern poker face up. There was something different about running in a game rather than running for conditioning. Bronson's drills helped, don't get me wrong, but the adrenaline and the stakes and all of it made you run harder. You had a reason to, rather than just jogging in a circle for an hour.

Everybody on the field was running that way and had been the whole first half.

We pulled back to our side of the field. Slick put his hands on the back of his head, taking deep breaths to steady his heart rate.

"One goal," Damian said. "We can get one goal. We advance with just a tie, right?"

Martin nodded, downing one cone of water, re-filling it, and downing another.

"You'll get cramps."

"Shut up," Martin said to Chandler, muscles in his face tight.

I sipped at my water, eyes running down the sideline to their bench. We were making them fight for it. 1-0 at the half. Winnable, very winnable. We'd come close. Two shots on-goal—only barely blocked.

Oliver sat on their bench, elbows resting on his knees, staring down at the dirt. Not out of breath at all.

Slow, 64.

There was a second reason everyone was going as viciously as they were.

That reason was sitting across the field in the front row of the stands. There was a smattering of other campers in the bleachers, some Team Eleven guys and a mix of Team Five and Nine's players. This was their off day in the tournament, I figured, or else they were playing earlier or later. Regardless, it wasn't really them I cared about.

Sitting in front, clipboard in hand, jotting notes as fast as we had been running was a guy none of us recognized. That meant one thing and one thing only this week—a recruiter. He had a red polo shirt, far too crisp and grass-stain-less to have been at Weltmeister very long. One khaki-clad leg was folded over the other, creating a makeshift desk for his clipboard, and he periodically took pauses from writing to finger poke-type something on the small laptop he had on the seat next to him.

Ludwig sat near him. Every few minutes he would turn and stare at someone who tried to slide in closer and see what the recruiter was writing down. The someone in question would suddenly remember urgent business elsewhere.

I took a deep breath, heart rate starting to settle.

"We need to figure out something different," Chandler said, for once not a note of snark to his words.

"Agreed," Alejandro said.

"Hey," Freddie said, bumping into me. He let his hand settle on the small of my back for just a moment, my skin dancing where his fingers pressed the fabric of my jersey against my spine. In that moment, the thought of how Damian could certainly see—how everyone on the field could see—flickered into my mind. It was followed by the game, the score, Oliver, the mud on my cleats, the recruiter. Then it passed, and the feeling and the focus was just how nice it felt for a second before Freddie had to let go. "Are you okay?"

I chewed on my lip for a moment, the sounds of Chandler and Charles brainstorming fading to background noise. I caught my eyes on Oliver when I forced myself to attention again. He was still staring down at the dirt.

"Honestly? No. I'm...I'm kinda pissed."

I hadn't been pissed forty-five minutes ago. Forty-five minutes ago, I had been *ready*.

Forty-five minutes ago, we'd squared up.

Oliver stood directly opposite me across the field.

The first five minutes had probably been more intense than any other we'd had. For sure in the tournament, maybe the whole summer. They'd kicked off with a crisp pass to—no surprise—Oliver and he'd immediately begun driving it down the field. If I hadn't known it was not physically possible for this to occur, I would've told you that he had started dribbling the ball downfield before the center had even cleared the pass over to him. He was past Martin and bearing down my direction before Martin had started to cut him off.

This time I was prepared. I jockeyed with him, angling him out to the outside of the field.

His face had stayed blank, but I could see the gears turning in his head the same way they had when I'd seen him drilling those balls into the net over and over and over, taking note of which ones had just barely spun off-course. Thinking, planning, adjusting.

I wrestled with him to the side of the field. His feet flickered to try to goad me into planting my weight. I saw him overextend his gait, just by a hairsbreadth. I had a split-second to try to determine if it was a feint, if missing this would give him a clear shot on Mateo, if the fullbacks—if Freddie—would reposition in time—

Stop thinking and do it.

I lunged out, knocking the ball clear from him, only a few feet away, but clear nonetheless. He reached out, trying to hold possession—

–and planted his foot down in the mud. A divot in the ground, slick and soft.

Oliver put his weight down, twisted, and I could see his whole body clench as he started to fall. There was a *pop!* Just barely audible through the sounds of cleats hammering on the dirt around us.

For a moment I was still on the ball, hounding it and trying to recover it before it rolled out—with a throw-in at this point on the field they could—

Oliver let out a gasp, the sort of sound where you start to make noise and then bite down hard to shut yourself up.

I stumbled and turned back, the ball rolling off to the sidelines. I'd given them a throw-in, but I didn't care. A whistle blew multiple times in succession somewhere. Oliver kneeled on the ground, right leg wobbly, left one folded up underneath it.

"Damnit," He muttered under his breath, eyes blinking rapidly. I saw him dig his teeth into his lips for a moment and twist his head away from where the bleachers had a view as he adjusted his weight to get the pressure off his leg. "Damnit!"

He punched the ground, grimacing.

"Holy crap, are you okay?" I asked.

Oliver opened his mouth, face tight and eyes closed, nostrils flaring as he forced steady breaths. Before he could reply, Wilhelm had jogged up.

"Are you alright?" he asked, glancing between the two of us. His eyes went from Oliver's left leg—which I was now noticing was angled awkwardly. Wilhelm's eyes hardened into a scowl so deep it made every time he'd barked orders at us look like playtime. I took a step back without even meaning to. "Did you—"

"No," Oliver muttered, so quietly he had to say it again for Wilhelm to hear. "No. I slipped. It was all me. He didn't do anything."

Wilhelm stood still for a moment then blew the whistle again and gestured a bear's paw of a hand to the sidelines. Bronson came jogging over and the both of them hooked arms under Oliver's shoulders and helped him hobble off-field. A round of claps went up, though there was a clear undercurrent: ours felt just a touch too frenetic; theirs mournful.

Wilhelm made sure Oliver could hobble on his own weight and someone sent for the nurse. He turned back, motioning for play to resume after a moment, and we settled back in.

God, that had looked painful.

But I wasn't sure if Oliver had looked more in pain or more pissed off.

And I hated it, but I couldn't deny the part of me that was excited. Almost glad. It made me feel awful to even think that, but it was still true.

I wanted to beat him, damnit, I thought. Oliver sat on the bench, grimacing and moving his injured leg up onto the bench, propping it on someone's duffel bag.

Slow, 64.

From the sidelines, the recruiter kept writing.

I blinked.

"You okay?"

"Sorry," I said, back to Freddie. *Focus. You've got a game to win. The first two minutes don't matter now.* "Just...it's nothing. Let's just focus."

Without Oliver, they were playing a man down, but it had stayed a close game. Nobody else on Oliver's team was anywhere close to his skill level, but it seemed like instead of demoralizing them, it'd lit a fire under them. They'd scored a goal right after Oliver went out, catching Mateo completely out-of-position. I could see Slick fuming from across the field, but Victor had kept him from saying anything and rattling Mateo further. I could see Mateo shaking his head, muttering under his breath.

Once they got their surprise goal, Team Three had realized their win condition. They turtled and pulled back, adjusting for the man down. They had very little capability to score another goal, going down to one striker, but they were content to stall. All they needed was to stall.

"How are we losing to a team with a man down?" Charles said, throwing his cup on the ground. "This is insane. They lost their only good player, and we—"

"It's alright," Miles said. "We can—"

"No! It's not alright? How bad do we suck to—"

"We don't suck," I said. I felt most of the eyes of Team Six turn on me. "And we shouldn't change anything up."

"Because our current strategy is working so well," Chandler said. "Brilliant, Cook, truly the mind of Clausew-."

"No," I cut him off before he could make whatever pretentious reference he was going to make, trying to keep the heat out of my voice. I felt Freddie moving up to my right, a look of—not quite confusion on his face.

Something closer to concern, eyebrows furrowed, blonde hair plastered to his face. He gave me a small nod. "Look at them," I said, pointing over to their bench.

A few of Team Three's players were huddled around the bench, still panting hard four or five minutes into halftime. Oliver was speaking to two or three of them, pointing at spots on the field and periodically at a few of our team members. I could see the grimace on his face, making his features seem sharper and more severe. I knew what he was feeling. He could see what was going wrong, and how to fix it, but he couldn't do anything.

"So what?" Victor said.

"So what," I said, "Is they're more winded than we are. They're having to play a man down and it's wearing on them."

"May not have noticed," Chandler said, "We're a bit tired too."

"A *bit*," I said back. "But hear me out. We make drastic changes and try to switch things up, we're probably going to spend the first ten minutes of the second half just getting adjusted. That's ten minutes they're recuperating and not getting pressed as hard. We need to keep the pressure on them. Constantly. I don't think they can sustain the pace we're running them at. And they're banking on it getting to our heads, which it seems is working pretty well."

Chandler didn't have anything to say to that.

"I agree with Kit," Freddie said, breaking the quiet of cleats digging into mud and water being slurped.

There was something about him being willing to take the heat from the team for agreeing with me that made me smile, despite how pissed I was at the game. I kept catching myself clenching and had to remind myself to loosen up.

Damian looked between us. He raised an eyebrow and suppressed a smirk. "I agree as well," he said.

"What if we're wrong?" Martin said. "We're losing to a team that is a man down."

"That man," Slick added, "is their best player, too. Top ten. I don't know if any of the rest of them even break top twenty."

Something about Damian's smirk and the venom in Martin's words and the whole damn day made the words come out harder and faster than I meant them to. "You may not have noticed, geniuses, the only numbers that matter right now are 1 and 0. Unless either of you has a better plan?"

Martin said nothing, and Slick muttered something under his breath in Korean. Undoubtedly, it was kind.

"We got this, guys, don't take it out on each other," Freddie said.

"Deep breaths, everyone," Miles said, tiptoeing into the conversation. "We're all stressed. But it's extremely winnable."

I turned to look at Chandler before he could retort. He caught my gaze, started to open his mouth, then sighed and stayed quiet.

"We're not losing this game," I said, looking at their bench. "This is a game we win. We just need to outwork them and they'll slip up. We exploit that."

There was a murmur of grumbling and muttering and everyone took their last sip of water, re-tied cleats, took a quick moment to stretch or warm up on a ball.

Freddie stayed close but didn't come draw up near me again. He talked to Charles about something I couldn't quite hear.

After two or three more minutes, which I spent breathing and thinking about where we needed to be on the field, Wilhelm blew the whistle again and we jogged back out. As I went past Wilhelm, I could feel his eyes on me. *Does he still think I fouled Oliver?*

Great. One more thing.

I took another deep breath, whose oxygen my body was still very much craving, and shook my head. One thing at a time. Probably nothing. Just focus on the game.

We set into positions. I glanced at Martin, who was still tense, jaw set and any hint of joking gone from his face.

Chandler was on the far side of the field, murmuring something to Miles behind him, who nodded.

Damnit. What if I was wrong? What if we had needed to swap something up?

I turned back around to look at Freddie, who gave me a tight-lipped smile.

I took a deep breath and Slick had kicked the ball off as soon as the whistle blew.

We moved forward.

We were playing the most aggressive game we had all summer. We'd fought hard, don't get me wrong—but this was the most we were looking to pressure the other team. Our sweeper was maybe fifteen feet from mid-field. At any given time they had the ball, in theory, we should've been able to push a 2 v 1. We did our best to make that happen. If they got past us on a breakaway, it would only be Charles between them and forty yards of open field to Mateo. Miles or Damian or Freddie could try to switch back, but it would be close.

That was not my focus.

I did not run all those damn sprints to lose to a team with a man down.

Or to lose with Oliver sitting on the bench, leg propped on top of a cooler and saddled with icepacks, staring at the game behind steepled hands. I had thought not getting the chance to prove myself would be worse—but part of me thought losing to him when he wasn't even playing might've stung more.

We moved. That's the only way to put it—there were no instances of me watching an exchange from across the field, trying to envision my position from the top-down to figure out where I needed to be to cut off their next play. Just running.

We worked possession around the field and probed our way through the dense cluster of fullbacks they had—a brick wall of a 5-3-1—and any time we got close to the goal box they just had too much mass in the way to make a clear shot.

They can't wall off everywhere. "Back!" I shouted to Alejandro, who was shifting to pass before the word had fully left my lips, as if he'd realized the play right as I'd started to speak.

Their defense rotated, Victor and Alejandro attempting to move down either flank. I pushed in a bit, testing the water, and two of their midfielders were starting to close in.

But it was slower than they had in the first half.

I didn't bother trying to gauge if I had a path to the goal or a clear shot to the strikers who might've had one instead. I passed to Martin, who stopped the ball with more precision than you would think his monstrous quads and calves capable of. He still looked absolutely pissed, but I could see something click behind his eyes. He sent it to Chandler, and the midfielders shifted to cut off Chandler's angles as soon as he had.

Chandler caught it and chipped it back over to Slick and I shifted into the path of the midfielders as I heard him trap the ball. He tapped it just barely down the field, pulling their defense inch by inch to the right wing to cover him.

I clocked Oliver on the bench, looking at the field the same way I assume a chess grandmaster looks at his board. Might've been my imagination, but I thought he gave me a slight nod.

Slick passed it back to me, and I kept the dance going. Me to Chandler, Chandler to Miles, Miles to Slick...

The first ten minutes of the half must have gone that way, interrupted only by brief, frantic flashes of movement in their goal box when we snuck a pass to one of the strikers. Their defense would sprint back to cover. Then the cycle repeated, their defense a little slower on the draw each time.

Are we burning too much time, I thought, trying to gauge the other team. *How much time is left? We need to score.*

"Kit!" I heard Miles shout, maneuvering around their striker—the one player on their team who still seemed to have the lion's share of his stamina left—and sending a pass over to me.

I caught the pass on my chest, dropping the ball to my feet and tapping it ahead once, twice.

Their midfielders were coming to cut me off, but I must have had two to three seconds more than I had before.

Two to three seconds is a very long time when you have the ball. I was used to milliseconds. I clocked Victor on the far left, sending it up and over their cluster of fullbacks.

Their defense had made a miscalculation—they'd seen the midfielders lagging to get me and two of them had pushed up to try cutting me off. I had an open stretch of twenty yards between me and the goal box. But there was no shot there of me scoring—literally—they just didn't know that I knew it.

Instead I made my best pass all summer.

It landed right at Victor's sprinting feet. He didn't take more than a second to size up the goal and send a wide curving shot out from the left corner of the field to the upper right of the goal.

The goalie had moved to wall off his angle, standing close by the left goalpost. He had zero chance of stopping it. The ball hit the back of the net.

"Yes!" Alejandro shouted, grinning.

I caught myself grinning too. 1-1.

I glanced over to their bench, where Oliver sat, stone-faced.

We repositioned as they setup for the kickoff. But something had changed. Before, they'd had their win condition set. It had been achievable. They may have known they could still get into the tournament unless we had an absolute blowout that game, but that wasn't the case for our team. They were down their best player and had been run ragged.

"Alejandro!" Slick shouted, jogging up. He swapped, and Alejandro settled in beside me.

The whistle blew.

The last fifteen minutes of that game were some of the best I played all summer. I set up five or six shots-on-goal, and even though we only scored once more, each of them had the defense scrambling, the goalie diving. We threatened to score almost constantly and must've kept them down to less than a minute of time spent on our half of the field.

The final whistle blew and a few of Team Three's guys almost dropped to the ground then and there. We ran into an impromptu mosh pit. There were back claps, someone rustled my hair a few times, Martin was back to laughing and loudly proclaiming how he never doubted it, and somewhere in the frenzy, I felt a few fingers slip around mine for a single, tight squeeze before pulling away.

We stayed in the huddle for a few minutes before pulling apart to grab our things and go grab dinner. I caught Oliver on the far side of the field, limping with the help of their other striker. The other striker clapped him on the back and shouldered his weight as they crossed a low divot where the ground was still muddy, saying something I couldn't hear.

I turned back to the group. It still felt like a win—like a very good win—but I wasn't so sure that it should've. We won against a team a man down. And it took us a long time to score. Was Team Three just better than we'd given them credit for? Did we suck?

Maybe it was just a random occurrence. A mix of momentum and energy and a dozen other things. Maybe there weren't necessarily big reasons for it.

As we pulled apart from the group, I grabbed my bag and started making my way back to the dorms, where I'd at least change out of muddy clothes and—

"Hey," I heard a voice say. One I didn't recognize.

I turned. It was the recruiter. I could not think of a starker contrast than my clothes, soaked with sweat or slide-tackle grass stains, and his polo shirt and khakis, which he may as well have been ironing while he was sitting on the sidelines.

"Oh, uh, hello. Are you looking for someone?"

He fumbled into his pocket for a moment, clipboard and laptop tucked into a messenger bag. He pulled out a card and handed it to me, which had his name. *Kyle Mayweather.*

Well, easily the least annoying of the Kyles I knew.

"Keep in touch," he said. "Wilhelm said you're a sophomore?"

I blinked. *Wait, hold on.* "Um, yes, yes sir. Going into my sophomore year, that is."

He nodded. "A lot of good positional play out there. Good patience. A lot of guys your age, they charge right in. You waited. Read the field. Made a smart play and not the first, obvious one."

"Oh, um, thank you. I really appreciate it."

He nodded, giving me a grin and a clap on the shoulder. "Stay in touch. Let me know if you're interested in learning more about our school, our programs, all that jazz."

"I—yeah, I mean, yes sir, for sure. Will do."

"Take care."

He strolled off, half-jogging to catch up with Ludwig, who greeted him with a smile and a half-hug, which was honestly more shocking to me than what had just happened.

I turned the card over in my hand and made a note to memorize the name and information or at least write it down somewhere else so I wouldn't lose it.

Wilhelm and this guy had talked about me?

I looked at the card, blinking a few times and rubbing my thumb over the tree printed on the card to make sure it was real and not some kind of heat-induced hallucination.

Stanford University.

I was still bewildered a solid hour after getting that card, but I didn't dwell on it (for once). There was still the post-victory high to be had, and we rode that high well through dinner (we were easily the loudest table in the dining hall that night) and our time after, where the coaches set up a projector for a movie night. The dining hall even mass-produced popcorn which was, against all odds, pretty good. Salt and butter and a hard-fought victory.

We watched the first half. Behind us, Martin talked over the movie; Chandler told him to be quiet so he could actually watch; Damian pointed out everyone else was talking too. Things had returned to homeostasis.

Freddie and I didn't have to plan it out ahead of time. We'd worked it out as wordlessly as some of our plays on the field. He got up and stepped away, slipping back through the field to the dorms. I gave him a ten minute head start and did the same, everyone else in the team either watching the movie, discussing, or frantically texting their girlfriend (guess who). I caught Damian eyeing me with a smirk as I slipped away, but he didn't say anything, just went back to throwing popcorn at the back of Charles' head.

I found Freddie in the dark of our secret dorm room, and greeted him with a kiss.

"Awesome game, man," he said, grinning wide.

"You too," I said back. And meant it—sometimes you say platitudes like that to a teammate when they sorta sucked, but Freddie had been on fire that game as well. It was so hard to put into words how good it felt to be doing something well—to be contributing to the team—versus some of my earlier games where I'd been mucking it all up.

We walked the empty hallways hand in hand, chatting about the game, the team, life. Occasionally he'd squeeze my hand mid-sentence or trace something or another into my palm with his fingernail and I'd need a second to remember what I was saying.

I didn't know if I should tell him about the recruiter thing or not. A part of me just liked whatever it was we had and whatever it was we were doing, and that felt like some great big abstraction that might change things up. I mean, I'm sure he would've been excited—and I think I wanted him to be excited, but there was also no way to talk about a college recruiter wanting me to stay in touch without bringing up, you know. A college recruiter hadn't talked to Freddie.

And, you know, college.

I shook my head. That was years away. *Just focus on tonight, then the tournament, then*...the ants-crawling feeling started to come back. At some point, the future would be a thing, right? Was I supposed to—was this—

Freddie squeezed my hand and I took a deep breath. It didn't matter for tonight. Later.

As we rounded the corner on the bottom floor, we came to a door that had been locked previously—we'd tested every doorknob just to see what else there was. Mostly cleaning closets or things like that.

This door, however, was propped open this time.

I felt the hair on the back of my neck go up. *Who else had been in here?*

"Hey, wasn't that door—"

"Yeah," I muttered, hand slipping from Freddie's as I walked up, easing it open. The door squeaked and whined as I opened it and looked inside.

It was a storage room.

I mean, I don't really know what I expected, but something cooler.

"Looks like an AV room or something," Freddie said, glancing around. "They've got spare projectors and stuff."

Freddie walked inside, looking around. "Man, some of this stuff is pretty old. I thought this was a rich kid's school or something."

There was some sinking feeling in the back of my mind, but the soreness of my legs and the sluggish feeling that seeps into your muscles after a hard, hard workout seemed to be slowing it down. My hand still felt warm from where Freddie had held it, and I-

"Oh crap. This is where they got the movie projector from," I said.

Freddie's head tilted to the side, eyes widening when the realization hit him a second later. "Oh. Um. Let's—not be here," Freddie said, turning to the door.

I moved back, one hand grabbing the door handle and the other reaching out for Freddie's. He took it, hurrying up behind me.

Before I could swing the storage room door open, however, I heard another swing open down at the end of the hall shortly before it slammed shut.

Followed by the sounds of heavy footsteps.

Chapter Sixteen

"This is pretty bad," Freddie murmured.

An understatement.

The footsteps were getting louder, and closer, and it took my brain a second to process those two facts, and the fact that they were coming to *us*, and that meant all kinds of really bad things when they got here. Did I want it to be Wilhelm? Ludwig? Which one was going to be worse?

If we got caught, it'd be—they might bench us a game from the tournament. Team Three had struggled with a man down. With two down, we would stand absolutely no chance.

I turned around in the storage room. The basement hallway was a long straight shot. There was no chance we could duck out and into another room, and I had zero doubts whoever it was planned on coming into the room where we were. For a single, idiotic second, my brain was convinced it was a good idea to grab Freddie's hand and blitz down the hallway and just hope whoever was there had their hands full and couldn't snag us or catch our faces.

Then I remembered either Ludwig or Wilhelm would take up almost the entire width of the hallway, and Wilhelm had that weird knack of recognizing each and every one of us from across the field. We didn't stand a chance.

"Kit, what do we do?" Freddie said.

I turned back around, looking the storage room over as best I could in the dark. It was pretty close to the worst place you could ask for to hide. There was a heavy duty vacuum for cleaning the halls, some cleaning spray bottles still in boxes, and spare school supplies. There were a few classroom desks flipped and put into the corner and some crates of spare parts for fixing the bunk beds.

I stepped over to the boxes and tried to look around, seeing if there was something—anything. Even if we ducked behind something, our feet would be sticking out below, or otherwise we'd be in clear sight when they walked past to put the project equipment back up on the far shelf. We could try to stay flat against the wall and just duck past as they came through, but I gave that pretty much the same odds as the coach being happy to see us when they walked in. There were rolling white boards which could hide our upper bodies, but our legs would be sticking out like we were in a *Scooby-Doo* episode, and we didn't have the time to clutter it up.

"Kit," Freddie said, his tone urgent. We had ten seconds. Maybe. I could feel his fingers digging into my arm, and my brain felt mired in a dozen different sensations at once—the feeling of Freddie's hand on my arm, the thundering in my chest that was making all my fingers and toes jittery, my legs shaky, the steady footsteps louder and louder, the dust in the air wrinkling my nose, making my eyes water—

I looked around the room one more time. There was absolutely nowhere in here you could hide two people. Even if we were out of sight when he came in, nothing was positioned for us to be out of sight when he turned back around. There was no way to hide us both—

It clicked.

The footsteps were way too close to risk talking. I turned and made eye contact with Freddie and nodded my head to the side of the doorframe the door would close back on. He slid past me and looked down, making sure he didn't step on any clutter and make a sudden noise.

Because of that, Freddie didn't notice what I was doing and try to stop me.

I turned and reached into one of the boxes, grabbing a set of markers and tearing them open. I grabbed the edge of one of the white boards and started jotting x's and o's down as quick as I could, then scribbling a big rectangle all around them.

The steps were maybe five feet from the door now, and every instinct in my brain was shrieking there was still a chance for me to try to duck somewhere and hide, to get out of sight, that maybe we'd catch a lucky break and they'd be on their phone, not paying attention.

I took a deep breath and forced myself to stay there, trying to make my drawing on the white board look like I'd been at this for a while and not just feverishly scrawled everything out in the last ten seconds.

I caught Freddie's eyes, flat against the wall beside the door. He caught on to what I was doing and waved a hand for me to come over, gesturing at the empty spot beside him.

"I owe you," I mouthed at him. The door opened and I went still.

In the moment between the door opening and everything going to hell, it occurred to me I was technically still grounded for sneaking out, and mom and dad were probably not going to be pleased about this development.

The door swung open, nearly smacking into Freddie, and Bronson stepped through.

"Ahh!" Bronson said, stepping through the door, flinching, and dropping the projector box in his hand. He seemed to realize his mistake as soon as it left his fingers. On reflex, he brought a thigh up to intercept it, gingerly as if it were an incoming pass, and grabbed it back again before it could crash and break. This just knocked most of the stuff out of the box across the floor. I winced. Hopefully nothing expensive was cracked. I didn't think that would help my sentencing. "What the hell—I mean—what, what? Why are you here?"

"Uh, sorry," I said, doing my best to sound meek and apologetic. It wasn't difficult. "I—um, I just wanted to clear my head and—"

"Do it your in your dorm or something, you—" Bronson took a deep breath and massaged at his face. I hadn't considered that he was probably just expecting an empty room and this might've been mildly unsettling. "I—how did you even get in here?"

I kept my eyes away from Freddie, doing his best to melt into the gray brick wall, and instead on Bronson, not meeting his. I was doing my best to look remorseful. This was, uh, incredibly easy for me to do. "The door was left unlocked."

Bronson's head cocked for a moment, and I could see the gears turning. *If he has to lock and unlock the doors he for sure knows which ones were and weren't locked*, I realized. *If I get caught in a lie on top of sneaking out I am utterly screwed here.* I was still trying to cover the window entrance, as if there was some chance I'd even get to sneak back out with Freddie again before the summer was over. "I'm sorry, sir," I said. *Get his mind off the doors.* "I just, um—" I took a deep breath.

I didn't lie a lot. I mean, about having my room cleaned or something, sure, but not like this, not when there was actual stuff at risk. Bronson still stood in the door, kneeling to grab all the stuff off the floor. I realized I should've been helping and not brainstorming excuses and I scrambled over to help him, but he'd gotten most of the stuff back in the box.

"I'm sorry," I said. I gestured to the board. "I just—" *You need to keep him off looking around the room. Get him out of this room as fast as you can and Freddie can make it out of this.* "It's just I had a scout talk—to me today and I needed—I wanted to get ready for the next game, I just needed some space and some of the other guys on my team were asking about it and I—"

The words started tumbling out faster and more authentically than I meant. I mean, the other guys asking wasn't true, but as I said the thing about the scout I could feel Freddie's eyes on me and my cheeks grew redder than they had already been. *Should I have told him?* I thought, before realizing it wasn't my main problem right now. If I screwed this up and got Freddie caught, Bronson was going to be doubly pissed. The universe had already sent me a break by sending Bronson and not—

"What's going on in there?" someone bellowed down the hall, accent thick.

Damnit.

"I, um, I just wanted to look over the game we had against Team Three and figure out what I could've done better and sorta—you know, think things over."

Bronson looked at the white board, and then back at me, and finally at the *Stanford University* card I had pulled out and showed to him. I could feel Freddie's eyes on it just the same, and though I had to force myself not to look in his direction, I could see the expression of terror on his face melt into something closer to confusion. Almost hurt.

"This way," Bronson said, putting the box down on a folding table and starting to turn the other way, where he'd catch Freddie—

I didn't really have time to think of something better. I dropped to the side against one of the tables, knocking a bunch of stuff over and making a general commotion.

"Cook, I swear," Bronson muttered, rubbing at his temples. He turned back to face me, his vision probably twenty degrees off from where he would've clocked Freddie, standing against the wall, doing his best to look like an inanimate object. "We don't own this stuff, okay? We have to pay back St. Michael's."

"Sorry, sorry," I said, grabbing things and putting them back on the table as quickly as possible.

"Is someone—" Wilhelm stepped to the door.

I had mentioned before in the game with Team Three there was a moment where Wilhelm thought I had intentionally fouled Oliver to try to get him out of the game, and he had stared at me with the sort of vitriol that I can really only compare to the looks somebody gets from their classmates when they remind the teacher to assign homework (which for the record, I never did). And even that was a poor approximation.

The wrinkles in his face deepened like they'd been carved out by hatchets, and I could see his face reddening to match mine. I think my red was more of an embarrassed blush and his was the color a bull saw right before it charged. He let out a single huff with flared nostrils.

I turned my head down and gathered up the boxes of paper towels I'd knocked over and stacked them back up on the table haphazardly, trying to—

"No. Organize them the way they were." Wilhelm said, each word clipped and tight like a boxer's jab. "You put it back the right way and fix your mess."

"Yes sir," I said, reshuffling the boxes, aligning them properly. I could feel both Wilhelm and Bronson's eyes boring into my back, which was fine by me. Bronson was standing right next to the door, and Wilhelm just on the other side of the threshold. If they didn't turn directly in that direction, Freddie would be fine, they wouldn't notice him—

"Enough. Come this way."

"Yes, sir."

I almost thought I clocked a bit of pity on Bronson's face, and maybe even a flicker of fear himself. If I'd just gotten caught by him, maybe I could've talked my way out, but that ship had sailed.

I walked out of the room as quickly as I could, and Wilhelm slammed the door behind me hard enough to cause a mild displacement of the building's foundations.

Bronson grabbed a walkie-talkie and radioed a quick message to Ludwig, telling him to meet up with us in the courtyard.

I would've said my luck could not have gotten worse, but they didn't turn back or go into the storage room again. That was something. Maybe that was everything.

In one of my lit classes we had to learn about Greek mythology, and the three old ladies who spun and wove and cut the cloth of life and death—the *Moirai*, whose name I had to pretend not to know when I took the class with Kyle so he wouldn't roast me for being a nerd.

Anyways, if two of the ladies had been German, and the other one an ultra-marathon runner, I would've felt like I was watching those three take a chainsaw to the thread that kept me alive.

"Are you out of your mind?" Ludwig said.

"Ludwig," Bronson said. I appreciated the effort, but it was pretty futile.

"Do you understand you cannot go walking around at night wherever you want? That we have a responsibility for every child at this camp? What do you think happens if you wander off and get hurt?"

"I'm sorry," I repeated. I meant it, too. I mean—I guess. I was probably sorry I got caught. It was worth it to spend the time with Freddie. I just hoped the coaches were talking loudly enough to keep Mateo from wandering around the corner on speakerphone with his girlfriend.

"First," Wilhelm said, "I seem to remember you promising me you would not cause problems. That you sneaking out after curfew was a mistake you would only make one time. At what point did you stop being a man of your word?"

I had nothing to say to that. I'd just...thought we wouldn't get caught.

"Second. Did it occur to you," Wilhelm continued, his tone methodical, surgical. That was more terrifying to me than Ludwig's explosive anger. I felt like Wilhelm was taking his time and really trying to contemplate what the punishment should be, whereas Ludwig was just getting the rant out of his system. I'd taken rants from coaches before, but it was worse when they slept on it and came back to you with something perfectly prepared.

Beyond that, I remembered Wilhelm pulling me aside after that game with Team Thirteen. He'd taken the time to try to help me out. And, I guess, talked to a recruiter about me. And I repaid that by immediately pissing him off and disappointing him.

He continued. "—that if you were caught, or punished, or sent home from Weltmeister, that Coaches Bronson and Ludwig and myself—we could lose our jobs? Did it occur to you that if you get punished or hurt messing around in the basement, your team is a man down for the rest of the tournament? That any recruiting opportunities they may have had would be done? All their hard work all summer wasted?"

I hadn't.

The thought hadn't occurred to me. For the seniors—Mateo, Miles, Slick, Victor, Alejandro—this was it. If they benched me even for one game, we had almost no chance of progressing. They were going to have no chance to showcase what they could do.

They were going to be livid. And somewhere under that, there were my prospects. If that Stanford guy was still hanging around, was he going to change his mind after seeing me sit the bench for what was clearly some kind of screw-up outside the game? Every sprint I ran or test I did well on was going to amount to absolutely nothing there.

"I didn't," I said, my voice soft. I wasn't really having to pretend or lie or think two steps ahead at this point. I wasn't totally sure I could if I wanted to. I was just reeling in how badly I had screwed up. I had just meant to hang out with Freddie, get time alone.

"For that reason, and that reason *alone,* I am not going to bench you the rest of the tournament," Wilhelm said.

"Though you deserve it," Ludwig said.

Wilhelm said nothing for a moment, and I could feel my heart simultaneously trying to crawl its way up my throat and down into my stomach. "Possibly. But I'm not punishing his teammates because he is irresponsible."

"Thank you," I said, not able to get my voice above much more than a murmur.

Bronson stayed quiet for a moment, hand stroking his chin.

"Why were you down there?" Ludwig asked. This was the closest look I had gotten at his cauliflower ears and the small bend in his nose that could only have come from it being broken decades ago. I did not care to ever get this close a look again. "Stealing?"

Wilhelm snorted at that. "Of course not. Why would he steal folding chairs and erasers?" He turned to me. "Though I also want to know why."

I took a deep breath. For some reason I felt the urge to tell the truth, even though I knew that was really dumb—it would've dragged Freddie down into this mess with me and ruined the whole point of it all. But some part of me did want to say something, I guess, and in that moment I couldn't have fully told why. Instead, I did the smart thing. I told them what I'd started to try to tell Bronson. "I got talked to by a recruiter from Stanford after the game today. I was—I was thinking about the semifinals match and wanted to go over everything. I just needed some space to think stuff over and not be surrounded by everybody for a minute. I wanted to be ready for the quarterfinals if—if they're going to be watching."

A part of me, as I said it, couldn't shake the feeling that maybe they already knew about Freddie, and this was just a trap to catch me in a lie. But I knew that didn't make any sense, it was just the part of me that had freaked out about—well about everything.

Wilhelm did not roll his eyes, but I could see the muscles in his face strain as he fought the urge to. "You don't need to be alone," Wilhelm said. "You need to be with your team. Your team helped get you a talk with the recruiter. Your team is there when you are stressed. Walking around alone in the dark did not ever help anyone. Your team is what helped you."

Bronson's features seemed to soften slightly in my peripheral vision, but he said nothing. I glanced up at him and then back at Wilhelm's feet.

"Yes, sir."

He shook his head. "You," he said, "Have a great many opportunities ahead of you, and have worked very hard. Do not risk it all over something stupid like this again."

"I won't," I said, which was half true. I wouldn't risk it over something dumb.

I'd risk it over Freddie, though, I thought. And I realized it was true as I went to dismiss it, to tell myself I wasn't going to let Wilhelm down this last week of camp. But as much as this whole shakedown was making my stomach do acrobatics, I realized I'd take another ass-chewing of even greater severity tomorrow night if it was the only way to get time with Freddie.

"Good. Straight back to your dorm. If we catch you out again, you *will* be sent home. Your parents will be informed. And I will see to it that every recruiter I speak with from now until the end of time knows that you are unreliable and not someone who considers their team before themselves."

I tried not to shudder. "Yes, sir."

"Tomorrow," Wilhelm said, "We'll discuss punishment. At six a.m. You can think on what it may be and what your team should be worth to you tonight."

***

"Slow, 64."

I glared.

Oliver smirked.

My shoulders and arms and lower back and thighs were all aching. I was in good shape—God knows Bronson made sure of that—but I had not been doing training montage exercises all summer.

I'd asked Ludwig if I could fill the water coolers at the spigot right by the field and not all the way behind the dining hall. In response, he had given me the first smile I'd seen from him all summer.

I set the cooler down on the bench and took a minute to suck in air. It was like moving furniture—I'd had to do that when Patrick had moved into his dorm last summer.

Wilhelm blew the whistle and Team Three jogged out onto the field, taking positions. Oliver and I were left at the bench as they squared up against Team Ten.

His team had shifted the bench to be perpendicular to the field rather than parallel. Oliver could stretch his knee out straight on some duffel bags.

There were enough ice packs to risk hypothermia on his leg, and they'd given him some duffel bags to lean back on.

Despite that, the guy looked...tense.

I mean, I would've been pissed about not getting to play, but there was something deeper undercutting it.

"You good?" I asked. I kept my voice low. The bleachers weren't far behind us, but between the noise on the field and the noise of eliminated teams in the stands, I didn't think anyone would overhear.

"Clearly," Oliver said, with a tone that made Chandler look like a bleeding-heart. "Don't you have water to go fetch?"

I thought about snapping at him, and also thought about just walking away and filling up Team Ten's cooler before Ludwig saw me slacking (note: any movement which was not done at full speed was considered "slacking"), but instead I just stood there and didn't say anything. I also briefly considered picking up his ice packs and moving them out of his arms' reach, but I'm not proud of that.

Instead, I said nothing and waited him out.

He turned up to look at me for a minute. He was one of the older-looking kids at the camp. You know those guys who hit puberty at nine years old or something and look thirty by the time they graduate high school. He was like that. He met my gaze and then looked back to the field, chewing on the ice in his cup. "No. Obviously not. Look at my knee."

"Do they know what's wrong with it?"

Oliver shook his head, just barely. He spoke like he was talking about someone else, a stranger he'd never met, and not himself. "Not until I get an MRI. Nurse thinks it's a meniscus tear. She's probably right."

Meniscus tear was...not good. He was not playing again at Weltmeister. It wasn't the worst thing, though. He could probably heal, do some annoying PT exercises for a few months, and be in fighting shape for the latter half of his season at home if it wasn't too bad.

Of course, there was always the chance that it was too bad.

I studied him for a moment, expecting another barbed comment. He had put on his cleats even though he was sitting the bench. Old, two or three coats of paint worn through. Those things must've been about as sturdy as fuzzy bath slippers at this point. *No wonder he didn't have any traction out there.*

Still, I felt like I—like there was something I was missing. There was something deeper. Not that I wasn't taking this all seriously, just that he—it felt more than a game, and more than just the usual ego stuff.

Before I could say anything, he asked, not looking up in my direction from the field. "What'd you get punished for?"

I paused. I wasn't sure how much Freddie and I were—what we were telling people, I guess, though I didn't think Oliver had anyone he could tell. Frankly, I didn't think Oliver cared enough to tell anybody. He'd be gone and back off to his senior year in five or six more days anyway. "Sneaking out after hours," I said, finally, which was true.

Oliver didn't respond for a moment—his team had stolen the ball and had a brief, intense drive on the other team's goal before getting pushed back. "Hm. How'd they catch you?"

"Went looking in a room I wasn't supposed to, Bronson followed me in."

Oliver's brow furrowed. "Why were you inside one of the buildings? Were you trying to watch tape or something?"

"Not...exactly."

I wasn't sure if Oliver got what I was trying to say or not. He just went back to being quiet and watching the game.

I wasn't sure what to say to break the silence. I settled on more of the truth. "You played really well," I said. "All summer. Seriously. Not just saying that because you're hurt."

"Yeah. We'll see," he said, keeping his eyes on the field, chewing on another piece of ice. His tone was neutral and level, but he was crushing the ice with far more force than was strictly necessary. He had a clipboard and some notes next to him and I saw him jot down a few points in annoyingly neat handwriting.

After a moment, I watched his eyes go up to the bleachers on the far side of the field. I saw the Stanford recruiter and a few others sitting there. For the quarterfinals on, the coaches had laid out an area where none of the campers could eavesdrop, now that the bleachers were more packed than they had been before. There were probably ten or twelve recruiters there, all watching the field.

None watching Oliver.

I gave him a once-over again, looking at his old, worn cleats. I saw the duffel bag by his good leg, just as roughed-up, the carrying strap held together by duct tape.

I realized after a moment he'd stopped taking notes, and was just staring at the recruiters, lost in thought, chewing ice and shifting his knee ever so often.

"See you around, Oliver."

He didn't reply.

I went off to go get more water.

Chapter Seventeen

"Hey, Cook, let me talk to you for a sec."

"Not in the mood," I told Damian. For starters, I was completely drenched in sweat and had developed soreness in muscles I had not realized I had, thanks to lugging those stupid water coolers, then from playing in the quarterfinals, and then from lugging water coolers again. *How do these guys drink so much water and not puke all over the field? Why did Freddie and I have to go check out that stupid room?*

Second, I had more important things to sort out. I needed a shower, which meant having to go back to the hall shower like everyone else, so I was trying to get in there while most of the dorm was still at the field. Then I had to figure out, you know. Actual problems. "I'm going to—"

"Sneak off with Freddie?"

I was glad I had my back turned, because I'm certain my wide eyes and sudden paling was a bit of a tell. Also, I almost tripped and staggered a step or two, which probably didn't help.

"Um," I said, turning to face him.

Damian had an annoying smirk, more so than his baseline annoying smirk, and pushed his brown hair out of his eyes. "Yeah, I figured. You got busted for sneaking out... Freddie was late coming back the same night..." He shrugged.

"Yeah. Two and two at that point, I guess."

"I mean you're maybe a two, Freddie's an eight or nine. Dude's a catch."

"Ha. Ha."

Damian snickered. He glanced over his shoulder, making sure nobody was nearby. The rest of Team Six was chilling on the bleachers, watching the first semifinals match. Oliver's team had lost in the quarterfinals still man-down. "Anyway, listen, I just—you know. I just wanted to let you know I'm—uh, yeah. Cool with everything."

I had to play the words back in my head before I realized Damian had actually been cool about this. I spoke again after a slightly awkward pause. "Oh. Uh. Thanks. I mean it. You know."

"Yeah, man, it's—just don't rock the boat for games and stuff. Next game's not going to be as easy as the quarterfinals was."

That was an understatement. We'd pulled off a—well, I wouldn't call it an upset because we were seeded pretty close to one another, but Team Eleven had absolutely crumpled. None of us had a clue why. It wasn't like we suddenly played like gods or anything.

That said, none of us were questioning a 3-0 shutout after barely making it out of group stages.

"Wasn't planning on losing."

Damian tilted his head in a *touché* gesture. "Yeah, I meant like, you know. You get me."

I paused, trying to think through what to say. I didn't want to antagonize Damian here, because he could still be a massive pain in the ass if he chose to be, but also...he was a teammate. And he was acting like one, here, even if he was doing it in the most annoying fashion possible. I mean, if I'd found out anybody else on the team was having a secret...whatever Freddie and I had...I would've been really surprised, first, but I wouldn't have wanted to go around telling people.

"I appreciate it, man," I said, taking a deep breath and trying to think everything through. I hadn't expected good news. Given the last twenty-four hours, I'd been primed to expect more bad news, like maybe Messi getting drafted to play against us in the next match, or Wilhelm getting mad at me again. Something along those lines.

This was welcome news. An easy win and Damian being cool.

I didn't have good luck, you know?

I glanced around for rain clouds.

I took a moment and then said, "I just want to be sure, you know. You guys are going back home with Freddie, and I don't know how—if that sort of thing would cause problems, or if he wants people to know."

Damian pulled out a piece of gum and began chewing it. Smacking it, actually. I contained myself. "Yeah. No worries there. I'm not a gossip. Freddie's a good dude. I don't want to cause any problems for him."

I nodded. "Thanks."

"Same goes for you though, man."

"Huh?"

Damian shrugged. "Don't cause any problems for him. He's—he's too nice, you know? I mean I don't think you'll be a jackass. But, you know. Don't be a jackass." Damian stood up a bit straighter and met my eyes. "Don't hurt him."

"Wasn't planning on it," I said.

"Then we're square in my book." Damian extended a fist, which I bumped back. "Alright, now go shower. You reek. You should've dumped some of those water buckets on yourself."

"Thanks, Damian."

My luck held. I got off the field without being hit by one of Wilhelm's glares, and as I'd guessed, the dorm showers were empty. It was worth

taking a speed shower and missing watching the latter half of the last quarterfinals match to not be surrounded by sixty other people later tonight. I
could have tried to go back into the closed-off dorms—I didn't think they'd
gone and closed the window back shut, but there was no way for me to
walk around in that direction without looking incredibly suspicious.

And it wasn't worth getting sent home from Weltmeister over. Not with
only a few days left, and not when I'd given Wilhelm my word—after
breaking it once—that I wasn't going to cause any problems.

Still, it was a weird kind of...defeat to be back there. I mean, it should
have just been a normal showering situation. It just sucked to have to deal
with this again after having my own space for the last few weeks and for
thinking I was finally in the clear. I scrubbed as fast as I could, toweled off,
and got dressed back in casual clothes to go back to dinner. I glanced at
the book on my desk, Polaroids sent by my buddies at Brightbirch serving
as a bookmark. Said bookmark had still not moved any further. I made a
mental note to speedread to the end at some point, so when Dad quizzed
me on it I could give satisfactory answers.

If I finished the summer without finishing a book, I was pretty sure my
parents would want CAT scans done at the very least or assume there was
a body snatcher or brainwashing going on at Weltmeister.

My feet were autopiloting to the main exit where I could catch back up
with the guys. It wasn't that I was in a tense mood, or feeling particularly
lost, there was just a lot to think about. Semifinals. Trying to square things
up with Wilhelm. Weltmeister ending in a few days. Freddie, what happened next there. School starting up a few weeks after I got back. Trying
to—

"Hey," Freddie said.

I flinched. "Ah! Hey."

Freddie raised an eyebrow.

"Sorry," I shook my head. "I was a bit lost in thought."

"You don't say." Freddie gave me a small grin, but it didn't seem as lively as his little grins normally were. It flickered across his face, brightening his features for just a moment, and then was gone.

"You okay?" I asked. We were near the entrance to the dorms, standing under one of the archways. It was one of those places that was both very public and yet felt private, the noise from the field and the sounds of all the eliminated teams shouting in the distance, and the sounds of St. Michael's on the other side. Someone was always mowing the lawn or blowing leaves or doing something to keep the grounds meticulous. The archway was built the exact same as the one we'd first kissed under. *Has it only been a few weeks?*

I'd of course gotten to see Freddie in passing since we got busted in the closed-off dorms, but this was our first time one-on-one since then. I wasn't sure what to do, exactly.

Freddie started to look over his shoulder, then stopped, tense for a moment, and reached his hand out for mine. I took it lightly, keeping an eye for anybody coming nearby.

"I'm okay," Freddie said. "I, uh, thanks. Man. You—that was really dumb of you. I mean you could've gotten kicked out or told not to come back." He blinked. "Wait, they didn't tell you couldn't come back, did they?"

I shook my head. "No, no, I got chewed out like you wouldn't believe but nothing aside from being water boy the rest of camp. Much to Ludwig's chagrin. I think he wanted capital punishment."

Freddie smirked. "Yeah, I—thanks."

"I mean, you covered for me on the first day, you know? I owed you."

Freddie opened his mouth like he was going to say something, but the words got lost somewhere along the way. I just squeezed his hand instead, and he nodded. "Thanks," he said.

We stood there quietly for a moment, and Freddie looked out towards the direction of the field, though it didn't look like he was scanning for anybody coming nearby.

"I—you should've said something, you know? About Stanford. That's huge, dude. That's awesome."

"Thanks, I mean—I've got two years to go, so it's not like—"

"Don't put yourself down," Freddie said. "That's really cool."

I stopped. I was putting myself down, wasn't I?

I grinned. "Thanks."

There was a weird tension there, like—well, I guess I hadn't had this happen to me personally, but I'd been out with friends when they ran into their ex, and the conversation just suddenly feels really stilted. It felt a bit like that.

"I'm sorry I didn't tell you," I said, "It wasn't—I didn't mean anything by it, it had just happened that afternoon and I think I was still trying to get my head around it. I didn't want to—I don't know. I didn't want to jinx it, or have everybody talking about it, and then make stuff weird with the team, you know?"

"Yeah," Freddie said, chewing on his lip for a moment. "I mean, you weren't—you weren't worried about stuff being weird with me, were you?"

The truth is I think I was, a bit. I didn't think Freddie would be jealous, but I also...I mean, the absolute truth is I think I was better than Freddie. The scout had come to me and not anybody else. And I didn't want Freddie to feel bad about that. I didn't know a way to say *Hey Stanford may want me to come play for them* without coming off like I was bragging, or without...I guess rubbing in the fact that nobody else had gotten that card.

But as soon as I had articulated that in my head, I realized...this was Freddie. I hadn't heard anything like that—jealousy or being pissed at another teammate—from him all summer.

I guess I didn't know, one hundred percent, what it was, or if I was right or not. Standing in the three-hundred-degree heat, feeling Freddie's pulse between my fingers, I didn't really feel like delving in and dissecting whatever that was.

"I hadn't really thought it all through and just wanted to process it first," I said. "I hope—I hope I didn't...I didn't mean to keep secrets or anything from you."

Freddie gave me a smile, and it seemed like the stiltedness was melting away. "Okay. I want you to be able to tell me cool stuff, alright? Like that's really, really cool. You're still just a sophomore."

I gave him a grin, feeling my feet shift back and forth. It was my turn to look over at the field. "I—thanks."

"Man, you don't take a compliment."

"Oh, whatever."

There were whistle blasts in sharp succession, and a roar of noise.

"You ready for tomorrow?" Freddie asked, his fingers slipping from mine. In a few minutes, people would trickle back this way to get ready for dinner. This felt so much shorter compared to three or four hours at night, alone, the campus to ourselves. And at the end of that short time was tomorrow.

Tomorrow was semifinals. Tomorrow was one day closer to the end of camp.

"Yeah," I said. "You?"

Freddie smiled and gave me a nod. "Let's go grab dinner."

———————— ⚽ ————————

They'd just mowed the lawn. It had that fresh-cut smell. Grass is important in a lot of ways. Different kinds of fields have a different feel to them, and it affects how the ball moves. If you're playing on turf, it zips around a lot faster. Regular old grass, it's slower, easier to control. If they haven't taken great care of things and irrigated it properly, you can get muddy spots and holes. Even if you *have* taken great care of things, you can still get muddy spots and holes, as Oliver found out.

The bleachers had a good crowd to them—with only four teams left in competition, the eliminated teams were allowed to watch and cheer rather than doing any more death marches for Bronson as camp wrapped up. I'd heard rumors that someone had a pretty robust gambling operation going; I just hoped it wasn't Martin handling the money, or he wouldn't be able to afford the flight home.

All the scouts and recruiters were also able to watch every game now, so it looked like their numbers had increased. There was a three-row buffer of empty bleachers (enforced by periodic glares from Ludwig) to make sure nobody was peeking over any scout's shoulders, and all the remaining teams were gathered up there. They'd make noise, but nothing raucous, and it wasn't like there'd be a home field advantage for either team.

I dug my cleats into the dirt a bit, testing them, testing the dirt. Laces were tight. Shin guards and socks in place. I scrubbed a dirty spot off the side of my right cleat.

The conditions were as good as you could ask for.

Around me, there was a mixture of moods. Some were stoic—Martin, his game face on, the jokes gone. Victor and Charles, talking quietly in tense tones; and of course, Alejandro, completely silent, though that wasn't a surprise. A few were making nervous small talk, like Miles and Freddie. Chandler wouldn't stop talking, and neither would Damian, but both were still glancing across the field, clocking the same details I was. Which way was the wind blowing, where was the glare the most intense. Would the few clouds on the horizon come our way or blow on by?

I felt a hand brush along my arm a moment too long to be accidental.

"Ready?" I asked Freddie.

"We'll find out," Freddie said, though in a way that was more jovial than it was nervous.

I grinned and stood up.

"Everybody good to go?" Martin asked. He and Slick came jogging back over from the coin toss. Across the field, Eight's fullback and keeper jogged to their side. *Eight's keeper is either the first or second in rankings for keeper, I think.* He moved with the confidence to match—his team immediately stopped talking to look up at him.

"They won toss," Slick said, "They kick off, we take this side."

Chandler scrunched his nose. "Still think we should've taken the other side."

"You were outvoted," Martin said. "Anyways, anyone got anything they want to add?"

"It'll be a good game, everyone," Miles said. "Proud to play with all of you."

One or two people nodded, there were a few looks of discomfort—the way you get when someone compliments you and you just want to change subjects—and Chandler rolled his eyes.

"Best team I've had at Weltmeister by far," Mateo said.

"Jesus, this is turning into a Hallmark movie," Chandler said. "Let's get on the field."

We went out with a smattering of agreement with Chandler, others calling him annoying, or staying quiet and getting focused. It all melted away as we got to our positions, bouncing from foot to foot, doing any last stretches to limber up, triple-checking the placement of shin guards.

It was war from the first whistle.

Their striker kicked off with a quick, low pass over to their right-center midfielder, who rolled the ball under his foot for a moment as we turned up the pressure. He turned and drew his leg back for a pass to the wing as the rest of their midfield surged forward. *They're going for the blitz.*

As my team moved to cover, they were already starting to dive into our defensive third. Instead of sending it to the sprinting centers, he sent a cross to their left wing. The wing was positioned right by me, hovering a half step ahead of me, just barely avoiding being offsides.

I think the first week of summer, the lightning attack might've caught me off-guard.

But this was week six. I'd clocked that their left wing was the one player on the field their midfielder hadn't been looking around at as the centers ran to receive the pass.

As the ball dropped, I moved in, jumping for the header. Eight's midfielder did as well, and the ball ricocheted somewhere between the jumble of our foreheads. We landed, jostled but standing. I was off moving before he was—if only by a second. The ball had dropped a few feet from us, rolling to the touch line. I wasn't sure who'd touched it last, and I didn't think Wilhelm was going to be a particularly gracious ref to me.

"Kit!" I heard Slick shout, somewhere up and to my right. I had to stretch, lunging for the ball before it went out. I flicked it up to Slick before Eight's center and left wing could pincer me, and Slick snatched it up and drove downfield.

I reeled back, stabilizing and scanning the field. I needed to be up—I started angling myself behind Slick in case he needed an escape option. Their wing was hanging close to me, seemingly thinking the same thing that I was. He must've been a senior. He was perhaps an inch or two taller than me but filled out and muscular like a Spartan soldier, with the beginnings of facial hair along his chin and jaw. *I got lucky on that header,* I thought. *He's going to have the edge on those.*

I took a deep breath and did my best to think ahead, and not just let my body operate on reflex.

Slick was dancing with one of their fullbacks, juking back and forth, looking for the opening. Eight's left back was directly between Slick and the goal. He didn't have a way through. The defender had him close to the goal line and was too quick on his feet to get past. There was no shot on goal and his only pass out of there was back to the center of the field.

Slick reeled back for a kick, planting himself to hit the thing to kingdom come. *Ye-Joon, you can't possibly think you can—*

I took the half-second between seeing him set up for the kick and the ball going flying to think.

I caught onto what he was going for an instant before the ball cleared his foot. I ran up in case Slick screwed it up, leaving their left wing standing behind me. Slick angled the ball at the last moment, hitting fullback's knee and sending the ball flying out of bounds across their goal line six feet away.

Eight's keeper looked furious. Slick looked pleased with himself.

We set up for the corner kick, moving as fast as we could to keep the pressure on. Chandler let loose and sent it into the melee that was the goal box. Alejandro managed to wrestle through a defender and get his head on the ball.

I hovered back, not in a position to get to a rebound. Even if I did push up to contest it, I would just be leaving Goliath open for a pass from the keeper. *They're counting on us getting greedy and overextending so they can send it downfield.*

I took a breath and went the other way, moving backwards and making sure I had their wing and their center midfielder in my peripheral vision.

I'd guessed right again. Their keeper snagged Alejandro's header and kept moving forward in one motion, punting the ball with practiced ease. It went up, and up, and over.

The rest of the team immediately began backpedaling—I'd gotten in position a moment or two early and was trying to anticipate where that punt was dropping. If we were lucky, it would land at midfield.

"Mine!" Damian shouted, moving in and grabbing the ball.

Eight's striker was already running back to contest. I did my best to jockey against him and buy Damian time, but it felt like trying to nudge a Clydesdale off-course.

I like to think I'm decently fast, but this guy probably had the same number of track recruiters after him as he did soccer scouts. He could cover more ground than me once he got going, and no amount of hustle on my part was going to make his legs shorter. I wasn't going to outrun him.

I needed something else.

I moved off him and back towards the center of the field, throwing my hand up like I was going to receive the pass.

The distraction worked—Eight's striker hesitated for a half of a second, trying to glance from Damian to me to the ball to see if he'd been faked out. It was enough. Damian cleared it to Martin, who began driving the ball back into their half of the field.

The game had been going on for two minutes at most and it already felt like it had been at least a half an hour. The pace did not let up. The balance between our strikers and their defense led to a delicate dance. We would push forward and work possession, probing for a chink in their armor.

They would wait and counter with surgical passes downfield, trying to punish our defense if they moved even a few steps out of position. Their strikers were my least favorite kind to play against: dangerously fast. Both teams were just searching for one golden opportunity or one careless mistake. We had played games where we were in control, at a slower, methodical pace. We'd played others that were more frenetic, more of a constant, dynamic back-and-forth. Never had we been so heavily counterbalanced, pushing both teams to the limits.

When the whistle blew at the half, I didn't see anyone bar the goalies who wasn't breathing hard. We jogged back to the bench, jerseys muddied wherever they weren't soaked in sweat.

"Good work," Martin said, clapping Alejandro on the back.

"Very good," Freddie said. "Very good."

I made eye contact with him and gave him a small smile, which he returned. It was just a second or so. It stung a bit, too, because it reminded how much it was going to suck lying in my dorm bed tonight, rereading the same page a hundred times, wondering if they'd closed that unlocked window.

Focus on the game, Kit, I told myself. *You have all summer to spend with Freddie,* which...I guess was still true. It just so happened all summer was a handful of days. Of which only maybe five or six free hours were there to have one-on-one time—and even then, who knew what privacy we'd be able to get, if there'd be anything but sneaking handholding when nobody was passing by.

I shook my head, wiping the sweat from my face and taking another sip of water. *Focus.*

"What's on your mind?" Charles asked. It took me a moment to realize he was talking to me.

I glanced and saw Victor and Damian were looking to me as well. I looked over at Eight's bench, chewing on my lip. Their keeper was their strongest player and had shut down five or six shots on goal that might've caught any other team's goalie off-guard. When their offense caught a pass, they could blitz downfield, take a shot...then jog back and do it again without slowing down. They just needed to get lucky once. But, I suppose, they were thinking the same thing about us.

I looked back over at them, and at Freddie sitting on the bench, who gave me a small nod.

"Honestly you guys are all playing really well. Let's keep kicking ass."

We took a minute to catch our second wind. This was maybe the first time we had gone an entire halftime without anyone arguing, or Chandler speculating on the ways we could lose.

"What?" Victor asked me.

"Huh?"

"You're just standing there smiling like a weirdo."

Eh, he wasn't wrong. "Just got distracted. Let's get to the finals."

We set back up a minute or two later and Wilhelm blew the whistle again. It was our kickoff, now, and we took the initiative.

We'd gambled wrong on the positions of the field. The clouds had blown the opposite way, and the glare of sunlight came through periodically right into our eyes. I could already sense Chandler's smugness.

They'd adjusted their formation from the first half. The tall midfielder who'd been on me was now at center, and they'd swapped one of their strikers with one of their midfielders as well. I wasn't immediately sure what that meant, just that Martin would have his hands full.

As much of a war as the first half had been, the second was as intense, only sloppier as both teams started to erode, bit by bit. Strikers would hit the ball a second too slowly, or the fullbacks moved just a moment later than they needed to. There were more throw-ins from the ball getting bounced out-of-bounds, more fighting that went down to the mud...then it was right back up to keep going.

The ball would suddenly be sent out, either by a desperate jab or a pass that only had a half second's time to set up. There were through balls that could've passed for artillery strikes that sent us all sprinting back to contest, and each time we were a hairsbreadth slower to jog back than the last. As the minutes ticked on, we were still locked in a stalemate, back and forth, back and forth. *If it goes on like this to a shoot-out I don't know if Mateo can block more shots than their keeper. We need a goal now and not overtime.*

The ball came to my feet, courtesy of one of their fullbacks smacking it clear from Victor. I caught it on the inside of my thigh and dropped it down, moving forward with it. The midfielder the tall guy had swapped with sprinted in. I saw him look up at Wilhelm, then over at Bronson, at the players around us—

He's looking to see if the refs have a line of sight, I realized. I yanked the ball to the right as he drew near. I couldn't have said for sure, but my gut was telling me he was aiming for my foot and not the ball when he knifed his leg in. His foot hit my shin guard, but I managed to dodge the tackle and stay on my feet, leg throbbing.

You can hurt tomorrow. Win today.

Their midfielder recovered and moved in closer. The tall center who I'd covered the first half was moving to the side, interposing himself between Alejandro and me.

I can't stay here without taking an elbow to the ribs, and I can't move up without getting mobbed by half their team. I tapped the ball up once and then flicked it to Damian behind me with a heel kick.

Damian wasted no time in passing it over to Freddie. Freddie had a good two or three seconds before their strikers were going to be able to threaten him.

Freddie swished the hair clear from his eyes, face tight and eyes narrowed, and sent a clear pass down the field to Martin, who was already rushing ahead. He tapped it once, control over the ball tenuous as he thundered at full speed, and kicked it left to Chandler.

He was only a step behind where Martin had sent the ball, cleats pounding on the field and face completely flushed. Their midfielder moved in to guard Chandler—cautiously. Chandler had gotten one past that midfielder earlier, and judging from how clenched the guy's fists were, he didn't seem particularly inclined to let it happen again. I saw Chandler start to roll the ball from his left foot over to his right, shifting his weight to feint—

Eight's midfielder already knows that trick.

As Chandler committed to the move, the midfielder lunged and tapped the ball loose from under his left foot. He darted around Chandler and started to go back down the field, where Miles was thirty feet away and in no position to contest. Their center was running straight for Mateo.

"Miles! Go to goal!" I shouted, turning and running back. There were times to backpedal with your eyes on the ball and there were times to haul ass. This was a time to haul ass.

I started running before Eight's shin-kicker did, moving to close the space between me and our fullbacks. Their midfielder fired a through pass, curving the ball with the sort of ease and precision I would've only expected from Oliver at the batting cages, setting up his shots with no one around and all the time in the world.

The ball dropped in where the center was running. He was past Miles and pressed closer to the goal. Freddie was sprinting to stop him, but the center was faster, the distance between them growing with each second. I pushed my legs harder than I had on any of Bronson's runs.

"Mine!" I shouted. Charles read my mind and moved back, shifting to guard Mateo from the other striker running parallel to the center.

I closed in. He was covering more ground than I could with his stupid ostrich legs but I had less ground to cover. I had clocked where he was headed early.

He had an open run to the goal if he got past me. Charles couldn't push up to help pressure him without leaving the other striker wide open. Damian was off on the wing.

I was ten feet away. Eight. Five. I could see him tense, readying to react, pulling a leg back to knock a pass through to the other striker.

If I block it wrong, I'm just going to knock it into the goal myself.

I didn't have the time to try to duel him and wrestle it clear. He was going too fast, I couldn't try to control it, I just—

Stop overthinking.

I went for the slide tackle and knocked the ball clear from between his legs. He staggered over, trying to avoid tripping, only to spiral his arms and fall over a half second later.

I'd knocked it clear. The ball had rolled back out towards Miles, but their right midfielder was getting there first. He closed in, Miles a step behind, then two, then—

He reeled back and kicked.

I was too far away. The ball rocketed past me and to the tips of Mateo's fingers, where he jumped, trying to knock it clear, knock it anywhere but the goal.

It spun off his fingers and into the net.

I saw him land, cursing and shaking his hand, trying to massage it with the other.

Jammed fingers, I thought. *That's not good, we need to change up, if he's—*

The whistle blew. Goal, Team Eight. We needed to reposition as quickly as we could. If we set back up and threw everything at a drive to their goal we could tie it up.

"Mateo, are you alright?" I said. I didn't want to be rude, but we didn't have time to sit around. "Grab the ball and kick it over, we need to—"

The whistle blew again. But that wasn't right. They only blew it once after a scored goal, they—

The whistle blew one more time, loud and long.

I just came to a stop, huffing for air, and looked up at the clock above the stands. It was sitting at 90. Their goal came in extra time. Everything left of my spine was still aching from hitting the ground. I felt Freddie's hand on the hurt shoulder. A small squeeze.

The game was over.

Chapter Eighteen

"That's idiotic. You pull for the team that beat you, so you can say 'oh, hey, at least we lost to the champs."

"Hell no," Martin said, wolfing through a bag of popcorn. They'd provided some snacks for the teams watching the championship match. The coaches had grossly, grossly underestimated how much food we would go through. "Eight beat us. I hope they go in second."

"Why? So then we're the guys who lost to the guys who lost? That's not—"

I let Chandler and Martin continue the summer's final argument and chewed on my popcorn. It was the semi-stale, mass-produced kind that was probably popped like six months ago and waiting around in the meantime...and it was delicious. I think it was the salt. The Weltmeister gods had seen fit to have intermittent clouds, so the sun was only brutal in spurts. The salt, however, was delicious constantly.

I watched Eight's players standing by the bench. *It's hard to be really upset about how things went,* I thought. *We played well. They just played better.*

Ludwig had been going around with a duffel bag full of sunscreen and interrogating anyone who crossed his path as to whether or not they had applied sunscreen within the last hour. Chandler had noted they must not have wanted kids going back to their parents with their skin peeling off, which I supposed was a pretty Chandler way of viewing keeping us from getting sunburned. That said, it did feel like they'd assigned that particular task to Ludwig as some kind of bizarre practical joke. I'd never seen someone be scared into applying sunscreen before.

"Cook, give me some of your popcorn."

I turned and looked. The championship game was at the half so a few of the guys had gone up to use the bathroom. Damian was among the few who'd remained.

"No, you had your own bag." I glanced over at his feet. "You had *two* of your own bags."

"Yeah, popcorn's awesome. You've still got half a bag."

"I'm saving it."

Damian scrunched his eyes and probed my armor for any weak points. "You really aren't going to share any popcorn with your good friend Dami-"

I threw a piece of popcorn into his mouth as he was talking and turned my focus away as he started hacking and coughing.

"Nice," Mateo said from my other side. He had crumpled his bag and was tossing it absentmindedly between his hands. He was sprawled across two rows of bleachers. "See, you should've been keeper and let me score some goals."

"I'll stick to kicking. There's a reason I didn't play baseball." *Actually, there are several.*

Mateo grinned, squinting as the sun came back out. "Not going to miss this sun. So glad I'll be back in cool weather in a few more days."

I think if I'd heard Mateo say that at the start of the summer, I wouldn't have read much into it. But he was crumpling that empty bag in his hand with a little too much force.

Damian had shifted to asking Chandler for popcorn, his voice signif-icantly hoarser, and had only succeeded in drawing both Chandler and Martin's annoyance onto him. I let them be and shifted to Mateo.

"You glad to be going back?" I asked, trying to keep my voice neutral. I didn't want to cross any lines, but I also didn't want to, you know. Not say anything. And I wasn't totally sure what to follow that back up with.

Mateo shrugged. "I mean—I'm glad I don't have to do any more run-ning for a few weeks, yeah. But it's always a bit weird. And it's—you know. Last time." I could see his eyes trailing from Eight's keeper over to the recruiters, most of whom had spent the halftime jotting down notes and talking in low voices. A few had gotten up to stretch their legs or grab water—including the Stanford recruiter, who I hadn't been able to help but watch whenever he'd been near the field the last few days.

"You played seriously well all summer, man," I said. "You had some crazy saves. I mean...some that were actually, clinically insane."

Mateo grinned again. "Likewise, Cook. You really improved a lot. I thought you were going to keep us from getting out of group stages those first two weeks, you know? And look at you now. You've got one more year?"

"Two."

"Two, that's right. I keep forgetting," Mateo said. "Weltmeister's fun. It's even more fun heading back and crushing everybody who you played with before with everything you learned."

I suppose somewhere I'd considered that element, in passing, but the last few weeks of the summer had been so hectic it wasn't something I'd spent a lot of time thinking on. "Might actually get to play a few games on varsity," I said, more to myself than to Mateo.

"You were on JV before?" Mateo said. "And still came here?"

"Yeah, I was hoping to make it last year, but they wouldn't take a freshman. Some stupid school rule. For sure this year."

"For sure," Mateo agreed. "You're good. You've—you know, not like I'm an old man or anything, but for all the sprints and all the yelling, you do learn a lot here. I was surprised how much better I got even after I knew I was going to get better. If you just focus on what they tell you and actually listen, you'll be running circles around your high school team. There's always some dude who just gets mad at the coaches yelling at him and never takes their advice out of spite. And it's like...dude, you're doing all that training for nothing now, you know?" I caught a brief flicker of something I couldn't quite place on his features, but the sun came out and the glare made me blink before I could determine just what it was. "Recruiters will notice you."

There was the metal thumping of the rest of the team clambering back up the steps of the bleachers and sidling back in around us.

"Here, man," Mateo said, reaching over and pulling Chandler's notebook and pen out of his bag. Chandler was still trying to fend off Damian's haggling and did not notice this in the slightest. *Man, for the guy who warned me about the column sprints, I thought he was going to be way more perceptive than he was.* Mateo took a brief moment to snoop on whatever Chandler had been writing, smirked, and then ripped out a piece of paper. He scrawled, in messy, loopy handwriting, his name and email and a few other ways to reach him. "Let's stay in touch."

I gave him a grin and folded it, tucking it in my pocket. "Sure thing. You better make sure your girlfriend knows I'm just a guy from soccer camp before she sees you texting a new number."

Mateo sighed and rested his elbows on his knees. "Honestly, man? I'm not sure we'll still get married at this point."

Thank God the others sat back down at that point and drew Mateo's focus away from my expression. I was going to need to develop a poker face for next summer.

Freddie took a spot next to me—perhaps a hairsbreadth closer than would normally be comfortable in the July heat—and offered me his bottle of water, which I gladly took a sip from. His face was a bit pink, glistening, and there were a few splotches of unabsorbed sunscreen around the corners of his eyes and the tops of his ears. I wanted to reach over and wipe it off, but there were a lot of people around, and some of them Freddie would be dealing with for the rest of high school. So I kept my hands at my side, and Freddie's sunscreen stayed splotchy.

"Looks like Ludwig got ahold of you."

"Yeah," Freddie said, frantically rubbing at his ears and face to smooth the rest of the sunscreen out. It scrunched up his nose and made the wavy blond hair that hung low over his face bounce back and forth. I couldn't help but smile at how cute it was. "On the positive side, I shouldn't have wrinkles until I'm at least, like, seventy-five with all this crap on."

I turned back to the field, where the teams had lined up for kickoff. 1-1. A very close game. Could go either way.

Behind me, Miles was inserting himself in between Chandler and Martin, and Charles and Victor had taken up on the other side of Freddie, bemoaning their summer reading they hadn't started. Privately, I hadn't thought *Wuthering Heights* was that bad, but I determined sharing that fact would not endear either of them to me.

It reminded me that I kept forgetting obvious details—like the fact they were going back home together, or that I may never see Mateo again—and each time those little facts hit me I was never quite sure what to make of it. In a weird way it felt unfair. I was headed back on my own, so why did some of the other guys get to keep a part of this group? Why did the guys who came from overseas get a few more hours together on the bus to the airport?

I didn't know if it made me a jerk, or if it was me not giving them a fair chance even thinking it, but...how the hell was my team back home going to compare even if I did move up to varsity right away?

Across the stands were a swarm of familiar faces of people whose names I couldn't have told you, but I knew them by the way they played, or position, or how skilled they were. Giraffe guy, the fullback with a howitzer for a left leg. Aides and assistants who'd brought water coolers (before I was assigned that joyous task) and set up cones.

Well, there was one whose name I could place. One watching the game on the other side of the field, arms folded, leg propped.

I rested my hands in my pockets and felt the recruiter's business card. I was trying to keep my hands off of it so there wouldn't be any crinkles or sweat stains or anything for when I showed my parents, but at the same time, a part of me wanted to keep touching it just to make sure the whole thing hadn't been some heat-induced fever dream.

I looked through the stands as they kicked off. The Stanford recruiter wasn't there with the others. He must've been off grabbing a bottle of water or using the bathroom or something.

I waited a minute until there was a big drive downfield by Goliath, and the noise from the crowd started to pick up. When Martin started shouting, I leaned over to Freddie, pointing at the action on-field, and whispered, "Meet me by the arch in like ten minutes."

I pulled back and Freddie didn't show any visible reaction, but I felt his foot tap against mine twice.

After the play concluded—I wasn't about to be that guy who gets up in the middle of the action and blocks the view—I stood up and started sidling over to the stairs.

"Where are you going?" Slick asked, his voice a bit too fast and high-pitched. Slick had been going off to the bathroom about every fifteen minutes to try to force his hair back into rigidity, only for the sun and the sweat to make it wilt shortly thereafter. He, I think, was under the impression no one had figured this out.

"Grabbing a drink."

"Why didn't you go at halftime?" Martin asked.

"Because there was a line at halftime," I said, and moseyed on over.

I jogged down the steps and around to the concessions area, glancing for red. I clocked it.

Well, I mean, the red in this case was also the only person not wearing a jersey, and also the only person who wasn't in high school. So it maybe wasn't the hardest job to track him down.

"Um, excuse me, sir," I said, approaching the Stanford recruiter before I lost my nerve.

"Hm?" He turned and looked, visibly exasperated. For a minute I was unable to shake that feeling I had made a huge mistake, like when you're right next in line to get on a rollercoaster which looks much, much higher up from where you're standing than from where you got in line. *If I piss him off trying to do this I may just torpedo my own chances too. Always brilliant, Kit.* Instead, his eyes brightened a bit under his visor when he recognized me. Or so I hoped. "Ah...Kit. How's it going?"

"It's going great," I said. "I know you're busy and don't want to bother you, I just wanted to say that I think there's someone else you need to, uh, consider."

"Oh?"

"His name's Oliver. He's on Team Three."

The recruiter frowned for a moment, grabbing his notes and speed-reading. "Don't have a lot written down from anything in the final rounds. Injured in group stages, it looks like?"

"Yes—yes sir, but...he's probably still highly ranked, and to be honest, the rankings don't even do it justice. He was one of the best players here all summer. I don't think you'll be disappointed."

The recruiter didn't say anything for a moment, looking at his notes and taking in what I'd said. "Senior?"

"Yes sir. I'm—I mean, I wasn't on his team, I don't know his grades, but I'm willing to bet they're probably solid. He's a hard worker. The guy skipped events to go drill shots on goal."

Part of me thought it may be a gamble to tell a college recruiter Oliver cut events, but I figured that a leg injury had already put him firmly in the "hail Mary" category for applying to colleges.

"Thank you," he said, extending me a hand to shake. I took it and did my best to shake it firmly but not seem like I was trying too hard, which I feel like is always a really impossible needle to thread. "I'm looking forward to seeing more of you, Kit. Keep working hard. Email me if you'd ever like a tour. Or a t-shirt, even."

His tone implied that the t-shirt was supposed to be a really big deal, but I honestly felt like I'd look like a dork wearing a t-shirt for a school I hadn't been accepted to. This was probably not the venue to express those sentiments. I just nodded gratefully. "Will do, sir. Thank you."

He stepped away, and I stood for a moment, trying to calculate the time in my head. I could probably still get over to that arch in time to tell Freddie goodbye, and maybe we could swing back by fast enough to tell the other guys bye without it being super noticeable. If—

"Kit Cook," Wilhelm said from somewhere about eight inches behind me. It was mildly startling. "If you were harassing a recruiter after I explicitly told you all not to—and after you already have caused me a considerable headache and told me twice you will cause me no more trouble—I am going to be very displeased."

No good deed. I turned to look at Wilhelm, whose expression was inscrutable in much the same way sheer cliffs on the side of mountains are inscrutable. "No, sir. I—I honestly was telling him to consider Oliver for a scholarship, nothing for me. I feel like he didn't get a fair shake since he blew out his knee and, I mean...he's good. He deserved it. He may not have come up to me after that game if Oliver hadn't gotten sidelined in the first thirty seconds. He worked really hard."

Wilhelm gave me a look. "I would tell you that I could easily find out if you're not telling me the truth, but you're smart enough to know that."

I was not sure if that was a compliment, or if I was supposed to respond, so I just nodded and said nothing.

Wilhelm studied me for a moment, which gave me some sympathy for the salmon in a river that look up and see a bear standing over them. He extended a hand for me to shake, which I took after a second's delay of needing to process the gesture. I contemplated how fragile the bones in your hand are until he let go. "You performed well this summer. You improved a great deal. Work hard. Don't get into any more trouble. I expect to see you back here. And with better behavior."

I nodded. "Thank you, sir. Will do."

He gave me a nod and a grunt which I interpreted as my signal to leave. I did so promptly. I mean, I appreciated the kind words, but I also still felt like the ice was pretty thin there. Didn't feel inclined to start jumping up and down on it.

I jogged over to the academic buildings. There was a small smattering of other campers moving around and packing up final things, so it wasn't like I was very noticeably sneaking off or anything like that. We were strongly,

strongly encouraged to go and watch the final game, but a small number of guys every year procrastinated packing their things until about thirty-five minutes ahead of pick-up. It would seem no force in the universe could make high school guys pack their bags on time.

Even the short jog was enough to make sweat start running down my back and arms in earnest. The one positive of that long, bumpy ride in the Beast was going to be that no matter how much else failed in that Frankenstein of a van, the A/C remained strong.

I came to the archway. For one moment I couldn't shake the feeling he just wouldn't be there, that somehow he'd already gone or been picked up and missed the chance to say goodbye. Freddie was already waiting for me, looking out over the empty dorm building we'd briefly claimed for ourselves. There was a flurry of movement going in and out—some kind of maintenance work, preparing for the start of the school year in a few weeks.

Freddie looked over at me and then down at his watch. "Kit!" he said, his voice thick with a German accent, his face scrunched into a furious expression. "You are one minute late! Do you understand how disrespectful it is to be one minute late at my soccer camp!"

I meant to say something witty back, and considered a Ludwig impression in return, and also wanted to laugh, and wasn't sure which one to go with. And then I realized which one I went with didn't really matter and kissed him.

Maybe it was just the last day of Weltmeister heat. But it felt like we were melting.

We pulled away slowly, leaning against the cool bricks and watching the small trickle of people move back and forth from dorms to the field. In maybe another half hour, the game would wrap up, the closing ceremonies would commence, and parents would be here for pickup. My brain was whirling trying to figure out some way to squeeze extra time out of things, to find something I'd overlooked that might allow for another hour and a half, another few minutes.

"It," Freddie said, blinking a bit and looking to the dorm that had been empty except for us all summer, "sucks that this summer is ending."

"Yeah," I said. There was something curling around my chest and squeezing tight. I reached down for Freddie's hand, which helped the constricting feeling to go away. "What, um," I said. For a minute, I think, I meant to say *What the hell do we do next,* but I didn't want to say that, because there were a lot of different responses to that question and I wasn't sure any of them were—I mean, a lot of them could've been bad. He could've hesitated, or said nothing, or laughed, or I could've just felt his fingers recoil slightly in mine. Instead, I think the words tumbled into that feeling of trying to claw another few seconds to pull something together, like trying to desperately get the ball back into play in our last game, to just get a drive downfield. "—what, um, what—what are you going to do when you get home?"

Freddie took a long breath and danced his fingers against mine. I took my other hand and finally rubbed in the sunscreen spots he'd missed while he talked. "I...I am going to take a really long shower until someone cuts off the water and makes me get out. And then I'm going to sleep for a few days straight. And then when I wake up, we've got a tradition—well, I guess it's not a tradition for Weltmeister specifically, but whenever we get back from a school trip or big game or something—and for sure once before summer ends—we always go to this ice cream place, Brainfreeze, in my hometown and just sort of debrief everything. They've got really awesome waffle cones. They always make them fresh to order. It's the one place I've been to where the cone is better than the actual ice cream."

I nodded. "Yeah, I went to another Brainfreeze just like that. It's on the way home from Brightbirch, so every year my mom and dad would stop there. We wouldn't ever stop anywhere that was within an hour of Brightbirch, because dad would say, 'Kit, all the ice cream places near the camp are going to have long lines from all the other campers. We'll just go to that Brain place, there's never a line there.' And so I wind up waiting like two hours for ice cream anyway. That's my Dad for you."

I glanced back over at Freddie, who was frowning.

The thing around my chest tightened harder. "You okay? Is something wrong?"

"You said *another* Brainfreeze. Brainfreeze isn't a chain, I'm pretty sure?"

There was some realization there, but the heat and the end of the summer and the feeling I still got when I kissed Freddie for a while were making my brain run slower than it should've. "I—wait, you said it was—"

Freddie nodded. "How far away is Brainfreeze from where you live?"

"Maybe another hour or two after that?"

Freddie chewed on his lip. "I...I think we don't live, like....super far from each other."

That made me rock back a bit, thinking, because he wouldn't have said that unless he had also been thinking about wanting to see me after we left camp, and that meant, I mean, that—

"Do, uh," Freddie said, "Do you want to—" his hand was twitchy in mine, his free hand scratching at the back of his neck, "Do you want to...I mean we could see if..." Freddie suddenly started to talk, slowly at first, then all at once, and I realized the way he looked right now, jittery and bouncing a bit, eyes wanting to make and hold contact with mine but maybe afraid of what they'd find—that was probably just how I had looked the last time we talked under this arch. "I—I haven't ever had, like, a serious...you know, but I...I like this a lot. And I feel like we could... we could visit over the year, or even—we could still figure out a way and—I mean point is we...do you want to try to, you know. Be..." he stopped right before the last word, hesitating to take the plunge, "...boyfriends?"

He stopped and breathed suddenly, as if he'd been so determined to spill it all out that his mind had forgotten about side details like remembering to breathe. Freddie's blue eyes settled on mine, just slightly wide, the way they got right before a game—somewhere between fear and excitement and opportunity.

"Yes," I said a little too quickly, watching the sweat and sunscreen run down his face as it slowly stretched into a smile. "I would like that. A lot. I was scared to ask you the same thing, honestly." I didn't really know what you were supposed to say when you got officially into a relationship, so I kissed him again. That seemed to work.

When we pulled away, Freddie was smiling. "I'll have my license soon, I mean soon-ish, my birthday's in October, so if we—"

"Hey," I said. He stopped talking and his blue eyes, which were most of what I could see at the moment, looked up at mine, steady. "We'll figure it out, okay?"

Freddie gave me another grin. His hair was falling down in his eyes again. "Okay. Okay. Thanks. I was—I don't know. I guess worried you'd say no."

"I was worried you wouldn't want to."

Freddie leaned against me in a hug, head on my chest. My arms fell around him and my hands traced the places where his jersey bunched, flattening them against his back. "Yeah I...I don't know. This is fun."

"Bit weird at the start," I said, grinning, "But pretty fun after that."

Freddie laughed, which I felt more than I heard. "Yeah, we, uh, aren't exactly the smoothest."

"I'm okay with that."

Freddie turned and looked up. "Yeah, I think it worked out."

We stood there for a moment, and I don't know what Freddie was thinking, but at least for me it was just how much it sucked this only had a few more minutes. It was like the week before Kyle left for Colorado, just trying to hang as much as we could, and not discussing the obvious, or doing math to figure out how many hours were left, how many hours of sleep we could function on. With the exception that I hadn't ever kissed Kyle. That was kind of a big difference there.

"But like I said, we—I'll have my full license in a couple months, and we can visit on long weekends or something. We're not crazy far apart—our parents might even be willing to drive us before then."

I nodded. "Do I have to hang out with Damian if I come visit?"

Freddie laughed again. "No, I, uh, I don't think so."

"Okay, then I'll come visit."

"Ha ha. But for real, there's cool museums and stuff we can go to, some hiking...it'll be good."

"I can bring all my history homework and let you write my essays."

Freddie rolled his eyes, which I couldn't see with my view of the top of his head, but just knew he'd done. "Okay, sure, like you'd let anybody touch any of your essays."

Man, I really was not hard to read at all. "...yeah, guilty as charged."

We stood and talked about school, what we'd do on visits, Weltmeister, anything, everything, and I think there was just that massive relief, of this not having to end, of Freddie wanting to keep going too. I hadn't realized how tight my shoulders had been, or the weight that had settled on the back of my mind. I could feel Freddie unwinding against me too, sagging a bit with relief, his heart rate slowly going from a frantic hammering against my chest to a steady beat.

After a while, we could hear whistles. Maybe the last whistles of Weltmeister.

"We should probably get going," Freddie said, "Not sure they'll believe we were busy doing last-minute packing through the whole closing ceremony."

"Yeah," I said, "Yeah, we should. We could still get one last Wilhelm chewing-out session to close out the summer."

"You don't want to go look inside the storage room again?"

"Too soon."

Freddie grinned and squeezed me tight, lingering for a moment before pulling away. "Yeah. See you soon?"

I had his phone number written down on three separate pieces of paper stored in three separate places in my bag. It was going in my contacts as soon as I got back in the car. *We probably can't see each other before school starts, but Labor Day's not super far away.* "Really soon."

The awards ceremony was short and sweet. It was almost one o'clock and there was literally no one who wanted to be on that field. Even the winning team—Eight, which prompted exactly the argument in the bleachers behind me you're predicting it did—seemed like they were extremely ready to go celebrate somewhere not in direct sunlight.

Wilhelm gave a quick speech about how much everyone had improved, and how much everyone had learned, hard work, the usual. The guy was great at giving speeches in the sense of convincing you that your life expectancy was tied to how fast you ran your next lap, but I don't think he was going to be delivering any keynote addresses anytime soon. Ludwig nodded dutifully at important points beside Wilhelm; Bronson was smiling and looking entirely pleased with himself. He was in jeans.

"He is not human," Alejandro said beside me, staring at him.

At the end, there was a huge roar, a quick distribution of awards. I did not get any, and neither did anybody on the team, which we quietly and unilaterally agreed was absolute robbery, corruption, they probably bribed Ludwig, so on and so forth. Oliver studied the various "best offensive player", "best defensive player" winners—most of whom had made a killer showing in the tournament games—his face solemn, betraying little in the way of emotion. I noticed the Stanford recruiter watching him curiously as he did.

From there, it was an exodus to the parking lot. We had been told to bring our bags with us to the closing ceremony, and so the whole thing was chaos of everybody scrambling to get out as fast as they could, people forgetting things, frantic goodbyes. There weren't any tearful moments with Team Six. I think the seniors didn't want that, and the rest of us were probably going to see each other next year. Mateo was passing around his phone, getting everyone's information and promising to assemble a group chat, and also asking Victor what he could pick up at the airport for his girlfriend.

It was a jostle of people I'd played against and with and watched from the stands as we assembled back to the parking lot, and the usual absolute chaos of trying to pick out your mom and dad out of a couple hundred people. I settled for looking for the Beast, which was usually a lot easier to spot in a crowd than anything else. I clocked Freddie approaching his dad's SUV, who got out with ramrod posture, giving Freddie a handshake, and telling him to load his stuff in the back. I caught Freddie's eyes briefly and gave him a quick smile. Freddie was busy talking to his dad, but he spared me a glance, but I could see the gleam in his eyes, and that was good.

I heard the wheezing of the Beast's horn honking.

I blinked and turned. Mom and Dad *never* honked the horn, not even when somebody cut us off, that was—

"DUDE!" Kyle said, leaning out the driver's seat. "What's up?"

"Kyle?" I said. "I thought—"

"You thought wrong, dude! I'm staying with you for a week! Get in, I'm driving back, we're--"

"No," Dad said, "Get off the horn, you were raised with more sense than that."

"C'mon, Mr. Cook, I've got my learner's, this is—"

"Literally no chance."

Kyle sighed and clambered out, grabbing me in the hand-clasp bro-hug. "Oh, God, you're sweaty."

"Yeah, you sweat when you play real sports."

"Alright, listen, I'll go back to Colorado *tonight*, okay, I don't care—"

Before I could reply, Mom and Dad had both come for their hugs, and Mom said I had gotten too skinny, which Dad said was the point of camp, and had the food here been okay, and what had the final rankings been, and—

"Let me get your bags," Dad said, clapping me on the back and grabbing my stuff to hurl in the back. Mom went to open the hatch, telling him to make sure not to jostle Kyle's stuff, to which Dad replied there was zero chance Kyle brought anything breakable, and—

"Good summer, dude?" Kyle asked, still eyeing the driver's seat.

"Yeah," I said. "Really, really good."

Kyle frowned a bit, head cocked to the side. "What? Soccer's not that fun."

I glanced over at my folks, who were still talking and trying to shift bags. Dad was convinced he had a system for packing luggage in the back of a car, but the system was just, like, putting bags where there was open space. "Uh...maybe, wasn't, you know. All soccer."

My eyes had gone over to Freddie's car, which was nearly loaded, nearly on its way to go.

I could see the gears turning in Kyle's head out of my peripheral vision. "What, but there weren't any girl..." Kyle took a moment, following my gaze, then looking back at me, where I could feel my cheeks getting a bit redder. His smile slowly widened to Cheshire proportions. "Oh dude, let's go. You absolute snake, you drop this now when we're about to get in the car where we can't talk for the eighteen hour drive home? You're gonna make me wait out the entire Oregon Trail before I get to hear—"

"Okay guys," Dad said, slamming the hatch. The car rattled. "Let's hop in and get going and we can beat the traffic."

There was one lane in and out of St. Michael's. Unless he took the Beast off-roading I wasn't clear on how we were beating the line out.

"Sure thing, Dad," I said, sliding into the backseat beside Kyle. Mom had a cooler which I suspect was initially full of Gatorade and sandwiches but was now only partially full of Gatorade and sandwiches. "Dude, did you drink everything but the yellows in here, are you serious?"

"Look, I needed proper hydration after my flight, you know that—"

"You boys good back there?" Mom asked. "Did any of your German come in handy?"

"Oh, um, yeah, a lot, a lot." I took a deep breath, never once remembering a time the Beast's backseat had been this comfortable.

"Need anything before we hit the road?" Dad asked.

I glanced at the window.

"Yeah. You think we could still stop at Brainfreeze on the way home?"

Epilogue

As the cloud settled I found myself coated in a light mask of flour. I was able to easily brush it off my clothes but caught a glimpse of my face in the mirror. My powder covered face made me look like a lordling from renaissance France. I had been informed about many details on lordlings from renaissance France on runs with Bronson, which I had not ever thought I'd miss, let alone this soon.

I chuckled at myself and sent a quick photo of myself to Kyle with the caption:

"He likes his history...he better appreciate all this prep work I'm putting in."

I grabbed a kitchen towel to wipe off and checked the recipe again. It definitely just said "add flour" and nothing about slowing down the mixer. I thought baking cookies would be easier.

"Kit Kat," my mom called as she entered the kitchen. "Oh!" There was a brief pause as she observed the scene. You could always tell when Mom was thinking of the polite thing to say because she tried very hard not to look like she was thinking of the polite thing to say. "You, um, need some help dear? I thought you'd be ready to go by now." She tousled my hair and sent a few more clouds of flour into the air.

I winced and wiped my face with the back of my hand. "I got it mom, I want to make them myself."

"Okay, well get them in the oven soon, I'd like to be able to drop you off and be back in time for dinner." She glanced around. "Also, please wipe everything down. Maybe twice."

I'd gotten out of captain's practice for the next few days. Somehow it had leaked that the Stanford recruiter had called my coach to set up a few visits and the team was already acting like I was going to be this big star this year. We still had another week or so before official tryouts, but there was no way any trials they did would be tougher than Weltmeister. It also meant the seniors were already including me in things and being a bit more lenient, like letting me skip out a few days without giving me too much of a hard time.

I got the cookies in the oven and ran upstairs to throw together my weekend bag. At a certain point I had to give up on the dream of washing all the flour out of my hair. When I came back down my mom was waiting with a special tin in the kitchen.

I grabbed an oven mitt and pulled the cookies out of the oven, not waiting for them to cool before shoveling them into the tin, cracking more than a few.

"Thanks mom."

"I think it's sweet that you wanted to bring a gift to your new friend for hosting you."

My ears turned red and I tried to bury my face in working the lid of the tin securely onto the box to not give my reaction away. I was sure Mom could tell I was really excited, but hopefully not exactly why.

I really owed Kyle for this one. He had made sure I was aware of this debt, and often. During his surprise visit once we'd gotten back from camp, I told him all about Weltmeister and Freddie. He had found the part where we got caught by Bronson the most entertaining part of the story which was definitely not the part he was supposed to be focusing on, but whatever. At the end of his visit, he got that mischievous glint in his eye, and convinced my mom that a visit with some of my new friends from soccer camp before the end of the summer would be a good idea since I didn't really have many other friends at home.

Of course Kyle did me the biggest favor in a way that made me look like a massive loser to my Mom. Well worth it. She worked her magic.

"You ready to go?" Mom asked.

"Coming!" I grabbed the tin of cookies and went out the door.

Acknowledgements

Writing my first book has been the journey of my life and there are many people who helped get me here. If you know me you'll know that I like to be concise but have a tendency to be a bit verbose so I want to open with a big thank you to everyone who helped along the way. You all know who you are. Thank you for your feedback, your help editing, your enthusiasm and being there for me along the way to making this a reality. Though I may not be able to call out each and every one of you, know that you matter and I appreciate your help in getting here. With that concise blanket to cover me, there are a few special thinks I need to indulge.

First and foremost, thank you to my wonderful husband, for rekindling my love for storytelling and helping me find the space and time to write. This book would never have been possible without you.

Thank you to my parents for sending me off to summer camp and soccer camp every year to ensure I had a well-rounded experience growing up that helped me build the world of Weltmeister.

Thank you to all my friends and beta readers and a special shout-out to Paul, my first beta reader who couldn't put the book down. You gave me the confidence that my story was worth telling and for that I will be forever grateful.

Finally, thank you to all my readers – the simple act of picking up this book and taking time out of your life to read my story makes this all worthwhile.

About the author

Felix Fowler is a dynamic writer, weaving tales that resonate deeply with the human experience. His stories are full of humor, heart, and an undeniable authenticity—drawing from his own trials and the triumphs that came with them.

When he's not penning his latest novel, Felix can be found kicking up dust on the soccer field in a local pickup league, where the game brings out his competitive side and fuels his creativity. With a knack for creating relatable characters and compelling narratives, Felix's work continues to inspire and entertain readers everywhere.

You can connect with Felix at

www.felixfowler.com